W9-AFH-965

Astrid Lindgren

Twayne's World Authors Series

Children's Literature

Ruth K. MacDonald, Editor

Bay Path College

TWAS 851

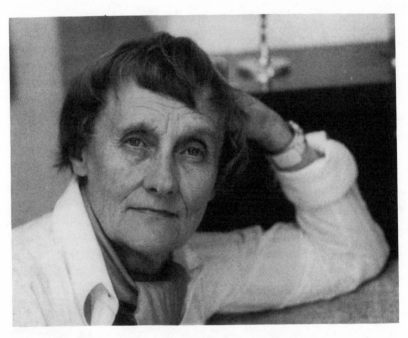

Astrid Lindgren. Photo by Jan Collsiöö. Copyright by

Astrid Lindgren

Eva-Maria Metcalf

Twayne Publishers • New York
Maxwell Macmillan Canada • Toronto
Maxwell Macmillan International • New York Oxford Singapore Sydney

Astrid Lindgren
Eva-Maria Metcalf

Copyright 1995 by Twayne Publishers

Twayne Publishers
Macmillan Publishing Company
866 Third Avenue
New York, New York 10022

Maxwell Macmillan Canada, Inc.
1200 Eglinton Avenue East
Suite 200
Don Mills, Ontario M3C 3N1

Library of Congress Cataloging-in-Publication Data

Metcalf, Eva-Maria.
Astrid Lindgren / Eva-Maria Metcalf.
p. cm.—(Twayne's world authors series; TWAS 851)
Includes bibliographical references and index.
ISBN 0-8057-4525-4
1. Lindgren, Astrid, 1907– . 2. Authors, Swedish—20th century—Biography. I.
Title. II. Series: Twayne's world authors series: TWAS 851. III. Series: Twayne's
world author's series. Children's literature.
PT9875.L598Z77 1994
839'.73'72—dc20   94-20503
                                                                          CIP
                                                                           AC

10 9 8 7 6 5 4 3 2 1

Printed in the United States of America.

Contents

Preface

Astrid Lindgren is the author of *Pippi Longstocking,* a book that rightfully brought her world fame. But as I will show in this introduction to her life and work, she is much more than that. Lindgren is one of the great storytellers of the twentieth century, and her international stature has grown steadily since the appearance of *Pippi* in 1945. To date she has published some 115 titles. Her work has been translated into sixty languages, and millions of copies of her books have been sold worldwide. In 1985, Lindgren became the most read Swedish author, when Swedish public libraries reported that her books had been borrowed 2 million times in that year alone. Beyond Lindgren the author there is also Lindgren the public figure who has raised her voice against excessive government bureaucracy, called for peace, and supported animal rights with considerable success. The list of her honorary doctorates, prizes, and awards is long indeed. Moreover, she has been honored by having thirty-four schools named for her in Germany alone, which is unprecedented for a living author. In short, there is no doubt about the high esteem in which Astrid Lindgren is held at home and abroad.

Nor is there any doubt about the genuine love readers show for her work as well as for the person who stands behind it. She receives sacks full of mail daily from children and adults who express their delight and appreciation. This wave of gratitude and goodwill, which spans generations, cultures, and social strata, echoes her unique sensitivity to the fundamental human needs and desires of all peoples. Lindgren's books are written in a spirit of love and respect for children and with a deep understanding of what it means to be a child. She shares with readers her sorrows and frustrations, her dreams and visions, her love and hate in powerful and well-crafted stories that display a convincing mix of humor and sentimentality, pragmatism and poetry, courage and compassion. Her readers vicariously experience the right amounts of freedom and security—a combination she firmly believes every child needs.

While Lindgren's stories are funny and full of suspense, they also touch the reader's innermost soul. They effortlessly merge the ephemeral with the archetypal, the local with the universal. Indeed, much of the attraction of Lindgren's stories lies in their polyvalence and complexity. Conflict and ambiguity are not only important structural elements for

Lindgren but are also paradigmatic of her overall creative endeavor. Seemingly irreconcilable opposites—resistance and compliance, truth and lies, nature and culture, childhood and adulthood—form a productive dialectical tension, leaving her narratives open to a great variety of readings and interpretations. It comes as no surprise, then, that critics have considered Pippi Longstocking and Emil to be harbingers of change as well as defendants of the status quo. Many of her shorter and novel-length fairy tales lend themselves to different readings depending on the reader's mindset and maturity.

Lindgren's stories are written in the twilight zone between engagement and escape, tradition and revolt. She writes to console her readers and help them escape from painful experiences while at the same time fostering strength and a sense of responsibility. By the same token, Lindgren writes to appease her inner child, or the part of herself that is horror-stricken at all the ugliness and evil that exist in this world, and she follows an inner drive to set things right by purposefully wielding her magic wand of fiction. Her powers of enchantment resemble those of her fictional characters Malin (in *My Nightingale is Singing*) and Pippi Longstocking, who find magic power in simple peas: Malin grows a singing tree from a pea, while Pippi transforms her peas into a wonder drug that will keep her forever young. The illusion Lindgren conjures up by escaping into realms of utopian love and beauty becomes the very device with which she confronts reality in her efforts to improve the world. Her social criticism, which is firmly embedded in a genuine love for the time and place of her childhood, takes on other forms as well. Through the protagonist's childishness, expressed in playful pranks and innocent (or not-so-innocent) laughter, she surreptitiously ridicules and subverts traditional patterns of thought and behavior in a joyous, performative, and altogether entertaining manner.

Throughout Lindgren's career as a children's book author—for roughly four decades—her work has heralded shifts in social and cultural discourse as they affect children's literature. At the time of their initial publication, many of her books were controversial, but a decade or two later they had become prototypes for new trends in children's literature. During a period of relative social conservatism in the 1940s and 1950s, Lindgren shocked and inspired critics and the public alike with *Pippi Longstocking* and *Karlsson-on-the-Roof*. She delighted children just as much then as she did thirty years later during a much more progressive and pragmatic era, when she once again stirred up emotions with her modern fairy tales *The Brothers Lionheart* and *Ronia, the Robber's Daughter*.

Lindgren's 'child within' seems to be an acute sensor for the compensatory needs of her readers. In the 1940s and 1950s, this sensor compelled her to undermine the still-current myth of sweet, innocent
childhood, rebelling against its limitations and calling for greater freedom for children and a recognition of children's rights. In the 1980s, at
the time of *The Brothers Lionheart,* her inner child sensed the need for a
new myth that could provide hope and security for her readers in a childhood world that has become increasingly decentered and demythified.

Given the sheer size of Astrid Lindgren's production and the broad
register of genres to which her books belong, this study must necessarily
focus on her most important contributions to children's literature.
Furthermore, my scope has been somewhat limited by what has been
translated into English. Among the translated works, I have, with a few
exceptions, concentrated mainly on those books that have become popular in the United States. Thus, Lindgren's early books for girls, which
she herself no longer considers noteworthy, have fallen by the wayside.
All the books belonging strictly to this genre—*Britt-Mari lättar sitt hjärta* (Confidences of Britt-Mari, 1944) and *Kerstin och jag* (Kerstin and I,
1945), neither of which has been translated into English, and the Kati
books (1950, 1952, 1954)—are quite outdated. Lindgren herself is not
very fond of them, and although they were progressive for their time and
genre and their style is brash and witty, they lack the timelessness,
depth, and intensity characteristic of her best work.

I have also excluded her early fairy tales and most of her picture
books, especially those that retell episodes from her books for older children in simplified versions. Aside from some additional insights into
questions of age stratification in her narrative, a more comprehensive
look at her picture books would do little to alter or expand my arguments. Once allowances are made for the specific expressive demands of
the medium in question, the messages and stylistic devices Lindgren
employs in her picture books and in the numerous adaptations and
dramatizations of her well-known stories for the theater and the screen
remain fundamentally the same.

My presentation of Lindgren's work is organized around major
themes and motifs that all her books share to a greater or lesser extent,
but of which some books seem to me more emblematic than others. My
analysis stresses the sociohistorical context of her work. I complement
this contextual analysis with a look at the translation and reception of
her work, an investigation of subtexts and intertexts, and by readings of
her most successful stories in an attempt to reveal Lindgren's narrative

techniques, specifically her use of humor and irony. Separate chapters are devoted to her Småland books, which include her realistic and somewhat idyllic stories for younger children and her detective and adventure stories for somewhat older readers; to her fantastic stories about Pippi Longstocking and Karlsson-on-the-Roof; and to her fantasy novels and fairy tales for all ages. In the first chapter I discuss Lindgren's life, making reference to how it has influenced her work. In the last, I distill and sum up the driving forces and the voice that have shaped her authorship by comparing the two great female heroes from her first and last major books, Pippi Longstocking and Ronia, the Robber's Daughter.

Acknowledgments

Support for this book has come from many directions, both at home and abroad. Closest to home, I would like to thank my husband, Michael Metcalf, for his consistent, yet never imposing, encouragement and support. My friend Miriam Butwin's editorial help in preparing the manuscript was valuable, indeed. Further afield, I would like to express my gratitude to the Children's Literature Association and the American-Scandinavian Foundation for providing me with a travel grant to visit Sweden in the summer of 1989. Across the Atlantic, my special thanks go to Lena Törnqvist at Svenska Barnboksinstitutet in Stockholm, where I received all the support and encouragement I could have asked for during my research stay. I would also like to thank Professor Vivi Edström for her warm collegiality in sharing her thoughts and ideas with me. Thanks go to Margareta Strömstedt as well, who gave me further perspectives on Astrid Lindgren the person and went out of her way to show me her Swedish television documentary about Lindgren.

I would like to express my appreciation to the publisher Rabén and Sjögren for its generosity in sending me all the books I did not have at the outset of this study, and I would like to thank Thimble Press and Bookbird, as well as Patricia Crampton and *Signal,* for the permission to reprint English translations of quotes by Astrid Lindgren.

For permission to use their illustrations my special thanks go to Björn Berg and Ilon Wikland, whose illustrations are an integral part of Lindgren's children's books in Sweden and in many foreign countries.

I also owe a debt of gratitude to Kerstin Kvint, Astrid Lindgren's agent, who welcomed me with open arms and provided much information about the publication of Lindgren's works and many insights into her private and working life. Last but not least, I would like to send a warm thank you to Astrid Lindgren, who subjected herself to yet another interview and made our meeting into a memorable moment in my life.

Chronology

1907   Astrid Ericsson born 14 November in Vimmerby, Små-land, Sweden. Second child of Samuel August and Hanna Ericsson (brother Gunnar born 1906; sisters Stina and Ingegerd born 1911 and 1916, respectively).

1923   Astrid Ericsson finishes school.

1924   Works for the Vimmerby newspaper (*Wimmerby Tidningen*).

1926   Moves to Stockholm.

1931   Marries Sture Lindgren.

1941   Lindgren family moves to apartment in Dalagatan where Astrid Lindgren has lived since.

1945   *Pippi Longstocking* (*Pippi Långstrump*); first prize, Rabén and Sjögren's Best Children's Book Competition (for *Pippi Longstocking*).

1946   Starts work as children's book editor at Rabén and Sjögren.

1947   *The Children of Noisy Village* (*Alla vi barn i Bullerbyn*).

1950   Nils Holgersson Medal for *Nils Karlsson-Pyssling: Sagor* (Nils Karlsson-Pyssling: Fairy Tales).

1951   *Bill Bergson Lives Dangerously* (*Mästerdetektiven Blomkvist lever farligt*).

1952   Sture Lindgren dies.

1954   *Mio, My Son* (*Mio min Mio*).

1955   *Karlsson-on-the-Roof* (*Lillebror och Karlsson på taket*).

1956   *Rasmus and the Vagabond* (*Rasmus på luffen*); Deutscher Jugendbuchpreis, Sonderpreis (German Prize for Children's Books, Special Award) for *Mio, My Son*.

1957   The Swedish State Award for Writers of High Literary Standard; Lindgren is the first children's literature author to receive award.

1958   Hans Christian Andersen Medal; Boys' Club of America Junior Book Award for *Rasmus and the Vagabond*.

1959   *New York Herald Tribune* Children's Spring Book Festival
       Award, shared with Anna Riwkin-Brick for *Sia lives on
       Kilimanjaro.*

1960   *Mischievous Meg (Madicken).*

1963   *Emil in the Soup Tureen (Emil i Lönneberga).*

1970   Retires as children's books editor from Rabén and
       Sjögren; Litteraturfrämjandets hederspris "Guldskep-
       pet" (Golden Ship Award of the Swedish Society for the
       Promotion of Literature); *Expressen's* Heffaklump
       Award (Sweden) for *Emil and Piggy Beast (Än lever Emil
       i Lönneberga).* Lewis Carroll Shelf Award for *Christmas in
       the Stable,* illustrated by Harald Wiberg.

1971   The Swedish Academy's Gold Medal.

1973   *The Brothers Lionheart (Bröderna Lejonhjärta);* honorary
       doctor, Linköping University, Sweden; Lewis Carroll
       Shelf Award for *Pippi Longstocking.*

1974   Smile Award for Russian radio adaptation of *Karlsson-
       on-the-Roof.*

1975   "Samuel August från Sevedstorp och Hanna i Hult"
       (Samuel August from Sevedstorp and Hanna in Hult),
       Silvergriffel (Dutch Award), Litteris et artibus (plaque
       presented by the king of Sweden).

1978   Friedenspreis des Deutschen Buchhandels (German
       Booksellers' Peace Award); Adelaide-Risto Award
       (Rome); International Writer's Prize (awarded by the
       Welsh Arts Council); honorary doctor of letters,
       Leicester University, England.

1979   Janusz Korczak Award for *The Brothers Lionheart.*

1981   *Ronia, the Robber's Daughter (Ronja Rövardotter).*

1984   Mildred L. Batchelder Award to Viking Press for *Ronia,
       the Robber's Daughter;* Dag Hammarskjöld Award
       (Sweden); John Hansson Award (United States).

1985   Illis Quorum (Gold Medal awarded by the Swedish
       Government); Silver Bear Award, Berlin, for the film *Ronia,
       the Robber's Daughter;* Loisirs jeune élu par l'enfant (French
       children's book award); Karen Blixen Award (from the
       Danish Academy); Jovanovic Zmaj Award (Yugoslavia).

1986   Selma Lagerlöf Award (Sweden); Swede of the Year (named by the Swedish Council of America).

1987   Leo Tolstoy International Gold Medal (awarded by the League of Soviet Organizations for International Friendship and Cultural Relations).

1989   Albert Schweitzer Medal (U.S. Animal Welfare Institute); honorary doctor, University of Warsaw.

1990   *Min ko vill ha roligt* (My Cow Wants to Have Fun).

1993   International Book Award (from the UNESCO International Book Committee).

Vitt, vitt i Västervik
och vått i Vimmerby.
Där traskar Astrid Lindgren
med vitt-vått paraply.

Astrid Lindgren portrayed in the 1984 Swedish picture book *Vitt: En historia från Kalmar län* (White: A story from Kalmar County), written by Lennart Hellsing and illustrated by Fibben Hald. The poem accompanying the illustration reads: White, white in Western Bay / And wet in Vimmerby / There goes Astrid Lindgren / With a white-wet umbrella.

Chapter One

Childhood Lived and Revisited: Life and Work

How long ago it must have been! Otherwise, how can the world have changed so much?
Could everything really be so different, in no more than a brief half-century? My childhood
was lived in a country that no longer exists, and where did it go?
—Astrid Lindgren, "I Remember . . ."

A Sense of Place and Community

"I was born in November 1907 in an old red house surrounded by apple trees."[1] So Astrid Lindgren presents herself to her readers in "Astrid Lindgren Talks about Herself," a brochure prepared for her Stockholm publisher, Rabén and Sjögren, in 1987. The setting of her childhood home at the edge of the small town of Vimmerby in Småland could not have been more traditionally Swedish. Many Swedes lived in a similar setting around the turn of the century. The red wooden house surrounded by apple trees has since become a Swedish icon for a wholesome and idyllic life in the countryside, contrasting sharply with living conditions for the majority of today's Swedes, who reside in big anonymous apartment blocks in suburbs and satellite cities. Lindgren's childhood home has assumed the same iconic function for her readers and herself, the more so because she remembers it providing all she needed for a happy childhood: love, beauty, freedom, and security. With its surroundings, its people, and its local traditions, her home has appeared in many guises in her children's books, a place with which many readers are more than willing to identify. Like Laura Ingalls Wilder's little house on the prairie, Lindgren's Noisy Village and Lönneberga, which are modeled on her childhood home, are important sites on the map of children's fiction. Set in a typically Swedish community at the turn of the century, Noisy Village and Lönneberga offer readers a mixture of security and adventure. Like Wilder's books, Lindgren's books about Emil, Noisy Village, and Mischievous Meg, as well as Rasmus and the Vagabond and Brenda

1

Brave, provide a subtly and concisely drawn ethnographic and cultural-historical background for fun-filled and funny childhood adventures.

Lindgren has made no secret of the fact that her childhood experiences are an integral part of her writing. As do the majority of good writers for children, Lindgren writes for and about the child within herself. It is thus important to take a close look at her childhood, as it reveals itself in her books, essays, and interviews, to create a portrait of the author that goes beyond a simple listing of facts and dates. This chapter is devoted to this task as well as to a less intensive examination of Lindgren's life as adolescent and adult. By occasionally drawing parallels between life and fiction, I do not, however, want to suggest a simple analogy of life and fiction, since I am well aware of the fault lines that exist between person, author, and narrator. Adult nostalgia and ulterior motives cloud and distort childhood experiences. Lindgren's childhood experiences and desires, as they are related in her books, are tempered and accentuated by the experiences and desires of later life, since all memories are also projections of personal needs and of current cultural norms and values. I will address these influences when discussing the makeup and message of her books.

Margareta Strömstedt's excellent biography of Astrid Lindgren—thus far available only in Swedish—has been a valuable resource for my own attempts to present the author behind the work.[2] Strömstedt cautiously and delicately reveals a few outlines of the private person behind the public persona, to whom few have gained access. Based on gleanings from Lindgren's work, Strömstedt's close friendship with the author, and many interviews with Lindgren as well as with relatives and friends, Strömstedt's book presents a many-faceted and insightful portrait.

Lindgren's autobiographical writings and various interviews round out my source material. My own experience as interviewer has not been different from that of many a predecessor who has come away with the best feelings but little if any new information. Lindgren is a warm and engaging conversationalist. Her answers are full of stories and anecdotes that seem fresh and new with each telling, although she has told them many times before. She surrounds herself with a personal lore that she uses to fend off further intrusions into her private life. By now, this tailor-made oral autobiography has assumed a life of its own, and an argument can be made that all lives, when told, become stories that hide as much as they reveal. The challenge is to reveal some of the hidden part. By combining the lore surrounding Lindgren with the factual evidence from her life—to the extent it is known—and, above all, by relating this information to the narrator's voice in her books, I hope to fill in the contours.

From the web of memories, needs, experiences, and values concerning childhood two things stand out as central for Lindgren. On the one hand is a sense of belonging and rootedness in her childhood community, on the other, a great sensitivity to the beauty of nature and the power of imagination. While it is not the least bit unusual for Lindgren to introduce herself to her readers by mentioning the date and place of her birth, the fact that she also provides detailed information about her family and the farm on which she grew up is quite interesting. It suggests the importance she attributes to her childhood surroundings and the sense of place and community they gave her.

Lindgren was the second of four children—Gunnar, Astrid, Stina, and Ingegerd—born to Samuel August Ericsson and his wife, Hanna. Throughout their lives her parents were farmers in Näs on the outskirts of Vimmerby, a small town in Småland, a region in central Sweden. Being a farmer's daughter has left a deep impression on her life and work. The family farm, of which only the farmhouses now remain, has a long history. It had been church property since 1411, and in 1895 her grandfather Samuel was selected by the local parson to work the land. He was succeeded by his son Samuel August, and he in turn by his son, Gunnar, Astrid's brother. Thus, the setting of her early years was characterized by close ties to the church, stability, continuity, and a sense of belonging. She was able to form deep roots, fostered by the love of her family and the stability of the rural community. During trying periods in her life Lindgren could always fall back on the strength and self-assurance she developed during these early years. It is here that a foundation of care and trust in life was established, which she, in turn, conveys to her readers by describing childhoods in settings not unlike that of her own. Even in stories in which the fictional characters go through hair-raising adventures, Lindgren's voice lends the narrative a steady undercurrent of stability and confidence.

In an essay dedicated to her parents, "Samuel August från Sevedstorp och Hanna i Hult" (Samuel August from Sevedstorp and Hanna from Hult), published independently in 1973 and as part of a collection of Lindgren's essays, *Mina påhitt* (My ideas), in 1984, Lindgren explains why her childhood was such a good and happy one. "We had two things that made our childhood into what it was—security and freedom. It was secure with these two who cared so much for each other and who were always there when we needed them, but who otherwise let us roam freely and happily on the marvelous playground we had at our childhood's Näs."[3] Lindgren may not have been conscious of these two preconditions for a happy childhood when she started writing children's books, but while writing for the child she once was, and in returning to her own childhood, she has given her readers the same combination of freedom and security. She takes them on wild excursions into the imaginary realm of play and adventure, all the while guiding them with the firm hand of a knowing and caring storyteller who is able to evoke the threatening in order to subdue it and to release chaos in order to fence it in.

Lindgren was born the year that King Oscar II of Sweden died, a time when monarchy was still strong and the rural community was steeped in tradition. Life during her childhood in Småland seemed ages apart from the life she encountered in Stockholm, where she moved in 1926 at the age of nineteen. Although as a writer she belongs to the second half of the twentieth century, her childhood memories date back to a time before electricity, the telephone, and other amenities of modern life, such as hot and cold running water. Lindgren herself always refers to it as the horse-and-buggy age, when the appearance of an automobile on the dirt roads was a rare and scary experience.

In a short essay entitled "I Remember . . . ," written mainly for an adult audience, Lindgren looks back at her youth with the eyes of an adult. She describes the return home from a family gathering—one of the few entertainments the Ericsson family could afford—with a good bit of nostalgia sobered by a tinge of irony and spiced with drama:

> It was fun to drive in the wagon, pulled by the team of May and Maud, to sit so high up and enjoy ourselves looking at all the things we drove past. The sun generally shone, and there was a good smell of horse and sun-warmed leather and resinous pine trees. How calm and peaceful it all was—unless one had the misfortune to meet an "ottomobile." Then mortal terror would strike the wagon. Papa would jump down and hold the horses by the reins . . . and we sat there quaking until the monster had puffed by. Afterwards the relief was great and then we became very excited, just fancy, we had seen an "ottomobile," and that was a rare and remarkable event.[4]

Småland, with its infertile and stony soil, was one of the most poverty-stricken regions of Sweden then and is known to this day for its hard-working and thrifty population. A glimpse into the hardships of everyday life in Småland is given in the Emil books. In *Emil's Pranks*, the narrator tells us: "Before Christmas comes one must face the cold, windy, dark autumn when there isn't much fun to be found anywhere. Alfred followed the oxen in pouring rain and plowed the stony fields. And Emil trudged after him, helping Alfred to shout at the oxen, which were sluggish and awkward and didn't understand what plowing was about."[5] A little closer to Christmas there is the big wash day in Katthult. "Lina and Krösa-Maja stood on the icy jetty by the brook and did the rinsing. Lina cried and blew on her frozen fingertips which were very painful" (90).

Hunger and starvation were widespread, and a great number of people who could no longer subsist off their tiny acres or did not have any land to begin with emigrated to the United States. One million inhabitants left Sweden for the United States between 1840 and 1930, and many of them came from Småland. There were also emigrants among Lindgren's relatives, and in her books set in Småland around the turn of the century she mentions emigration along with many other difficult facts of life. In *Madicken,* translated into a fine British edition as *Mardie's Adventures,* one of the prize possessions of Ida, who helps out with the wash and the cleaning in Mardie's family, are the photographs from America of her daughters Esther and Ruth: "They were fine ladies with beautiful, flowery clothes and their hair piled up in a bird's nest on their heads. Their photographs stood on Ida's desk but they themselves were in Chicago and would never come home again."[6]

In *Emil in the Soup Tureen* the emigration motif finds its way into the last episode and is picked up again at the beginning of *Emil's Pranks.* There, the reader is informed that the villagers are fed up with Emil's pranks and have collected money for the purpose of sending him to America, hoping to get rid of him soon and forever. Their effort fails, however, because Emil's mother won't hear of it. In real life, the Vimmerby community's effort to get rid of a disagreeable distant relative of Lindgren by the same means fell through as well. The relative had accepted the money and sailed to America but returned several weeks later, proclaiming loudly that he preferred to stay in Sweden (Strömstedt, 65).

This anecdote is only one of many in which the local lore of Vimmerby has found its way into Lindgren's stories. Not only are physical surroundings and events faithfully restored in her Småland books, even her language retains its local flavor. Lindgren, who seems to have inherited her keen memory and gift for storytelling from her father's side of the family, likes to enrich her narrative with familiar sayings and quick and witty retorts that originated among what she calls tongue-in-cheek the "rough peasantry" of her home village. Her best informant on local lore was her father. Many of his anecdotes and childhood experiences are immortalized in the Emil books. One of them is the catechism story in *Emil and Piggy Beast*. Because it belongs to a different time and place, it can't be retold to modern readers without a bit of background information. Thus, Lindgren slips on her teacher's hat and explains the existence and function of catechism hearings in nineteenth-century Sweden before she delves into the action. Lindgren's propensity to explain the traditions and norms of a bygone era are helpful to those who do not read the books in their original language and know little about Swedish culture.

Young and old, rich and poor came together under the auspices of the parson to be examined on their knowledge of the Bible, Lindgren tells us. Lina, the maid at Katthult, likes these periodic catechism hearings because they provide a welcome respite from her daily drudgery. But Bible knowledge is not Lina's strength, and when asked the names of "our first ancestors," she answers proudly "Thor and Freya" instead of Adam and Eve. Thor and Freya were two old Norse gods "whom the people in Småland worshiped long ago in heathen times, thousands of years before they'd ever heard of the Bible," Lindgren explains.[7] As the narrator observes, Lina is not that far from the truth, but in the Christian context her answer is naturally unacceptable and she becomes the laughing stock of the parish for a while. This episode illustrates the considerable influence the Lutheran State Church held in the country at the turn of the century. Lindgren was raised Lutheran, and reading the Bible and attending Sunday church services were facts of life. The need Lindgren felt to explain these traditions to modern-day Swedish children—and it is they whom Lindgren addresses first and foremost—as well as the ironic twist of the interchange between Lina and the parson, hints at the secularization Sweden underwent during the twentieth century and also sheds light on Lindgren's personal alienation from her childhood creed.

With "Samuel August från Sevedstorp och Hanna i Hult," Lindgren made an exception to her professional concentration on children's books. Told from an adult perspective to a largely adult audience, this tribute to her parents and their lifelong love, in the form of a short biography, reveals much about living conditions at Näs and family relationships. Together with "I Remember . . ." and a few other precious essays, it complements the children's stories, providing a rich source of background information about Lindgren's childhood and her first steps into adult life.

With humor and with deep love and understanding, Lindgren traces a lengthy courtship that led to the long married life of two special yet ordinary people whose wisdom, skill, and devotion to each other the daughter admires openly and somewhat jealously. This short tale is above all a declaration of love for her father, Samuel August Ericsson. Lindgren later said that she never loved anyone more. The quality of his character, described by Margareta Strömstedt, is echoed in his daughter's. "He was both naive and sharp-sighted, kind without being indulgent, respected but not feared, economical and generous, active and outgoing, and he had great sensitivity to the needs of others, in sum, he was an unusual conglomerate of a realist and a dreamer" (Strömstedt, 107).

One episode in "Samuel August" strikes me as paradigmatic of Lindgren's relationship to the world of her childhood as it is reflected again and again in her books. Standing outside her parents' bedroom door on the eve of her mother's death, she overhears their customary evening prayer (*Mina påhitt,* 218). In her adult life she remains an outsider to the world her parents represent, which is secure in itself and blessed by naive, unquestioning belief, but she can and does enter it by going back to her childhood days in her children's fiction. Besides giving us glimpses of the character and life of her parents, "Samuel August" provides a somewhat different portrayal of this frugal, patriarchal, and devoutly Lutheran childhood home, ruled by the Protestant work ethic, than do Lindgren's children's books. It is this document, if any, that provides an explanation for the many biblical references that run through her work.

In this narrative for adults Lindgren's recollections are not bent to fit a child's desire for excitement, action, and a happy ending, as is the case in her children's books, where the harsh realities of everyday life are submerged as a dark undercurrent that makes only the occasional unpleasant interruption of fun and games. The adult world Lindgren describes was austere and only occasionally interrupted by enjoyment. For the most part, only the storytelling, merriment, and song during holidays or family get-togethers would break the tedium of daily toil.

Many hands were needed on farms at that time, and children grew up in close contact with people of all sorts, sizes, and ages. And that, Lindgren reports, was instructive. "From them I learned—without their knowing it and without my knowing it—something about life's demands and how hard it can be to be a human being" ("I Remember . . . ," 158). Life in early nineteenth-century Småland was not easy for a landholding farmer and the conditions for the penniless who could no longer work were poorer still. The tramps and vagabonds roaming the

countryside are described almost identically in "I Remember . . ." and in
Lindgren's 1950 tale "Godnatt, Herr Luffare" (Good night, Mr.
Vagabond), from which the following observation is taken: "There were
different tramps. Kind and shilly-shally ones who timidly sat down on a
chair close to the door without saying a word. Verbose and talkative
tramps who bragged and invented stories. Drunk tramps who sometimes were in a good mood and sometimes drew a knife. And tramps
who were so full of lice that mother had to wipe the chair where they
had sat."[8]

Lindgren's early fairy tale *My Nightingale Is Singing* renders a full-
blown portrait of living conditions in a turn-of-the-century poorhouse in
Småland. The orphaned Maria meets a sorry sight when she enters the
"poorhouse," where she is to spend the rest of her life because nobody
wants her. In this "place of sighs" were gathered together "the old who
could no longer work, the sick, the spent and destitute, the half-crazed,
and homeless children whom no one would take care of."[9] They are all
crammed into a small cottage with little food, little warmth, and no
hope. Their life is filled with meanness and ugliness in the form of constant bickering, dirt, stench, and bedbugs. Every day these paupers go
round the parish begging a crust, among them Fuggy, "the dirtiest man
in the parish, whose name was used to frighten the children although he
was kind and decent and never harmed a soul" (2). Fuggy is based on a
pauper Lindgren remembers from her youth. His nickname was Jocke
Squint, and he too came to the kitchen door of the Ericsson farm regularly. "One-armed and covered with lice was Jocke Squint and he wore
an indescribable yellow coat. The food he received on his begging trips
would be stuffed into the pockets of his coat, and because the pockets
had holes in them, it all collected between coat and lining and lay round
Jocke Squint like a huge sausage" ("I Remember . . . ," 160).

Nature's Child

Maria in *My Nightingale Is Singing* has to go on begging excursions with
the others to get enough food to survive. She is hungry and dirty, to be
sure, but she suffers most of all from the bleakness of existence and the
total lack of anything beautiful and inspiring in and around the poorhouse. For "outside the window there was nothing but a bleak potato
field, no flowering apple trees and no clumps of lily-of-the-valley" (3).
Astrid Ericsson, like Maria, would have suffered from the lack of natural
beauty:

The beauty of Småland at apple-blossom time is evoked over and over again in Lindgren's books. Illustration by Ilon Wikland from *Mio, min Mio* (*Mio, My Son*).

But if anyone asks me what I remember from my childhood days, my first thought is not in fact of the people. I think first of the *nature* that enfolded my days then and filled them so intensely that as an adult one can scarcely understand it. The mounds of strawberries, the fields of liverwort, the meadows full of cowslips, the billberry patches, the woods with the pink bells of linnea in the moss, the pastures round Näs, where we knew every stick and stone, the water-lilies in the streams, the ditches, slopes and trees—all these I remember better than the people. ("I Remember . . . ," 167)

The beauty of nature continues to touch Lindgren deeply. Thus, a breathtaking sunrise observed from a train in Dalarna on a cold winter's morning resounded in her soul and awakened feelings and associations that led to the conception of *The Brothers Lionheart*. Lindgren's affection for and closeness to nature, which goes far beyond mere appreciation, also become apparent within the narrative itself. Descriptions of nature—though short in the books for younger readers in order not to test their patience—are among the most beautiful, highly poetic passages in her books.

Her later writings, especially, contain gems of natural description. Lindgren uses them not just as scenery or stage setting. Instead, she makes them an integral part of the narrative as expressions and reinforcements of a protagonist's deep emotions. The landscape of Småland and the Stockholm archipelago, where she spent most summers after moving to Stockholm in 1926, form the physical and emotional backdrop for most of her books. The dreamland or paradise through which Rasmus wanders with Paradise-Oskar and to which Mio, the Brothers Lionheart, and Mattias and Anna from *Sunnanäng* (South Wind Meadow) are drawn is a sublimation of a warm and sunny day in Småland. Love of nature resounds in all of Lindgren's books, from *The Children of Noisy Village* to *Ronia, the Robber's Daughter.*

The nimble and enterprising young Astrid Ericsson lived in tune with nature and on nature's premises. The farm as well as the surrounding fields and woods became a familiar and exhilarating playground for her, holding real dangers and delights. She could climb trees as easily as her brainchild Pippi Longstocking. Even in her seventies Astrid Lindgren had lost neither the ability nor the desire to climb a tree. There is a snapshot of two elderly and enterprising ladies, Astrid Lindgren and her good friend Elsa Olenius, about to climb a tree. Admittedly, this photograph was probably staged, but it expresses the thrill of heights and the desire to cast off the earthbound state.

Lindgren's delight in the thrill of danger is reflected in various balancing acts performed by her fictional characters on tightropes, school roofs, barns, and trees. The sight of the "owl tree" by her childhood home still fills the adult Lindgren with memories of the sensations of climbing. "And each time I see its rugged trunk I can remember in my hands and feet which moves were needed and which bulges one stepped on in order to come up and how it felt on the soles of my feet" (*Mina påhitt,* 263). This hollow tree, Lindgren says, is the prototype for Pippi's climbing tree. It reappears in *Noisy Village,* for here Bill, in a grand experiment, makes the owls hatch a chicken egg for him, just as Astrid's brother Gunnar had done.

"Stones and trees were almost as close to us as living beings and it was nature that sheltered and nourished our games and dreams," Lindgren recalls ("I Remember . . . ," 167). She opens her essay "Are There Different Trees?" with Karin Boye's statement, "For me a tree is as much alive as you are—a personality." She recalls her grandmother's cherry tree, "the like of which could only have existed in paradise, no place else" (*Mina påhitt,* 255). She vividly recalls the intense pleasure she experienced as a child, getting up early in the morning before everyone else and walking barefoot in the grass, still wet with morning dew, to find a few shiny green Astrachan apples underneath a big tree. Pleasure, enchantment, consolation, and excitement—all these experiences she derived from nature in childhood—have found their way into her books, where they are imperceptibly interwoven with the romantic discourse about childhood. The child becomes a mediator between nature and culture, and the child's state of oneness with nature enchants an increasingly disenchanted world.

Nature provides Lindgren with an escape from all that is wrong and sick in civilized life, and she uses this topos deliberately, like Rousseau, as an invocation against the alienation of modern life. Loss of nature parallels the loss of childhood, and the modern scientific mind's objectification and neglect of nature is blamed for the loss of wholeness and wisdom in our lives. Lindgren's special relationship with nature and her true love and respect for it, dating back to her childhood days, are revealed in her essay about trees in which she cites a poem by Edith Södergran. In the essay Södergran's childhood trees reproach her for having become an adult and "unworthy" because "the key to all secrets lies in the grass by the raspberry bushes" (*Mina påhitt,* 262).

Lindgren still claims to hold the key to the "secret garden" of childhood. The sublimated memories of her childhood, memories of people and nature, which forge a productive tension between vitality and rootedness, make up the blueprints from which she creates the models for a more livable life. This childhood utopia reverberates in her realistically colored narratives about Emil, Rasmus, Mischievous Meg, and the Noisy Village and Scarecrow Island children, as well as in her fantastic stories about Pippi and Karlsson. She evokes this utopia in her early fairy tales and in the novels *Mio, My Son, The Brothers Lionheart,* and *Ronia, the Robber's Daughter,* and her love of it is reflected in her social activism. A line can be drawn from Lindgren's early and enduring love of nature to her fervent support for ecological and animal rights issues later in life.

Stories and the Written Word

For Maria in *My Nightingale Is Singing,* pleasure, enchantment, and salvation come as much through culture as through nature, or rather through their mutual enrichment. On one of her begging excursions to the parsonage, something wonderful happens to Maria, Lindgren tells us. "Then and there, in the parson's kitchen, Maria received something beautiful for her heart's comfort. Someone was reading a story aloud to the parson's children in the next room . . . words flooded through the half-open door, words so beautiful that she began to tremble. She had never known before that words could be beautiful, but now she knew, and they sank into her soul like morning dew on the fields in the summer" (10). The beauty of the words instills in Maria a longing so great that it enchants both her and those around her.

Lindgren points to an equally remarkable experience she had as a young child around five years of age, when Edith, the daughter of a farmhand, read her a fairy tale in her parents' kitchen, an incident that left an indelible mark in her memory. The effect of this tale "moved my childish soul in a way that's never stopped," as Lindgren puts it. "Until then I was a little animal sucking in only that which was *nature* with my eyes, ears, and all my senses" (*Mina påhitt,* 240). The sudden awareness of the power and magic of words became a love affair with stories and books and the whole realm of the imaginary early on in her life.

Her love of books was a very tangible one to begin with. When Astrid Ericsson bought her first book, she wondered why she did not faint for pure joy: "I can still remember how these books smelled when they arrived fresh from the printer. Yes, I started by smelling them, and there was no lovelier scent in all the world. It was full of foretaste and anticipation."[10] Britta, Anna, and Lisa in Noisy Village share the same kind of pleasure and anticipation on the way home from school: "Britta took her book out of her schoolbag and smelled it. She let all of us smell it. New books smell so good that you can tell how much fun it's going to be to read them."[11] All three succumb to the lure of the story and finish the book on their way home, although Britta had wanted to save it for Christmas Eve. Based on her own experiences, Lindgren asserts that there is no substitute for the book to make a child's imagination grow.

As a girl, Astrid Ericsson became a voracious reader. From the Trojan Wars to Robinson Crusoe and Jules Verne, from Huck Finn to Anne of Green Gables, she imbibed just about everything the local library provided and she could get her hands on. About Anne of Green Gables she remembers, "Oh, my unforgettable one, forever, you will be riding the cart with Matthew Cuthbert beneath the flowering apple trees of Avonlea! How I lived with that girl!" Astrid and her siblings not only read, they actively recreated, they *lived* the books. "A whole summer, my sisters and I played at Anne of Green Gables in the big sawdust heap at the sawmill. I was Diana Barry, and the pond at the manure heap was the Dark Reflecting Waves" (*Something,* 128). "To think," Lindgren writes, "that there is a time in a person's life when she reads with such intensity and devotion" (*Mina påhitt*, 242). A child's ability to become completely absorbed in a book and to take a naive, uncritical approach to it still fascinates Lindgren and is one of the reasons she writes for children.

There is a small yet decisive step between the retelling and adaptation of stories that takes place in child's play and the actual creation of stories out of the preexisting tapestry of narratives. Lindgren not only read and reenacted stories, she could also tell and write them. Her genius was soon noticed in school, where she was jokingly nicknamed Vimmerby's Selma Lagerlöf, the by-then famous author of *Nils Holgersson's Wonderful Journey*, published in 1907, the year of Lindgren's birth. As it happened, Astrid Lindgren did follow in her footsteps.

Troubled Years: The End of Childhood

But to begin with, partly out of shame and partly out of spite, Lindgren vowed that she would never write a book. She kept her word until 1944, even though, as she admitted later, she had felt the urge somewhere deep down inside. What finally made her change her mind, she reports, was the weather. The following anecdote has been told so many times that it has become part of the Lindgren lore. As such, it is still worth retelling here. I will let the author speak for herself:

> In 1941 my seven year old daughter Karin had pneumonia. Every night when I sat by her bed, she would beg me to tell her a story. One evening, completely exhausted, I asked her what she would like to hear, and she answered, "Tell me a story about Pippi Longstrump (Longstocking)!" (she made up the name right on the spot). I didn't ask who Pippi Longstocking was, I just started telling a story about her. And because she had such a funny name, she turned out to be a funny little girl. Pippi was a hit with Karin and later with her friends; I had to tell the story over and over again.
>
> One snowy March evening in 1944 I was taking a walk in central Stockholm. Under the newly-fallen snow was a layer of slippery ice, and I fell, spraining my ankle. It was quite a while before I was up and about again, and to pass the time I started writing down the Pippi stories (in shorthand—I still always write my books first in shorthand, which I know from my secretarial days). ("Lindgren Talks," 3)

Two and a half decades had passed between Lindgren's intense reading as a child and her first attempt at her writing. Some years in between had been difficult ones indeed, and it may be that childhood seemed even brighter in retrospect because it was followed by a dark and troublesome period. Lindgren never tires of telling her readers that her childhood at Näs was a happy one. This statement has been reiterated so many times that it has become a cliché. Her childhood memories have come to merge imperceptibly with the childhood she depicts in the Noisy Village series, where the narrator's selection process eliminates much boredom and drudgery and instead concentrates on fun-filled summer vacation days and special occasions. Bearing in mind Freudian theories about repression and the denial of painful childhood experiences, readers and critics started doubting the one-sidedness of Lindgren's assurances and have uncovered a darker side of sadness and melancholy in her stories. Despair and despondency form the point of departure for the fantasies of Maria, Mio, Malin, and Karl Lionheart, and the dark side of life—in the shape of villains, rogues, poverty, meanness, and dangers—is a counterpoint to the carefree playfulness and naive trust that dominate most of her realistic books. In this blend of melancholy and playful, childish exuberance lies much of the magic quality of Lindgren's books.

Certainly, Lindgren's childhood was not altogether cheery, bright, and happy. But seen against the background of hardships she witnessed later in life—both her own and those of others—her childhood stands in positive relief as a time in which she was allowed to live to the fullest. Yet the darker years, following childhood, have left an indelible mark on her literary production. Puberty for Lindgren was the death of childhood, but not the birth of reason.

The death of childhood at the brink of adolescence took Astrid Ericsson by surprise. She recalls the shock and the sense of loss she experienced one spring when she could no longer play with other children and realized that she had outgrown childhood. Later in life she dismissed her teenage years as a period when she had nothing but crazy ideas in her head. It was a time of revolt against the unquestioning obedience that had been expected of her. She became a "flapper" (*jazzböna*) and cut her hair short, unheard of for a farmer's daughter. "The teens were only a state of existence, soundless and lifeless. I was often melancholy," Lindgren recalls (Strömstedt, 184). Although she is generous with recollections from her childhood, memories of her middle and late teens are sparse and lackluster.

While working on her first children's books, Lindgren discovered that writing was one way of reclaiming her childhood. She realized "it was as much fun to write books as it was to read them" (*Mina påhitt*, 245). For Lindgren, writing for and about children works somewhat like the chililug pills that Pippi, Tommy, and Annika swallow at the end of *Pippi in the South Seas* in order not to grow up. Writing enables Lindgren to revisit and relive her childhood experiences as she immerses herself in the fictional world she creates, and in this world she stays eternally young, whereas in real life grown-ups cannot play and have fun. Despite the pills, expressing the fictional children's and the real author's desire to remain a child forever, the very end of *Pippi in the South Seas,* the last of the Pippi books, clearly represents a good-bye to childhood. This good-bye is delivered, so typically for Lindgren, with a comforting reassurance that childhood can live on in a transformed state. Pippi, the wild spirit of childhood, will always stay with Tommy and Annika in the realm of make-believe, that is, the place where a simple pea can become a chililug pill:

> Pippi was inside. She would always be there. That was a comforting thought. The years would go by, but Pippi and Tommy and Annika would not grow up. That is, of course, if the strength hadn't gone out of the chililug pills. There would be new springs and summers, new autumns and winters, but their games would go on. Tomorrow they would build a snow hut and make a ski slope from the roof of Villa Villekulla, and when spring came they would climb the hollow oak where soda pop spouted up. . . . And the most wonderful, comforting thought was that Pippi would always be in Villa Villekulla.[12]

The chililug pills have not lost their potency. Generations of young readers have followed Pippi into the realm of make-believe and are likely to do so for quite a while yet. On a realistic level the last volume about Pippi ends on a melancholy note that foreshadows the end of childhood for Tommy and Annika. It is a dark, cold winter night. Not aware of being observed, Pippi sits all alone at the table with her head propped against her arms and stares at the little flickering flame of a candle in front of her. She is far removed from Tommy and Annika, and no contact can be established. " 'If she would only look in this direction we would wave to her,' said Tommy. But Pippi continued to stare straight ahead with a dreamy look. Then she blew out the light" (125).

When Astrid Ericsson finished school, with excellent grades and proficiency in three foreign languages (German, English, and French), she got a job at the local newspaper, *Wimmerby Tidningen,* because she had a talent for writing. There she wrote reviews and articles of local interest and gained some insight into the world of politics. She read Charles Dickens, August Strindberg, Knut Hamsun, and Erich Maria Remarque and moved yet another step toward adulthood when she discovered that

the world was not the way it should be. At nineteen, Astrid Ericsson left
her hometown for Stockholm. She was pregnant, unmarried, and unwill-
ing to marry the baby's father, which at that time was socially unacceptable, even disastrous, in the small-town atmosphere of Vimmerby. She
decided to make it on her own and raise her son, Lars, who was born in
1926, as a single mother, a courageous step. Because she was initially
unable to support both herself and her child, however, she had to give up
her son to a Danish foster mother for the first years of his life. These early
Stockholm years were hard. She took courses in stenography and soon
found a position as a secretary, but her salary provided her with a meager
living. For a long time, she felt devastatingly alone. Her income barely
covered her food, her rent, and the longed-for train rides to Copenhagen
to visit her son. Often enough, toward the end of the pay period, she was
forced to go hungry. No wonder Knut Hamsun's novel *Hunger* provided
one of her most intense reading experiences at that time. She could truly
identify with the narrator, who observes, "How gaily and lightly these
people I met carried their radiant heads, and swung themselves through
life as through a ball-room! There was no sorrow in a single look I met,
no burden on any shoulder, perhaps not even a clouded thought, not a little hidden pain in any of the happy souls. And I, walking in the very
midst of these people, young and newly-fledged as I was, had already forgotten the very look of happiness."[13]

In 1930 Astrid Eriksson attempted to keep Lars with her in
Stockholm while she was working full time, but that, too, proved very
difficult, so her parents took him in until 1931. That year she married
Sture Lindgren, an executive with the Royal Swedish Automobile Club,
where she had worked writing travelogues and motoring guides. In
1934, her daughter Karin was born, and, true to her conviction that
small children need a parent at home, Lindgren became a full-time
homemaker.

Five Decades Devoted to Children's Fiction

Now and then, Lindgren took on secretarial and writing jobs, but she
had given up thoughts of a career for the time being. In 1944, however,
things took an abrupt turn, when she started writing down the stories
about Pippi Longstocking that were so popular with her children and
their friends. She sent the completed manuscript to Bonniers, then the
largest publishing house in Stockholm, where it was refused. But the
writing experience had whetted her appetite. Jotting down the episodes

about Pippi released the floodgates of her creativity. The same year she
entered a girl's book competition sponsored by the then small
Stockholm publishing house Rabén and Sjögren, submitting a much
more traditional manuscript called *Britt Mari lättar sitt hjärta*
(Confidences of Britt-Mari). With this entry she won second prize, much
to the chagrin of Hans Rabén, who had hoped for a known writer to
boost the image of the publishing house. Little did he know what a
boost Lindgren's submission to the next year's children's book competition would be. In a revised and tidied-up version, *Pippi Longstocking*
(1945) became an immediate success and was soon followed by *Pippi
Goes on Board* (1946) and *Pippi in the South Seas* (1948). The Pippi books
have by now reached what for Sweden is the astronomically high sales
figure of 1 million (in a country of 8 million inhabitants), and the rights
have been sold to publishers in fifty countries.

In 1946, Rabén and Sjögren announced a new competition for detective stories for young people. This time Astrid Lindgren shared first prize
with *Bill Bergson Master Detective* (*Mästerdetektiven Blomkvist*), and that
was the last time she entered a writing competition. She needed no more
incentives. From the late 1940s to the 1970s, she wrote at least one
book a year, all of them published by Rabén and Sjögren. She became
editor and head of the children's book department there in 1946, a position she held until 1970. By then Rabén and Sjögren had become the
largest publisher of children's books in Sweden, and it is no secret that
Lindgren had a large share in this development.

With Pippi, Lindgren reached instantaneous fame at home and soon
thereafter abroad as well. The Pippi books were followed in tight
sequence by a great number and variety of books, such as the Bill
Bergson mystery series, the Noisy Village books for younger children,
Karlsson-on-the-Roof, short fairy and fantasy tales, and the long fairy tale
Mio, My Son. With each successive book Lindgren consolidated her fame
and popularity. She was a well-established writer when she received the
Hans Christian Andersen Award in 1958, the highest international
recognition bestowed on a children's book author. Some of her best
work—the Emil and Madicken books, her great novels *The Brothers
Lionheart* and *Ronia, the Robber's Daughter*—were still to come. Her acceptance speech for the Andersen Award was a tribute to children's books in
general and to those aspects of children's fiction she valued most.
Reading her arguments in defense of "good" books in conjunction with
her narratives about her own childhood, it becomes evident how deeply
her thoughts are anchored in her own early reading experience:

Present-day children see films, listen to the radio, watch television, read serial strips—this can all be quite pleasant, but it has very little to do with imagination. A child, alone with his book, creates for himself, somewhere in the secret recesses of the soul, his own pictures which surpass all else. Such pictures are necessary for humanity. On that day that the children's imagination no longer has the strength to create them, on that day humanity will be the poorer. All great things that have happened in the world, happened first of all in someone's imagination, and the aspect of the world of tomorrow depends largely on the extent of the power of imagination in those who are just now learning to read. This is why children must have books, and why there must be people . . . who really care what kind of books are put into the children's hands. (*Something*, 130)

When Lindgren made these comments in 1958, the culture of images was only slowly beginning to encroach upon the culture of print. As the visual media have grown in importance, so has Lindgren's acceptance of them, as well as her realization that pictures can also stir the imagination, although they do it differently. Most of her books have been made into films for the big and the small screen, and Lindgren wrote most of the scripts and participated actively in the books' adaptation to the screen. "Children have an obsession with images and pictures," Lindgren said in a 1987 interview, remembering the forceful impression some pictures made on her when she was young.[14] These experiences, too, have found their way into Lindgren's fiction. Two pictures in grandfather's room have a powerful hold on Lisa, Lindgren's fictional alter ego in Noisy Village. One is a dramatic depiction of Jonah in the stomach of the whale, and the other shows a snake that has escaped from a zoo and is squeezing a man to death. Lisa responds to their drama and sensationalism with, "Maybe they're not exactly pretty, but they're scary and exciting" (*Children of Noisy Village*, 35). In *Mardie's Adventures,* Mardie and Lisbet are also fascinated by "the awful pictures over Ida's bed," which Mardie nonetheless considers "the best pictures I've seen in my life" (64). The girls shiver at the depiction of a fire-spitting mountain and people running to escape the fire and at the other, equally "dreadful" one of men drowning in a flood of brandy.

While Lisa, Mardie, and Lisbet experience the thrill and drama of the pictures vicariously and from a safe distance, other protagonists enter the illusionary realm of the pictures. In her fantasy tale "Junker Nils av Eka" (Squire Nils of Eka), Nils, the oldest son of a crofter's family, is fascinated by the picture of a beautiful castle on the lowered window shade, one of his family's treasures. Nils is hovering between life and death. Borderlines between the real and the imaginary break down, and, inspired by the picture, he enters its heroic world of the quest romance. In his dreams he does battle for his lord and eventually sacrifices his life, but in real life he recovers from his illness as the ominous call of the cuckoo bird slowly vanishes into the distance.[15]

Lindgren says she likes seeing her protagonists in moving pictures, "especially if the films are as good as Tage Danielsson's film about Ronia, the Robber's Daughter." But she adds, "I do not see *my* books on the screen, it is true. I see something else." She continues, as if to convince herself, "No, pictures are very good for children, because then they can see how things look. Not all of them have such imagination that they can see what I saw when I sat and wrote the stories" (Rosenqvist, 5).

Nevertheless, the children who come to know Lindgren's stories on film are missing out on much. While reading, children use their imagination to visually enrich the text. Film, by joining image and narrative, limits the viewer's creative impulse. "When a child reads a book," Lindgren writes, "he or she has to create his or her own pictures, which are more lovely and beautiful than anything you can ever see on TV" (*Something*, 133). Because of its constant presence and ready availability, Lindgren finds television damaging on the whole. She admits willingly that she grew up in a world different from the one populated by today's children in Sweden or in any rich, postindustrial nation and that her childhood experiences are a thing of the past. This may also explain Lindgren's move away from realistic stories toward heroic epics and fantasy tales—especially for older children—in her late authorship.

With her imagination, curiosity, and sense of wonder she can still relate to children of the 1990s. She admits, however, that she can no longer speak to adolescents. "I can't write for teenagers now—I don't know enough about them. They're completely unlike the Bergson children—there's no resemblance at all" (*Something*, 133). Few of today's teenagers (or even preteens), reared on *Beverly Hills 90210, Melrose Place,* and *The Simpsons,* could relate to the games of make-believe practiced by the teenage protagonists in Lindgren's detective stories about Bill Bergson, published in the 1940s and 1950s. These books have aged disproportionately and are now read by a much younger age group than originally intended. The games of older children are imbricated with cultural codes and expressions of contemporary popular culture to a greater degree than those of younger children. For that reason these books have not traveled as well as those for younger readers.

What Lindgren seems to resent most about image culture encroaching on print culture is its discouragement of active, creative imagination on the part of the viewer and its promotion of pacifying consumerism. In the talk I had with her about this issue she expressed disdain for the superficial glossiness of the "trash culture," whose pernicious influence she wants to counteract with her books and films. Here, the adult Lindgren is at odds with her younger spokespersons Lisa and Mardie, who admired cheap calendar prints, then the equivalent of today's popular commercial images. Yet there is a difference, which resides in the intensity and overwhelming presence of readymade images today.

Against the flood of images Lindgren sets the rich world of narrative with its roots in the distant past of oral culture and modern literary traditions. All of Lindgren's books—and she has experimented with a great variety of genres—are written with one unmistakable voice. Its integral elements are her intellectual strength, her compassion and humor, and her stylistic sensitivity. These traits form a unique alloy with the passion, boundless imagination, and strict moral demands of the child within, and, above all, with her intense childhood experiences. Because of the intensity of her narrative, Lindgren's texts are still compelling, even when measured against the glossiness of the image culture. Based on her own personal experience, it is not surprising to see Lindgren defend the idea that books are the primary source of growth for the child's imagination, a notion that runs like a red thread through all her statements on this matter, right up to the present.

The continued popularity of her books testifies to the fact that Lindgren's stories engage the imagination of her readers. Far from being escapist, her stories are anchored in everyday concerns, openly or covertly addressing ethical questions and fostering critical thinking. These qualities have certainly contributed to the number of awards and prizes Lindgren received for her writings over the years. In 1971 she received the Swedish Academy's Gold Medal, in 1975 the Dutch Silver Pen Award, in 1985 the Danish Karen Blixen Award, in 1986 the Swedish Selma Lagerlöf Award, and in 1987 the Russian Leo Tolstoy International Gold Medal, just to mention some of the more prestigious ones. Many prizes, like the Peace Prize of the German Booksellers' Association (1978), the Polish Janusz Korczak Prize (1979), the Swedish Dag Hammarskjöld Award (1984), and the American Albert Schweitzer Medal (1989), do not primarily recognize her literary achievement but her humanitarian engagement, which has become more pronounced and less confined to her fiction later in her life.

Lindgren never remarried after her husband's death in 1958 and she stayed on in the family apartment once the children had grown up and moved out. Although she has made millions in royalties and could have afforded a fairly luxurious life-style (or a well-appointed home in Switzerland or on the French Riviera in order to evade the exceedingly high marginal taxes in Sweden, as many rich and famous Swedes have chosen to do), she chose to pay her taxes faithfully and to remain in the same unpretentious apartment on Dalagatan in Stockholm, where she has lived since the 1930s. Her adult life itself has in many ways been an extension of her formative years. Honesty, hard work, and a simple, frugal life-style characterized life on her parent's farm. During the twenty-four years Lindgren worked as an editor at Rabén and Sjögren, she spent her early mornings writing her own books, film manuscripts, theater adaptations, radio plays, lectures, and correspondence. Afternoons she spent at her editorial job with the publishing house and evenings with her family.

Most summers were spent with family and friends on a small island in the archipelago outside of Stockholm, where the Lindgren family had bought one of the many typical wooden summer homes. Lindgren would take advantage of the peace and quiet at dawn and write many chapters of her books sitting on the small balcony overlooking other skerries in the Baltic. It took some thirty summers in Stockholm's archipelago, however, before she felt comfortable enough to use the life and landscape of the Stockholm archipelago as the setting for *Seacrow Island*. Lindgren's most basic precept for her creative activity is "truthfulness" in the artistic sense of the word. As a writer she remains true to herself, her notions, and emotions. Each story she tells presupposes a deep personal involvement. Her books are not the result of study and uninvolved observation or simply faithfulness of reproduction. She writes, as it were, with all her senses, and the truthfulness she talks about is a distillation of stimuli from the world around her that she transforms into her own voice. Thus, the antimaterialist undercurrent in her prose, for which the Melkerson family in *Seacrow Island* is an obvious example, is based on personal conviction.

Champion of the Voiceless and Powerless

Lindgren practices what she preaches. With her unassuming and straightforward manner, her courage, integrity, and compassion, she is not only viewed as Sweden's premier storyteller but is also highly

If pigs could speak up for themselves . . . Illustration by Björn Berg from *Min ko vill ha roligt* (My cow wants to have fun).

respected as a human being and citizen. She has gained this respect largely through her open political engagement since her retirement from Rabén and Sjögren in 1972. But, in effect, her humanitarian political engagement dates back to World War II, although it then assumed a rather clandestine character. For several years she worked for an organization that secretly helped German Jews emigrate, and she confided her outrage at the Nazi regime and cruelties committed during the war to the diary she kept during the war. All of her stories, in one way or another, condemn violence, oppression, and the abuse of power.

Lindgren has even used the same strategy and stylistic means in her fiction and her public protests. As an author of children's books she slipped into the trickster's or the underdog's role innumerable times; she has employed exactly the same technique in her newspaper polemics. The revealing, liberating gaze from below proved to be suitable tool in the limelight of political quarrels. She was no stranger to the media when she launched her first public protest in the 1970s. For years she had worked off and on for newspapers and magazines, and in the 1950s she was a rather famous radio personality, appearing on programs for children as well as for adults.

Her first step into the public arena as a renowned author occurred in 1976. In March of that year, after a 102 percent tax had been levied on her income, Lindgren published a satirical fairy tale about the witch Pomperipossa in Monismania in a large Stockholm daily. The tale contained biting criticism of the ruling Social Democrats and found a resounding echo among the public. The ensuing debate was credited by some with bringing to an end the forty-year rule of the Social Democrats in that fall's elections. What Lindgren attacked was not so much the steep taxes—although the absurdity of her situation helped make a point—as a thoroughly bureaucratized, self-serving party apparatus that no longer resembled the Social Democratic movement she remembered from her youth and whose ideals of true democracy and social justice she cherishes. The government at that time did not recognize the tale's explosive power; finance minister Gunnar Sträng advised Lindgren to stick to what she knew, namely, writing tales for children. Lindgren—as little at a loss for words as Pippi Longstocking—suggested that they trade jobs. To her the reason was clear: Sträng was not good at arithmetic, but she considered him to be very good at telling fairy tales.

Lindgren's refreshing disrespect for authority is based on her deep respect for humanity. In a conversation with Sybil Gräfin Schönfeldt in June 1984, Lindgren reaffirmed her egalitarian attitude: "I don't care. It makes no difference to me whether I meet a queen or a cleaning lady. I can't judge people by what they are. I see them as the children they once were, and I am Astrid from Småland, a farmer's daughter from beginning to end. . . . That is also the reason why I do not regard (important) people as anything special."[16] Lindgren's view from an odd angle, or rather from the perspective of a child, reveals the emperor's new clothes. It penetrates right to the core of people, instantly deflates any pretentiousness, and erases the barriers erected by status and prestige.

The farmer's daughter from Småland, who by the 1980s was not only the nation's number one storyteller, but its conscience as well, took on the government again in the spring of 1985. Her open letters to the minister of agriculture protesting the mistreatment of farm animals appeared in major Stockholm newspapers. This time, having learned a lesson from 1976, the government listened. Her three years of public engagement in animal rights issues resulted in "Lex Lindgren," the Animal Protection Act, promulgated in June 1988. The law, however, did not meet Lindgren's expectations; many of her demands had been watered down. "Should I be flattered that they've named this toothless law after me?" she asked.[17]

Nevertheless, much had been gained since the spring of 1985, when veterinarian Kristina Forslund, along with millions of other Swedes, read Lindgren's tale about a fiery, lovesick cow published in Stockholm's largest daily, *Dagens Nyheter*. While the anecdotal tale itself seems rather mundane (about a cow going out in search of a bull in the middle of a snowstorm), its effect was somewhat remarkable, in that it made the reader consider the feelings of the animal. What began as a somewhat tongue-in-cheek anecdote against artificial insemination soon grew into a full-fledged campaign for a decent life for domestic animals. Once Lindgren, under the guidance of Kristina Forslund, had familiarized herself with the dismal conditions under which factory animals were kept and slaughtered in large-scale operations, and once she became aware of the extent and severity of animal abuse hidden from public view, she could not be stopped. Letter after letter appeared in *Dagens Nyheter* and *Expressen* against legalized and institutionalized cruelty against domestic animals based on greed and shortsightedness.

Rabén and Sjögren published a collection of these letters in 1990 under the title *Min ko vill ha roligt* (My cow wants to have fun). This book does not necessarily distinguish itself by its literary quality. It is a report of work in progress and, as such, it is not as carefully composed as her other books. The unifying elements in the collection are Lindgren's persistence, devotion to the cause, and her skillful use of satire. In one letter, composed as a fairy tale for grown-ups, the farmer's daughter from Näs talks about a dream she had. God comes down to earth and realizes that its people have gravely abused their God-given power over animals. Being as appalled and as helpless as Brecht's gods in *The Good Woman of Setzuan*, God dissolves into smoke and leaves the responsibility for change to the minister of agriculture, to whom Lindgren had been sending her message all along. In her dream, the minister promises to do what he can to clean up animal husbandry in Sweden, to which Lindgren adds, "preferably before the 1988 elections," just to be sure her message is heard. The letter, first published 23 March 1988 in *Expressen*, ends in typical Lindgren fashion, never giving up hope, even when the odds are stacked against you: "Just then I woke up. Alack and alas, of course I had been dreaming. It was all just a dream! But who knows? Maybe it will turn out to be a dream that comes true? Hoping in all confidence, Astrid Lindgren."

If we continue to obey the laws of efficiency and profitability in animal husbandry and if we objectify animals by treating them as production units, Lindgren argues, nothing will change, and animals will continue to suffer. Pigs will continue to bite off each other's tails, and chickens will continue to pluck out each other's feathers. Her answer is clear: technology must be adapted to the needs of the animals, not the reverse. Only with a caring attitude toward all living creatures can this earth become a more peaceful and humane place.

As with her engagement in the rights and well-being of children, Lindgren bases her animal-rights protests on personal experience. The somewhat idealized small-scale animal husbandry she witnessed in her childhood on her family's and neighbors' farms, where most farmers loved, respected, and cared for their animals, forms the concrete basis of her protest and continues to be her source of inspiration. Lindgren does admit that not everything was rosy then and that there is no way leading back to small-scale preindustrial farming. What she finds more than anything else in those bygone days is something much more fundamental: a basic respect for life that should remain the guiding principle even in large-scale operations.

Lindgren's concern for the humane treatment of animals can be found in all of her work. Pippi, for example, gets furious at a farmer who mistreats his oxen, and—in her usual manner of confronting villains—throws him high up in the air to teach him a lesson. Like all of Pippi's victims, the farmer mends his ways. Lindgren does not have the brawn of her brainchild, but with persistence and wit she managed in an equally playful-serious way to stun the agricultural establishment and politicians alike. In an almost fairy tale-like development—one she had envisioned in her dream—she brought about a change in Swedish agricultural policies.

Lindgren has stepped into the public arena with open letters on other occasions and for other causes. Relying on the weight of her prominence but never officially claiming more than common sense and a child's unspoiled sensitivity, she has reached out to those in power, mindful of her early realization that everyone is no more or less human. Yet we should all try to follow Pippi's adage that the more powerful we are, the better we should act, indirectly recalled in Lindgren's address upon receiving the German Peace Prize in 1978:

> I can still remember very well what a shock it was for me—I was very young at the time—when it became clear to me that the men who were

Lindgren's protests against the mistreatment of farm animals led to a new Swedish farm animal protection law in 1989. Illustration by Björn Berg from *Min ko vill ha roligt* (My cow wants to have fun).

governing the world were not superior beings with supernatural talents and divine wisdom, that they were people with the same human weaknesses as I. But they had power and could at any time make fateful decisions depending on the impulses and forces which they were influenced by. If the circumstances were particularly unfortunate, this could lead to war, merely because a single person was obsessed by power or revenge, by vanity or avarice, or—and this seems to be most common—by blind belief in violence as the most effective remedy in all situations. Accordingly, a good and level-headed individual could occasionally prevent catastrophes, for the very reason that he was good and level-headed and renounced violence. (*Something,* 133)

Now in her eighties, Lindgren is still going strong despite impaired eyesight, which has left her virtually blind and makes work and daily life cumbersome. Projects keep piling up on her desk. Requests for adaptations of her books to the stage and screen keep coming in. In the late 1980s her early fairy tales were turned into a series of short films, and in 1990 *Emil* was performed at Kungliga Dramatiska Teatern in Stockholm, one of Sweden's most prestigious stages. Open letters and editorials in the Swedish press about the need for better animal protection laws have consumed much of her time over the last several years. Throughout her life, Lindgren has had a keen eye for injustices and exploitation. Her children's books, however, remain the most eloquent testimony to her cause. They document her deep concern for the welfare of every living being on this planet, especially those who are likely victims of the abuse of power because they cannot speak up for themselves.

Ready for another prank, Emil strolls through the småland landscape with his friend
Alfred, the farmhand at Katthult. Illustration by Björn Berg from *Nya hyss av Emil i
Lönneberga* (*Emil's Pranks*)

Chapter Two

The Småland Books:
From Noisy Village to Emil's Pranks

My Småland—is it not a land to be loved?
—Astrid Lindgren, *Mitt Småland*

Intensity of Experience

This chapter is devoted to those books most immediately and concretely related to Astrid Lindgren's childhood experiences in Småland. Because of their common theme and background, I have chosen to group them together and to refer to them as the Småland books. Included are the books about Noisy Village (*The Children of Noisy Village* [1947] and *Happy Times in Noisy Village* [1949]),[1] Emil (*Emil in the Soup Tureen* [1963], *Emil's Pranks* [1966], *Emil and Piggy Beast* [1970]),[2] Bill Bergson and his gang (*Bill Bergson, Master Detective* [1946], *Bill Bergson Lives Dangerously* [1951], *Bill Bergson and the White Rose Rescue* [1953]), and Mischievous Meg (*Mischievous Meg* [1960]—translated as *Mardie's Adventures* in England—and *Mardie to the Rescue* [1976]—translated and published only in England), as well as *Rasmus and the Vagabond* (1956). The story collections *Kajsa Kavat* (Brenda Brave) and *Sunnanäng* (South Wind Meadow) belong here as well, but since neither collection has been translated into English, I will touch on them only briefly.

The Småland books span Lindgren's writing career from the 1940s to the 1980s. Thus, Lindgren has repeatedly and over a long span of time returned to this setting, which seems closest and dearest to her heart. Her first Småland books are the detective stories about Bill Bergson and the Noisy Village books. They appeared in close succession, sandwiched between the fantastic stories about Pippi Longstocking. The books about Noisy Village are among her favorites, along with the Emil and Meg stories. Although the Småland books differ in the age group they address and belong to different genres and categories, they all have one important thing in common: a concrete historical setting dating back to the

author's own childhood. All are based on recollections of events, emotions, and local lore from Lindgren's childhood in rural and small-town
Småland.

Except for the mystery stories about Bill Bergson and Rasmus the
Vagabond, the Småland books consist of loosely connected episodes
about growing up in Småland about a century ago. They portray fun-
filled days and exciting childhood adventures in vivid colors and strong
brush strokes. For the most part, readers participate in the joys, games,
and excitements of the young protagonists' ordinary daily lives, summer
and winter, on holidays and workdays. Play and imagination dominate
the narrative, which is nonetheless firmly placed within a specific and
recognizable cultural-historical setting. In Lindgren's fictionalized childhood recollections millions of readers have thus been able to vicariously
relive parts of her childhood, altered and embellished as it is by the
mechanisms of the author's memory, the dictates of her creative impulse,
and the demands of self-censorship. They are transplanted to a different
world, yet meet fictional characters with whose feelings and desires they
can identify.

"How can a rascal from Småland like Emil speak directly to Japanese
children . . . and how can the life of six happy children which does not
contain more drama than pulling out a loose tooth or haunting each
other in the barn become a favorite reading for Western European children, who are used to the strong impulses of modern mass culture?"[3]
Lena Törnqvist posed this question in a tribute to Astrid Lindgren on
her eightieth birthday in November 1987, referring to the popularity of
the Emil books and the Noisy Village series. A close look at the recurring themes and stylistic techniques may provide at least a partial answer
to Törnqvist's question about their continued and widespread popularity.
In an essay that appears in *Mina påhitt,* "A Small Chat with a Future
Children's Book Author," Lindgren brings the novice writer into her creative workshop.[4] Lindgren's advice to the novice is not meant to be read
as a manual on how to become a good writer, a process forever shrouded
in secrets. Inspiration and creativity can be neither taught nor controlled. "To be honest," Lindgren asserts, "I believe one becomes a writer
the same way one becomes an Arab or Chinese" (*Mina påhitt,* 248).
Nevertheless, she suggests some elementary rules all writers for children
should follow. They should know that while children have limited experience, they often "know more than one suspects" (*Mina påhitt,* 249).
Content and language should form a harmonious unity. Her advice to
the novice, based on nearly a quarter-century of manuscript evaluation

and editing for Rabén & Sjögren, seems simple: "Write freely straight from your heart about anything you want and however you would like to express it" (*Mina påhitt,* 250).

Most important to the author is freedom, Lindgren contends; freedom to find one's very own voice and to break away from prevailing conventions. "[W]ithout freedom the flower of poetry wilts wherever it may grow," Lindgren writes. "Don't ask yourself, what should a good children's book look like today or tomorrow?" (*Mina påhitt,* 250). That kind of question will necessarily lead the writer in the direction of didacticism, trendiness, and parochialism. The one restriction on the author's freedom she imposes is simplicity of style. Her own guideline has been the Schopenhauer dictum, "Man brauche gewöhnliche Worte und sage ungewöhnliche Dinge" (Use common words to say uncommon things) (*Mina påhitt,* 249). Lindgren has always written straight from her heart and allowed herself the freedom to let poetry's flower bloom. Her prose is simple, strong, and beautiful. Style and content form a harmonic unity, and she speaks directly to the child in a language the child can understand. Most of Lindgren's children's books are told from the child's point of view with great humor and compassion, which gives them the directness and immediacy to which so many child readers respond.

Lindgren has never consciously followed a trend; if anything, she is a trend setter. It is nevertheless possible to discern a shift in social concerns as well as cultural codes in a chronological review of her books. Traditional gender stereotypes, for example, have become less rigid over time in her realistic narrative, reflecting changes in social behavior and discourse. Thus, in a picture book from 1986, Emil's little sister, Ida, who in the original Emil books is as unlike him as she could be in her well-adjusted mellow sweetness, comes up with pranks of her own. Lindgren's fantastic protagonists, on the other hand, have always been anything but traditional in their behavior, gender-based or otherwise, and Pippi is the prime example.

In the first chapter I highlighted the intensity of impressions and the felicitous combination of freedom and security Lindgren experienced in her own childhood. A close look at the Småland books will show how these conditions are reflected in the narrative's style and content and how they are interlaced with preconceived beliefs about childhood and ideas on childhood education Lindgren acquired later in life.

One characteristic of the Småland books can hardly be overlooked: the importance of merrymaking and play and the desire to experiment and venture out into the unknown and potentially dangerous. By means of a variety of rhetorical devices, as well as through a deliberate choice of plot and story line, Lindgren conjures up intense emotions of both happiness and horror in her readers, while simultaneously providing them with a safety net of loving relationships and comfortable environments. Thus, after horrifying encounters with ghosts, robbers, and their own mortality, readers and protagonists are brought back to the security of a familiar place or a warm embrace. Some of the Småland books, especially the Noisy Village group, have been criticized as being too serene and idyllic. To some extent this criticism is warranted, and I will examine the degree to which the Småland books present an idyllicized picture or a realistic portrayal of a Småland childhood around the turn of the century. The three Swedish books about Noisy Village appeared in 1947, 1949, and 1952, but more than a decade passed before they were published in the United States. In 1961, Rabén and Sjögren published a compilation of all three called *Bullerbyboken*, on which the American Noisy Village stories seem to be based. They were published by Viking under the title *The Children of Noisy Village* (1962) and *Happy Times in Noisy Village* (1963). Only thirty-three of the forty-four Swedish episodes were included in the two books, and the order in which the episodes appear was scrambled to suit the new format. Generally, those episodes with the most action were chosen for American readers. Since I did not have access to the Astrid Lindgren files at Viking, I can only surmise the reasons that lay behind the alteration of the original text.

Some of the episodes omitted in the American edition contain Swedish customs and cultural details that may have constituted barriers for American readers if unexplained, such as "När vi slutade skolan" (When we finished school) or "Vi tittar på Näcken" (We look at the water-sprite). (Who knows, the nakedness of Karl sitting on a stone in the middle of a brook playing his flute and impersonating a Swedish Pan or water-sprite, may have constituted an additional barrier, as it still does in pictorial representations for American children's books in the 1990s.) On the other hand, the Midsummer and Christmas celebrations and the crayfish catching at the lake also contain culturally determined material, yet those episodes were included. The chapters in which the Swedish children play wild Indians were most likely omitted because their game was considered socially and culturally offensive to an American audience in the 1960s.

I cannot find any apparent reason why other wonderfully funny episodes were left by the wayside, except for economic considerations or perhaps the personal preference of the American editor. These include "Vi gallrar rovor och får en kattunge" (We thin out beets and get a kitten), about making boring farm work fun by inventing games and a secret language; "Anna och jag vet inte själva vad vi gör" (Anna and I don't know ourselves what we are doing), about Anna's and Lisa's make-believe excursion into the fairy-tale world among the wild flowers at the brook and their attempts to conjure up a prince by kissing a frog; and "Vi letar efter skatten" (We look for the treasure), about a treasure hunt on a deserted island where the boys lure the girls and the girls get their revenge. Fortunately, the general mood of the stories remains the same despite the cuts, and the episodic character of the books limits the impact of the repositioning of chapters on the reader's overall impression.

Compared with translations of adult literature of the same stature, translations of children's literature have often been carried out with a good deal of indifference and only limited respect for the original text. Unfortunately, some of Lindgren's books have fared no better. Uninspired and careless translations may also be partly to blame for the relative obscurity of some of her books in the United States. It is no doubt difficult to find a fitting equivalent for Emil's Småland dialect, so the translator opted for standard English, which detracts from the book's local flavor. The language is also "cleaned up." This leads to such oddities as Lindgren's aside to readers of *Emil's Pranks* that she does not want to teach them more shocking words than they already know, after Alfred, the farmhand, has just uttered the word "codswallop." A closer equivalent to the Swedish *det skiter vi i* would be "bullshit," a word that despite the author's excuses was most likely considered improper (127). Treatment of Lindgren's books about Madicken, known as Mischievous Meg in American translation, is another case in point. Besides seemingly pointless name changes and an age change for Meg (Madicken) from seven in the original to ten in translation, the American publisher deleted one complete chapter from the first book and chose not to publish the second book at all.

Translations are of necessity one step removed from the original telling of the stories, yet in most English versions of the Småland books the intensity of the lived experience shines through, if somewhat muted. The intensity of telling reflects children's propensity for extremes and the total involvement with which they play, read, or do anything else, for that matter. One need only compare the noise and activity level of a group of children in a room or on a bus with that of a similar group of adults. The intensity of the child's reading experience is one of the reasons Lindgren finds it so appealing to write for children.

I want to write for readers who can work miracles. Children work miracles when they read. They take our poor sentences and words and give
them a life which in themselves they do not have. The author alone does
not create all the mystical essence contained within the pages of a book.
The reader must help. But the author of books for adults has no willing
little helpers at his disposal as we have. His readers do not work miracles.
It is the child and *only* the child who has the imagination to build a fairy
castle if you provide him with a few small bricks. (*Something*, 130)

Incidentally, this statement was written in 1958, long before any
reader-response theory had become an issue in literary criticism.
Although it is true that the text comes to life only in the mind of the
reader and with the reader's cognitive and emotional involvement, the
author provides the "bricks" in the form of printed words on the page,
and those words may be more or less well formed and more or less
inspiring for imaginary constructs. Lindgren's "bricks" are easy building
materials, and they also come in different shapes and sizes according to
the age group of the implied reader, who in each case is first and foremost the child within:

This girl I write for is rather hard to please: she knows exactly what she
wants, and what she doesn't want. When she is six I may tell a very simple little story about a boy who gets angry with his mother and moves
out into the yard. When she is eight she might want to hear about an
enormously strong girl who can lift a horse on one outstretched arm and
eat a whole big cream cake all by herself. When she is eleven she suddenly wants to hear about a boy who wanders on the roads in the company
of a tramp. "But it must be exciting," she says. "Not too exciting," I say.
"Yes, I want crooks," she says, "two terrible ones who nearly kill
Rasmus." "You've got very poor taste," I say, "I think it was better when
you were younger." "If my taste has got worse, perhaps it's because I'm
growing up," she says, "I want my crooks." I give in. (*Something*, 130)

If finding the right ideas, mood, rhythm, and plot development for a
story is an unconscious process in which Lindgren follows a guiding
inner voice, articulating these elements clearly and effectively is a conscious process that involves both aesthetic deliberations and many revisions before she is content with the outcome. Her memory is a
precondition for her ability to reach out and touch readers. Lindgren
remembers not only facts and events, she remembers the feelings and
emotions, perceptions and misperceptions, sights, sounds, and smells of
the different stages of childhood:

In memory—what does not lie slumbering there from a vanished childhood's scent and taste and sights and sounds! At any moment it can all
wake up and feel almost as it did then . . . no, now I am lying, not at all
as it did then! But I have not yet completely forgotten, I can still recap-
ture the scents and remember the bliss of that briar rose in the oxpen
which showed me for the first time what beauty was; I can still hear the
rasping of the corncrake out in the rye on summer evenings and the hoot-
ing of the owls over in the owl tree through springtime nights; I still
know exactly how it feels to come in from biting cold and snow to a
warm barn; I know how a calf's tongue feels against my hand and how
rabbits smell; the smell of a coach-house and the sound of milk streaming
down into the pail, and the feel of baby chicks' feet when you take one,
newly hatched, in your hands. These are not such remarkable things to
remember. What is remarkable is the intensity with which one experienced it all when one was new to this earth. ("I Remember . . . ," 168)

Such memories of childhood's intense perceptions and desires, paired
with Lindgren's ability to record these feelings with sensitivity and exac-
titude in the fictional children she has created, distinguish her stories.
Her childlike attitude of delight in all aspects of the world surrounding
her transforms itself into words that evoke strong feelings and impulses
in the child reader. Lindgren is a preeminent writer for younger children,
and many of these books have become classics because in them the ever-
lasting and boundless spirit of childhood becomes manifest. Pippi, for
certain, is the supreme representative of the spirit of childhood that, one
should not forget, is in itself a product of modern Western culture and a
deeply entrenched myth. The inner child that Lindgren listens to while
writing is as much a product of culture as of nature. The vibrant, energetic, creative, and self-assured person that Lindgren presents in Pippi—
if we disregard her fantastic characteristics—corresponds to the
innermost desires of readers and at the same time represents an ideal,
desired state of being for both children and adults.

Pippi is not the only fictional character to represent this childhood
spirit; in a more realistic manner Emil and Meg, the Noisy Village children, and Bill Bergson's gang possess it as well. At the age of five, Emil
is as strong as a young ox and just about as enterprising as Pippi. Both
share unlimited energy, curiosity, and self-assurance. The decisive difference between the two is that Emil lives in a realistic setting and is forced
to undermine his parents' authority to get his way, whereas Pippi is
totally free and independent. About Emil we are told that he "wanted to
boss his father and mother and the entire household, in fact the whole of

Lönneberga itself, but the Lönnebergans weren't going to put up with that."[5] Pippi, on the other hand, does not have to put up with townspeople, institutions, or conventions. All children in the Småland books are more or less curious, enthusiastic, positive, cheerful, buoyant, capable, imaginative, energetic, and enterprising, and thereby lend the persons, places, and events in these books a special aura.

For what is at the heart of Lindgren's Småland books is not Småland around the turn of the century—although it receives a loving and accurate portrayal—but the rendition of colorful, lively, and happy childhoods at that particular time and place. Much of the plot development and style of these books is based on the indomitable childhood spirit that gets Emil and Mischievous Meg into so much trouble, but they persevere and end up the better for it. We are reminded throughout the Emil books that he will be a prominent member of society when he grows up, and it is hard to doubt it, given his success in every sphere of life at a tender age.

How does Lindgren convey the intensity of feeling, sometimes bordering on euphoria, in her narrative? Many exclamation marks and expressions of wonder and surprise suggest a surplus of high emotion, and her books abound with emphatic "oh's." Unfortunately, some of those exclamations have been sacrificed in translation from Swedish, taking away a measure of the intensity typical of Lindgren's narrative style. To illustrate how tone and voice lose intensity in the American translation, I have chosen one of many possible examples from *Mischievous Meg* to compare with its British counterpart, *Mardie's Adventures*. In my estimation, Patricia Crampton's British translation is far better than its American counterpart, for it retains much of the tone and rhythm of the original. The American version lacks much of the original's stylistic exuberance and so does not quite reflect the original's spirit. When Meg's (Mardie's) mother, while talking to the teacher, finds out that her daughter has invented naughty Richard to put herself in a better light, the narrator in the British translation describes Mardie's reaction: "Oh, how she missed Richard, now he had gone!" (*Mardie's Adventures*, 25). The American translation, on the other hand, is comparatively flat: "Meg was already missing Richard terribly."[6]

Emphatic repetition is another of Lindgren's stylistic trademarks. After the shock of believing her sister captured by a slave trader—the result of a game of make-believe—Meg is overjoyed to have her sister back again: "Oh, everything was perfect! Meg was so happy that Betsy was her sister and was lying there, safe at home and not in some miserable slave-dealer's power" (139). The British version is again more emphatic and much closer to the original: "Oh, how lovely everything was, thought Mardie. She was happy, happy, happy because Lisbet was lying there and was her sister and in Junedale, not in the power of some wicked slave-trader" (155).

In *Happy Times in Noisy Village,* Anna, Britta, and Lisa find a wild strawberry patch and vow they will "never, never, never tell it to anyone."[7] Examples of emphatic repetition articulating utmost intensity of feeling and assuring deep emotional involvement on the part of the reader are plentiful in Lindgren's work. Lindgren knows how to pull out all the stops to build up the reader's expectation. Especially in the Emil books she uses the tried and true method of foreshadowing what may come in order to increase the tension and excitement. Most of the mischief Emil gets into is announced in the previous chapter or in the chapter title. Thus, one chapter in *Emil and Piggy Beast* is called "Tuesday, the Tenth of August When Emil Put the Frog in the Lunch Basket and He Behaved So Badly that I Hardly Dare Write about It" (77). In *Emil's Pranks,* another eventful day, Wednesday, the thirty-first of October, concludes with:

> Perhaps you may think that Emil gave up getting into mischief because he now had a horse, but that wasn't the case. He rode Lukas for three whole days, but the third day, which was November 3, he was ready to get up to his pranks again. Guess what he did—ha, ha, it makes me laugh whenever I think about it. Well, on that particular day he—no! Stop! I promised his mother never to tell what he did on November 3, because soon after that the Lönnebergians collected all that cash, you remember, and wanted to send Emil to America. Emil's mother didn't want to remember it and never even wrote about it in her notebook, so why should I give it away? No, instead you shall hear what Emil did on Boxing Day that year. (81)

Remarks about the 3 November mischief that the narrator withholds from the reader run through all three Emil books, and not even in the last of them is the reader's curiosity stilled; this piece of mischief will always remain a secret. By preannouncing and by withholding information from the reader Lindgren tightly controls the flow of tension in the narrative. The immediacy of the oral taleteller's voice, quite perceptible in the above paragraph, is another way for Lindgren to grab hold of her reader/listener and intensify the reading/listening experience. She also knows how to heighten the dramatic aspects of the narrative by means of contrast and suspense on matters ranging all the way from Olaf's loose tooth, and whether it will come out or not, to the question of whether Bill Bergson and his gang will succeed in catching the criminals.

The chapter in *Emil's Pranks* about the "Clean Sweep" provides a good illustration of Lindgren's emphatic narration and her use of suspense. The episode builds up slowly from a dark, gloomy, uneventful fall day when members of the family are peacefully sitting around the kitchen table doing their chores. The children are playing with the cat underneath the table, and everyone is listening to Krösa-Maja tell frightful stories about werewolves. These stories immediately set off a spark in Emil's imagination and rouse the reader's interest. From this point on, tension builds in waves until Emil catches the "werewolf" in the wolf pit he has dug out by the woodshed.

The werewolf is actually the much hated, mean, and selfish superintendent of the poorhouse who "goes about like a roaring lion in the sheepfold" (94) and "howls like a dog" (117). She can only be caught on a moonlit night when werewolves are said to be about. Mistaking the superintendent for a werewolf reminds the reader subtly, and with a little twist of irony, that werewolves do exist, if in a slightly more human form than folktales and horror tales lead us to believe. They also remind us that Emil achieved what he set out to do, which he does with great frequency. When Emil, the little farm boy with his wooden toy rifle, corners the big, mean superintendent in the wolf pit, we are reminded of a heroic knight's victory over a homely and horrible beast. Lindgren uses the paradigm of the heroic tale in a down-to-earth and humorous way, making the most of its dramatic action to enhance the reader's ultimate satisfaction. This episode also bears traits of the underdog story, so popular in folktales and children's literature.

But before Emil and the reader achieve their ultimate satisfaction of deriding the superintendent and teaching her a lesson, tension has peaked in a parallel plot about the "Great Clean Sweep at Katthult." In this episode, Emil and his sister, Ida, decide to invite the community's paupers for Christmas dinner after their parents have left home. Lindgren employs contrast, enumeration, and repetition as stylistic tools to heighten suspense and intensity. Thus, the reader who first hears about hunger and depravity among the paupers in the poorhouse is pulled into the debauchery of the legendary Grand Clean Sweep at Katthult by means of the long list of delicacies arduously prepared by Emil's mother for the Christmas smorgasbord and now dished up for the paupers. While "those little paupers from the poorhouse" sit around the

table waiting very patiently, their eyes filling with tears, Emil and Ida
fetch from the larder one by one:

> A dish of black pudding
> A dish of pork sausages
> A dish of liver paste
> A dish of headcheese
> A dish of meatballs
> A dish of veal cutlets
> A dish of spareribs of pork
> A dish of oatmeal sausages
> A dish of potato sausages
> A dish of salmagundi
> A dish of salt beef
> A dish of ox tongue
> A huge ham
> A dish of cheesecake
> A plate of rye bread
> A plate of syrup bread
> A crate of juniper berry drinks
> A can of milk
> A bowl of rice pudding
> A bowl of cream cheese
> A dish of preserved plums
> An apple pie
> A jug of cream
> A jug of strawberry juice
> A jug of pear ginger
> And a suckling pig garnished with sugar. (*Pranks*, 110–11)

Expectations build with each dish, and the exuberant wealth of wonderful dishes (and wonderful they are for a Swedish palate from
Småland) stands in sharp contrast to the emaciated, hungry paupers
who, once they believe this miracle is really occurring, start digging in.
The subsequent consumption of the food is described with dramatic
intensity, and the growing bodily satisfaction of the paupers is counter-
balanced by the mounting mental anxiety of the children faced with the
unexpectedly rapid depletion of their resources. Now the tables are
turned and they stand aghast as they watch the food vanish: Ida "heard
the chomping and crunching and lip smacking and guzzling all around
the table. It was as though a herd of beasts of prey had flung themselves
at the bowls and dishes and plates" (*Pranks*, 112).

A similar list can be found in *Bill Bergson and the White Rose Rescue,*
where Bill and Anders, who haven't seen any food for quite a while, load
up secretly in Bill's father's grocery store. Their consumption of food
rivals that of the paupers at Emil and Ida's feast:

> How they ate! They cut thick slices of smoked ham and ate. They
> chopped off chunks of the best salami and ate. They pulled apart a large
> fragrant loaf of rye bread and ate. They peeled off the foil of small trian-
> gular pieces of cheese and ate. They thrust their hands into a box of
> raisins and ate. They took some chocolate bars from the candy counter
> and ate. They ate and ate and ate. It was the meal of their lifetime, and
> they would never forget it.[8]

Eating—and especially eating candy, sweet rolls, and other delicacies—is a matter of great pleasure for children, Lindgren knows, and
they should not be deprived of experiencing this pleasure vicariously
while reading. There is, I believe, not one among Lindgren's major books
in which food is not mentioned specifically and in detail, particularly if it
is a desired item. From Pippi's pancakes and copious supply of candy,
which ends in an excess of candy eating, to the Bread that Satisfies
Hunger in *Mio, My Son* and Ronia's intense appreciation of her mother's
bread in *Ronia, the Robber's Daughter,* food is not just consumed but
becomes a matter of intense pleasure and satisfaction and a symbol of
the children's appetite for life.

Nature is experienced with equal intensity, and Lindgren's narrative
often assumes lyric qualities. The freshness and enchantment of an early
summer morning lingers in the picture Lindgren draws of the children of
Noisy Village coming back from a night of catching crayfish in the lake.
"There was dew in the grass, and there were spiderwebs here and there
and they sparkled like diamonds" (*Children of Noisy Village,* 123). In
Emil's Pranks the reflection of the red August moon on the calm, warm
lake suggests the warmth and affection between Alfred and Emil; there
is no need for further articulation between the two: "They swam among
the waterlilies in the warm lake water, and up in the sky the moon shone
for them like a red lantern" (40). These islands of quiet contemplation
also serve as a counterweight to the action and excitement surrounding
Emil's feats, which dominate the books about him. "It was a glorious
evening of the kind you only get in Småland; all the hedges were in
bloom, blackbirds sang, mosquitoes hummed, and the perch were biting
well. Alfred and Emil sat there and saw their float bob on the shining
water. They didn't talk much, but were very happy all the same"

(*Pranks*, 127). A similar peace rests over Mardie's Junedale in *Mardie's Adventures*, when after an exciting day filled with altercations the two sisters are happy to be with each other. In contrast to the male friendship associated with the activity of fishing, this imagery is encoded with traditionally feminine metaphors:

> Now it was night at Junedale, now the red house by the stream was asleep. The sun had gone down, dusk had fallen among the birches, a blue-dusk, for it was Spring. It was now that the narcissus shone their whitest and smelled their sweetest, it was now that the birches looked their loveliest in their thin green veils under the Spring sky, so cool and clear. And it was quiet. The air had been full of birdsong, but now all the little birds were asleep in their nests and holes. (155)

There are few better ways to describe the closeness and comfort Mardie and Lisbet feel at this moment. By capping the preceding sibling rivalries with a description of nature at peace, heightened and paralleled by the two girls snuggling up to each other in bed, Lindgren makes sure that not their fights but their closeness will linger in the minds of readers as they close the book.

Fun and Games

Running errands for Mom is usually not very much fun, but Anna and Lisa make the best of it in a spirited Noisy Village episode in which the girls go shopping. The plot, in which the girls forget some of the groceries and have to return to the store several times, is not very exciting, if one gets right down to it. Indeed, it is rather annoying for those involved. But Anna and Lisa take it in stride, turning their shopping experience into play by inventing songs and games on the way. What makes this episode funny is the cumulative nature of the narrative. Three times (as is the rule in the European folktale) the girls have to return to the store after reaching the crossroads (an ominous place in the folktale), the place where they stop and think for a while after having ambled along in a world of their own. Besides enhancing the tension of the narrative, the predictable repetition puts readers in a position of superiority from which they can laugh both at and with the girls.

Fun, as experienced by the children in Noisy Village, is frequently nonspecific. This general sensation has its source in the children's enthusiasm, can be evoked by almost anything, and finds its release in repeated expressions of delight. Lisa, the narrator, provides ample assurances in the first volume, *The Children of Noisy Village*. At least fifteen times, Lisa declares—and it sounds almost like an incantation—"we have such fun . . ." or "it is such fun. . . . "These exclamations occur mostly in such strategic places as a chapter heading or a passage at the beginning of a chapter. For readers these assurances fulfill the same function as the reminders about Emil's mischief, putting them in the right mindset.

Childlike exuberance and farce share certain characteristics: exaggeration for the fun of it. Especially in Lindgren's books for younger readers, characters and events are overdrawn and hyperbolized to the extent that they become farcical. The most prominent examples of this are the Pippi and Emil books. The fact that Emil gets his head stuck twice in the same soup tureen is as much slapstick as his father's predictable yelling and nonsensical economic sense. The comedy in the Emil books is an amalgam of unfettered childlike curiosity and a misguided desire to help; both get Emil into trouble. In the Noisy Village books and *Mischievous Meg* as well the protagonists' unsuppressed curiosity and desire for experimentation propel the action and result in situation comedy. Emil expresses it his way. When asked by the farmhand Alfred if he intends to get into more mischief the next day, he replies: "I don't know, I never know till afterwards" (*Pranks,* 128).

With words like "happy," "noisy," "pranks," and "mischievous" in their titles, the Småland books announce the boisterous merriment they have in store for their readers. The level of action is high in all books, and what is happening is invariably funny and exciting. Fun lies in the prickly sensation of anticipation that holidays and special events carry with them, but most of all it lies in the euphoria of play. In her book *En lek för ögat* (A play for the eye), Margareta Rönnberg points out the enormous importance that play has in Lindgren's writings and in their film adaptations. She argues that play stretches the limits of body and mind.[9] The movement up—away from the ground to a higher elevation—and out—away from the enclosing walls and conventions of home and tradition—are important features of play in Lindgren's books mirroring psychological growth and development.

Whatever the underlying causes, Lindgren's fictional characters seem to have a preference for wider perspectives and a larger perimeter of action. The children in the Småland books climb trees, balance on rooftops, and hoist each other up the flagpole, as Emil does with Little Ida, because she wants to see the neighboring hamlet of Mariannelund. Ida, by the way, is not the least bit frightened by substituting for the flag; on the contrary, she thoroughly enjoys her elevated position. This predilection for high places is shared by Pippi as well. She outshines even her monkey in agility as she balances across a narrow beam high up in the air leading to a burning house and plays tag with the police on a rooftop. Her attempt to fly as she is jumping off a rather high cliff during the children's picnic is echoed in a similar attempt by Meg. But whereas the superchild gets up, brushing her knees as if nothing had happened, blaming her failure on forgetting to wave her arms and the presence of too many pancakes in her stomach, the more realistically drawn Meg ends up in bed with a concussion. Karlsson, another childhood spirit and distant cousin of Peter Pan, lives on a rooftop and can fly, thanks to the little propeller on his back.

The vitality and liveliness of the children in Noisy Village is at times unrestrained and "high-flying." But most of the fun consists of harmless gaiety, which creates the playful atmosphere that is almost programmatic for these books. The six Noisy Village children, whose individual characters are very different, feel elated or devastated, curious or silly; they mock and tease each other, but never experience any lingering hard feelings, for life, seen strictly from the child's perspective, presents itself in an eternal present that contains within itself the promise of new challenges and exciting adventures.

Everything is play in Noisy Village. Life seems one long, extended holiday with short interruptions of everyday grayness. If we take Lindgren's word, the persistent presence of play is based on her own experience. "We played all the time, morning, noon, and night, just like the children in Noisy Village. It is true what is written there" (*Mitt Småland,* 10). This observation is somewhat modified and expanded in "Samuel August från Sevedstorp och Hanna i Hult," Lindgren's tribute to her parents:

> Surely, we were brought up with discipline and in admonishment of the Lord, as was the custom at that time, but in our games we were wonderfully free and never supervised. And we played, and played, and played so it was a miracle that we didn't play ourselves to pieces. We climbed like monkeys in trees and on roofs, we jumped from piles of boards and haystacks so that our entrails started groaning, we were in mortal danger when we crawled through our subterranean passages in the big pile of sawdust, we swam in the brook long before we could swim, oblivious to our mother's warning that we should not go out "any deeper than up to the navel." Still, all four of us survived. (*Mina påhitt,* 216)

Reflections of the creative and uncontrolled play of the four siblings at Näs surface in *Pippi Longstocking,* just as they do in almost every episode

of the Noisy Village books and *Mischievous Meg*. Games that Pippi makes
up were played by the Ericsson children, who played "don't touch the
floor" in the big bedroom of Näs when the weather was bad outside.
Astrid's brother, Gunnar, was a "thing-finder" long before Pippi.
Because of her own childhood experiences, Lindgren equates childhood
with an abundance of imaginative play, and her stories revive the freedom of play that was lost together with childhood. It may be true that
this freedom was more intensely felt eighty years ago when ideas about
rearing children were stricter and more authoritarian, and when children
could throw off the shackles of convention and strict discipline only
while at play. Playful imagination became a compensatory expression of
freedom in the face of narrowly defined rules and truths. Now that the
education of the average child has been liberalized and a multiplicity of
values has stretched rules, morals, and truths, the need to escape into the
free and wild world of play and adventure may not be quite as great. In
any case, the chances for playful escape in real life have been narrowed
for many middle-class children, whose play-life has become more organized and structured and has come under greater supervision. By going
back in time Lindgren offers her readers the chance to partake at least
mentally in the free and imaginative play she once experienced.

In "Samuel August från Sevedstorp och Hanna i Hult," Lindgren
points out that life was not only play (*Mina påhitt*, 217). By the age of
six, children had to go out in the fields to thin beets, a chore reflected in
one of the episodes omitted from *The Children of Noisy Village*. Work
around the farm was plentiful and included the children, who were thus
socialized into and made part of the adult world. Besides hardship, however, work gave them natural recognition and responsibility, leading
both to self-assurance and a sense of belonging.

Work, too, became engulfed in the exuberant spirit of childhood.
School and fieldwork, the long walk home from school, and errands to
the store all assume an aura of fun, wonder, and excitement in the
Småland books. If set to a boring physical task they have to perform, the
protagonists let their minds take them off in airy heights, or they invent
another coping mechanism, they simply redefine work as play. Just like
Pippi, who turns every chore into play and hence does not know any
chores, the children from the Småland books try to do the same to avoid
boredom and drudgery. This playful attitude lends to work an air of
extravagance and allows hardship to dissolve into laughter. When the
children of Noisy Village without much luck try to sell their cherries on
the main highway, which is still a dirt road, the passing cars whirl up big

clouds of dust. Since it does not help to complain about the dust, they simply decide to like the dust and to dislike sunshine and birdsong. So each time a car passes, enveloping them in dust so they can hardly breathe or see each other, they exclaim, "What wonderful dust!" and explode in laughter (*Happy Times,* 98).

For the Noisy Village children, a routine occurrence like the walk home from school is animated by play, storytelling, and competition. Karl, Bill, and Lisa, Olaf, Britta, and Anna see who can hold his or her breath the longest, climb trees to look at bird's nests, and walk on the fence or in the ditch, for only boring grown-ups can have invented the idea that one must walk only on the road (they share this opinion with Pippi). The reasonable, prudent, and moderate is anathema to the spirit of play; play should be immoderate and excessive, far removed from the boring middle-of-the-road that the children eschew. How else could a big rock in the middle of the shoemaker's inundated meadow become a ship drifting in the ocean with sailors in danger of death by starvation, as it does for the six children on their way home from school? Such games presuppose a wealth of imagination, joining together bits of cultural narrative from the oral and literary tradition shared by readers and protagonists. Besides the ever-present playful exuberance, Lindgren's use of many folkloric motifs and paradigms that transcend cultural borders may explain the popularity of her books in other countries and cultures as well.

Imagination and the children's desire to act it out physically can prove dangerously explosive at times. Meg, who gets her ideas "as fast as a pig can blink" (10), attempts to fly, parachuting off the woodshed roof, umbrella in hand, and suffers a concussion. The passageways and caves burrowed deep in the hay by the Noisy Village boys would most likely not meet any builder's or parent's safety standards. Karl stretches the limits of the permissible and narrowly escapes death when he falls through the ice while skating too close to a hole. Although the protagonists unconsciously invite close encounters with death, these stories do not resemble cautionary tales; the exact opposite is the case. Even when children overstep their bounds, things turn out right in the end. Lindgren's books celebrate rather than punish the carefree exuberance of childhood. Readers thus experience vicarious thrills and adventures— guilt-free.

In the Bill Bergson books the adventures and the danger are more real. In these books thieves and murderers are not relegated to the imaginary world of the protagonists as they are in Noisy Village; Bill Bergson and his friends encounter them in real life. The opening lines of *Bill Bergson, Master Detective* are ominous enough: "Blood! No doubt about it!"[10] (No matter that this blood happens to be from a small cut on his thumb and that it is the only blood that flows in this volume.) The two sequels to this story are a little more hard-core: in *Bill Bergson and the White Rose Rescue* blood does flow in the end, when the thieves are caught, and in *Bill Bergson Lives Dangerously* Eva-Lotta witnesses a murder. In 1951, when the latter book was written, murder was considered an inappropriate topic in a book for teens (who were not considered "young adults" then). But Lindgren has never done or written the appropriate thing; she has written only what feels right to her, often in opposition to accepted ideas and conventions. In the following passage from *Bill Bergson Lives Dangerously,* Lindgren ridicules a then popular discourse about sweet, helpless girls. At fifteen, Eva-Lotta has left childhood behind, and with it the protective sphere that Lindgren believes should be a natural part of childhood but that should not be artificially prolonged by society, especially in the case of girls. She considers as criminal as the crime itself the syrupy words of a small-town journalist describing her as a picture of girlish innocence, safely returned to the family haven that resembles paradise. By revealing the falseness of this cliché-ridden description of Eva-Lotta in the newspaper, Lindgren attacks head-on glossy childhood and family myths:

> . . . our sweet little Eva-Lotta, who today is playing among the flowers in her father's and mother's garden and seems to have forgotten all about the horrible adventures last Wednesday out there on the windswept Prairie. . . . Well, where could she forget, where could she feel secure, if not here—in the home of her father and mother, in the familiar environment where she was reared, where the aroma of newly baked bread from her father's bakery seems to vouch for the existence of a safe and secure everyday world which cannot be upset by any bloody outrages in the world of crime. (114–15)

Freedom and Security

The narrator's treatment of the journalist's comments shows how far removed Lindgren already was in the 1940s and 1950s from a cheap, idyllicized image of adolescent girlhood. Only for young children does she perceive a real need for protection and security; that need, however, is of paramount concern to her. That is why her younger protagonists always return unhurt to the security of a loving family or friend or to a

Meg (Madicken/Mardie) and Betsy (Lisabet) enjoy a lovely hot summer day by the creek in Junedale. Illustration by Ilon Wikland from *Madicken*, the original Swedish edition of *Mischievous Meg*.

familiar and cozy place after encounters with villains and rogues. For the most part, encounters with ghosts, robbers, and pirates take place in the children's fantasy world, while they themselves are secure.

Betsy enjoys the warmth and comfort of her sister's presence and a peaceful spring evening at June Hill when she asks to hear a ghost story. At this point horror stories are a welcome contrast to the girls' comfort and security, as well as a reinforcement of it. "'Meggie,' said Betsy, and put her cold little feet against Meg's warm ones. 'Meggie, tell me more about ghosts and robbers'" (*Mischievous Meg,* 139). (Or in the less prudish British version, which more closely captures the original Swedish wording, "'Mardie,' said Lisbet, pushing her cold little feet in under Mardie's legs. 'Tell me about ghosts and murderers and war!'" [*Mardie's Adventures,* 156].) Meg/Mardie willingly obliges with a story most likely resembling the one Mardie tells her little sister at the beginning of *Mardie to the Rescue,* a story that makes Lisbet shiver with excitement.

"'He comes creeping along softly, softly, softly through the jungle, and when he sees a missionary—gulp—the cannibal sinks his teeth into him before the missionary has heard a single sound.'"[11] Just like Mardie, Lindgren delivers suspenseful and thrilling stories within a well-defined and comforting framework for the younger readers and listeners. That Ida's pictures of a fire-spitting volcano and a horrible brandy flood hang over the bed in her "marvelously cozy" cottage is equally significant.

Telling ghost stories is a popular pastime in both the Noisy Village and the Emil books. These stories belong to the rich oral lore that children used to hear from their grandmothers or other older women. A village gossip who is not a little superstitious, Krösa-Maja is a much-welcome entertainer on long, dark fall and winter afternoons within the security and comfort of the kitchen in Katthult. Young and old listen to her stories about "murderers, thieves, ghosts, and spooks, . . . about throats being cut, ghastly calamities from fire, appalling tragedies, fatal illnesses, or dangerous beasts" (*Pranks,* 85).

As a child, Lindgren herself heard many such stories from her grandmother, and the thrill she experienced then lives on in her fiction. The story *The Ghost of Skinny Jack,* published in picture-book format in the United States in 1988, is a retelling of one of these stories that remained permanently engraved in her memory. In Scandinavian folklore, stories about ghosts, trolls, and other elemental beings abound; most of them end tragically, and so does this story. It is indicative of Lindgren's attitude toward her young audience that she does not simply retell the ghost story; she reshapes it with the intimacy and skill of the oral taleteller, making special amends to the mindset of the young and impressionable child, who does not distinguish between fiction and reality as neatly as do older children.

The task of a good taleteller is keeping the lines between fiction and reality fluid, so that protagonists and readers can transgress them with ease. In the case of tales for young children, Lindgren solidifies the fluid borders in the end. To control the setting in which the tale is received, she frames it with a story in which Skinny Jack comes alive in a little girl's imagination during her walk through the dark woods. Lindgren appeases the readers' minds and brings them back from the imaginary to fictional reality when the little girl's father appears and saves her from the clutches of Skinny Jack. The story ends happily, like the song they sing on the way home: "Home sweet home, and Father near, Home to everything that's dear." Or almost. Normalcy has not quite returned, and in a little coda, the brother has to calm his little sister's remaining fears that she may have gone mad with fright like the maid in the ghost story.

Meg/Mardie is still quite impressionable, and even stories from the Bible turn into horrifying experiences for her, thanks largely to Ida's emphatic renditions. She hears stories about David and Goliath, Moses in the bulrushes, Daniel in the lion's den, King Herod murdering so many little boys in Judea, and Joseph in the well. Even for Mardie borders between fiction and reality can disintegrate in the heat of a game of make-believe, as it does in the Joseph-in-the-well episode, or when Abe tries to fool her by pretending to be a ghost.

In *Rasmus and the Vagabond*, Rasmus, who spends a few free and exciting summer weeks together with a tramp named Oscar after escaping from an orphanage, also finds the security of the safe and loving home he had been longing for when he and the tramp finally end up at Oscar's little cottage. Their life on the road, however, is filled with danger and excitement that ranges from witnessing an armed robbery to enjoying life at a fair. Freedom is the wonderful aspect of a tramp's life that reveals itself to Rasmus in an instant when Oscar assures him, "Tramps can sleep any time," and Rasmus soon realizes, "You could do exactly what you pleased. You could eat and sleep and go exactly where you pleased. You were free, wonderfully free, like a bird in the forest."[12] From a materialistic and commonsensical standpoint, life in Paradise Oscar's little cottage does not seem as favorable a deal as life with the wealthy and handsome farmer Nielson and his equally handsome and friendly wife, a choice Rasmus turns down. The allure of a life with Oscar lies in the unique combination of the real and true love that exists between the two, a familiar comfort he feels at Oscar's place, but, above all, in the promise of freedom and adventure on the road in springs and summers to come. As it turns out, Rasmus makes the wiser choice, for he gets both freedom and security by choosing Oscar and his wife over the well-appointed, boringly sedate farmer's family.

To an American radio audience Lindgren once said about *Rasmus and the Vagabond:* "When I wrote the book I had a feeling that Oscar was an intimate friend of mine and that I had really met him when I was a child. To us children the tramps represented adventure, and it was natural for me to choose a tramp as a hero in an adventure book. . . . To my surprise he chose to stay with Oscar, and I think it was the best thing he could do. Because I knew Oscar since I was a child myself."[13] With a wondrous blend of pragmatism and illusion Rasmus follows his dream and chooses the exact balance of freedom and security that Lindgren had experienced as a child.

It is true that Lindgren writes for the child she once was, the child that still remains alive inside of her, but she also writes to satisfy her adult self, who is appalled at the carelessness and thoughtlessness adults display toward children and who thus writes in selective and corrective ways about the free and happy child she once was. A case in point is her protectiveness of young readers in her retelling of *Skinny Jack*. Ulla Lundqvist's book about Pippi Longstocking, *århundadets barn* (The child of the century), sheds some light on the historical, social, and ideological context within which *Pippi Longstocking* was created, and which is equally applicable to Lindgren's other books from that period. Lundqvist emphasizes the great influence that educational debates in Sweden in the 1930s and 1940s had on Lindgren's thinking and writing for and about children. Lindgren was familiar with the ideas of the progressive and reformist school in pedagogy inspired by the writings of Ellen Key, Alexander Sutherland Neill, and Bertrand Russell, as is evident from her letter to the editor of *Dagens Nyheter* in December 1939. This excerpt from that letter reveals Lindgren's attitude toward children and her indignation at then current pedagogical ideas:

> It is not easy to be a child! No, it is difficult, immensely difficult. What does it mean to be a child? It means that they have to go to bed, get up, get dressed, eat food, brush their teeth, and wipe their noses when it suits the adults not when it suits them. It means that they have to eat hard bread when they would rather have eaten soft bread. It means that they have to run down to the store to buy a gas coupon just at the point when they have settled down with Edgar T. Lawrence. It also means that they have to listen to the most personal reprimands from all kinds of adults concerning looks, state of health, dress, and projects for the future. I have often wondered what would happen if one treated grown-ups the same way.[14]

Lindgren's writing is based on the conviction that all human beings deserve respect, be they old or young, poor or rich. But since reality was and largely remains otherwise, Lindgren created a fictional counterworld in which children are granted respect or in which they possess the freedom and strength to claim it. It is indicative that her own choice of reading material for the hypothetical child in the article was Mark Twain's *Huckleberry Finn*, which the newspaper editor replaced with Edgar T. Lawrence.

Strong, independent, imaginative, and assertive protagonists in her books function as both wish fulfillment and inspiration. Emil, who at his tender age outshines his father as a knowledgeable farmer and good businessman, is strong-willed and unintimidated by authority. His spirit and curiosity cannot be broken by any amount of punishment. The punishment, it has to be said, is unusually mild for a time when the rod was used frequently, for after each bit of mischief Emil is sent to the toolshed to "think over" his misdeeds carefully. He does, but he also uses his time in the shed creatively by carving wooden men. These carvings—the results of his mischief—instill in him a sense of pride so that, in the very last episode from 1985, he bequeaths his entire collection to his children, just as Lindgren proudly bequeaths the results of her creative endeavors, based on youthful exuberance, to her readers.

Not only in the depiction of punishment does Lindgren veer slightly from the educational customs of the early twentieth century. Her portrayal of the parent-child relationship also contains corrective measures. A more open, democratic, and understanding atmosphere reigns than could have been true in the realistic equivalent of Noisy Village or June Hill. Parents in Noisy Village—to the extent they appear at all—adhere closely to the ideal behavior envisioned by free education. They represent the ideas of the innovative pedagogy of the 1930s and 1940s, which was based on the bourgeois nuclear family with its greater potential for intimacy and closeness. As Margareta Strömstedt points out in her biography of Lindgren, it seems highly unlikely that the fathers of Noisy Village would have taken a toboggan ride with their children (Strömstedt, 99). In a farming society this would have been considered frivolous and out of place. Emil's father represents this attitude when he scoffs at the thought of joining a snowball fight with the children in *Inget knussel, sa Emil i Lönneberga* (No stinginess, said Emil).

What *is* true to life, according to the oral history Strömstedt collected, is the firm foundation of love and trust that most of Lindgren's characters experience either in life or in fantasy. Without the love and understanding of his mother, Emil might not be the contented and enterprising fellow he is. She runs off with him to the toolshed to protect him from his father's rage, which was likely to end in corporal punishment. Most important, she loves him. Her avowal, "Emil's a dear fellow, and we love him just as he is," is repeated several times and forms a foundation of trust and confidence that gives Emil the strength to explore the world around him freely and the self-confidence to follow through on things he has envisioned. Emil is "living" proof of Lindgren's deep conviction that every child will turn out well if he or she is given the right amount of freedom and security:

> If children nowadays lack sensibility and common sense, don't blame "free" education! Free education does not preclude firmness. Nor does it preclude children having affection and respect for their parents. And—

most important of all—it means that parents also respect their children. Respect for the child, that is what I wish adults had to a greater extent. Treat them with approximately the same respect that you are compelled to show your fellow adults. Give children love, more love, and even more love. Then the sensibility will come on its own. That was my position during the debate around Pippi Longstocking and that is what I still stand for.[15]

Lindgren made this statement in a 1985 interview, when the educational climate in Sweden had shifted in a more conservative direction and she felt the need to speak up for the rights of children. Unperturbed by changing theories in child psychology, she proclaims her commonsensical approach to child education, which she has done far more eloquently and with few traces of didacticism in all her books. Like Emil's mother, Mardie's mother also emphatically proclaims her unconditional love for her two daughters, who have both gotten into trouble and feel pangs of guilt. When Mardie asks her mother, "Do you like us all the same?" her mother finds the only answer that will soothe the girls' fears of a withdrawal of love, "Of course I do! You little sillies, whatever you dream up, nothing can change that. Nothing ever, ever!" (*Rescue*, 23). Would any child or adult not want to be loved like that?

The education at June Hill/Junedale and in Noisy Village is characteristic of the "helping mode," Lloyd deMause's ultimate stage of development in the parent-child relationship.[16] The atmosphere between the generations is nonrepressive, open, and loving. There are few serious conflicts between the generations, because the parents are aware of the children's need to live out their fantasies and aggressions. Mishaps are not punished, and even an occasional lie is tolerated.

The adult who sees everything through the eyes of the child is the main driving force that makes Lindgren "adulterate" her own childhood memories. An additional incentive to fill her stories with ideally tolerant and loving parents is her intent to "console the five-year-old remaining somewhere deep down in my soul below all the years' deposits" (*Mina påhitt*, 12). Thus, a sense of lack or imperfection is yet another impetus for the presentation of a mostly harmonious and happy world. One of these later improvements on a lived reality is *Lotta on Troublemaker Street*, a story for younger readers that takes up the motif Lindgren had used in "Pelle Moves to the Outhouse," a story from the Brenda Brave collection of tales. Lindgren describes the driving force behind these two episodes:

I decided like Pelle to move to the outhouse. For some reason, I've forgotten why. I thought I had been treated unjustly and wanted to teach all of them a lesson. I was convinced they would all come sobbing and begging me to move back home again. But nobody came. It was terrible. I had to move back on my own with the bitter feeling that nobody in the world cared. That's why Pelle's Mom does the right thing when Pelle acts in a similar way.[17]

Lotta also decides to move out of her parents' house, into the next door neighbor's attic, because she is furious and feels guilty about having taken her bad temper out on her sweater, into which she has cut holes with a pair of scissors. Toward evening she gets lonely and cries, but just in the nick of time her father appears and tells the sobbing Lotta that both he and her mother miss her very, very much and want her to move home. When Lotta comes home, her mother takes her in her arms and asks forgiveness for all the times she has treated her unfairly, whereupon Lotta also feels free to ask her mother's forgiveness for her bad mood and the abuse of her sweater. This scene resembles an illustration in a child psychology textbook—almost too picture-perfect to be believable. It is most assuredly written with an eye to the parents who read this story to their children, but it is also, as Lindgren tells us, meant to console the child within. That child wants picture-perfect parents at moments of distress.

Lindgren focuses on a child's life as it should be, and in that respect her books are compensatory. They are not so much based on nostalgia for her own childhood—although this sentiment surely exists—as on a longing for a better state of being. It is in her attempt to improve on reality that Lindgren's books leave the ground of realism. Bending her childhood memories, she softens the authoritarianism she experienced and stresses conviviality, mutual tolerance, and a deep sense of security instead. The purpose is twofold, both therapeutic and enlightening: to grant children a fictional escape into a better, happier world that at the same time serves as a blueprint for a more livable and humane future.

A loving and caring attitude toward her readers permeates Lindgren's books. Her own conviction that children need images and stories to nourish their imagination, and the illusion of a better world to nourish their sensitivity and hope, is in concordance with an unwritten law in children's literature that demands protection for the youngest from the harshest realities of life. In her predilection for and selection of the sunny side of life—summer, playfulness, adventure, intense joy, and freedom coupled with security—and in her loving depictions of natural beauty lie the same idyllicizing element that is present in much of children's literature. Lindgren wants to make readers feel good about themselves when they read her books, and, invariably, they do. Life in Noisy Village, on Emil's farm, with Meg's family, and even on the road with Rasmus becomes the childhood of their dreams, because life there is a completely satisfying adventure.

Utopia and Realism

The Småland of Lindgren's fiction resembles the paradise of Nangilima in *The Brothers Lionheart,* where grandfather Mathias awaits Rusky and Jonathan in his little cottage surrounded by apple trees. According to Jonathan, children there live in the days of campfires and sagas, "in days that were happy and full of games. The people played there; they worked, too, of course, and helped each other with everything, but they played a lot and sang and danced and told stories. . . . Sometimes, they scared the children with terribly cruel sagas about monsters like Karm and Katla, and about cruel men like Tengil. But afterward they laughed."[18] Real cruelty is barred from Lindgren's Småland or Nangilima. An aura of cheerfulness and guileless credulity surrounds that epoch's everyday life on the farm.

By anchoring her utopian vision in a concrete past, Lindgren creates a retrospective utopia. And a strangely realistic utopia it is. Emil, Mischievous Meg, and the children of Noisy Village take readers to turn-of-the-century Småland, a lifelike recreation of a lost society. The innocence of childhood is intimately linked to the innocence of Småland before industrialization and commercialization invaded the countryside.

Life on a Swedish farm or in a small town at the turn of the century could be made saccharine, yet Lindgren's world lacks the sentimentality one might expect of a nostalgic glance at past happiness. Accounting for this lack are her use of humor, her acknowledgment—however oblique-ly—of the dark side of life, and her narrative perspective. As I have already stressed, the Småland books are written from the perspective of a happy, sensitive, and self-confident child for whom life presents itself as a long series of adventures and challenges. The wide-eyed naivete and candor of the protagonists also accounts for the lighthearted, matter-of-fact portrayal of the darker side of life. Lindgren reasons along the same lines as Walter Benjamin in his essays on childhood: nothing human should remain hidden from children if they are to grow up as complete human beings. Early on, their naivete provides the necessary barriers; later, when these barriers come down, children are already prepared.[19]

Lisa, the narrator in the Noisy Village books, looks upon the world with a special mixture of brazenness and dreaminess, curiosity and self-centeredness, an attitude that both limits and broadens her perspective. The child's perspective screens out some "adult" realism based on historical and comparative knowledge, and replaces it with magic realism in which words can take on a life of their own. If we consider Lindgren's perspective derived from a fundamentally carefree and happy childhood, the portrayal of life in Noisy Village or in Lönneberga seems eminently realistic.

On the farm at Näs nothing was hidden from Astrid Ericsson's eyes. She and her siblings did not have the shielded childhood a bourgeois child from that period experienced. They were as close to the life and death of animals as to the people on the farm; they heard the crude language and coarse jokes of the farmhands; they saw the despondency of the poor and homeless first-hand; and they secretly read the love letters that the maids tucked away in a box in the attic. But they did not suffer (though the maids may have) and their minds were not corrupted.

The pain and suffering of others that enters the cheerful childhood world of Noisy Village only obliquely is not always acknowledged as such by the child protagonists, and it may not be acknowledged by readers either. But Lindgren does not conceal that life in Småland was filled with toil and hardship for the majority of the population. For the grown-up reader, who has access to greater life experience and means of comparison, everyday life in Noisy Village appears anything but rosy. Poverty, homelessness, and mean-spiritedness exist there as they do in the stories about Rasmus, Emil, and Mischievous Meg. But in all these books they affect the main protagonists only tangentially. The attentive reader can glean much about living conditions on a Swedish farm at the beginning of this century from the books about Emil and, to a lesser extent, from the Noisy Village books. In the Emil stories the narrator sometimes helps the reader along by explaining an old custom or artifact, but these are asides. The world in which Emil grows up comes alive with all its smells and sounds, emotions, and activities. Lindgren draws a colorful picture of the extended farm family, which included maids and farmhands, close and distant relatives, old people and children, all members of a close-knit community. In *Emil's Pranks* Lindgren allows us a glimpse into the Katthult kitchen on a dark and dreary fall afternoon.

Now the dark autumn days hung heavily over Katthult. The paraffin lamps in the kitchen had to be lit as early as three o'clock in the afternoon, and the family sat there together, doing their various jobs. Emil's mother had a spinning wheel going, and spun fine white wool to make stockings for Emil and Ida. Lina carded the wool, as did Krösa-Maja

when she was there. Emil's father soled shoes, thereby saving lots of
money which the village shoemaker would otherwise have had. Alfred
was no less diligent—he mended his own stockings. (84)

Maids and farmhands shared the small space and the available
resources with the farmer's family and became part of it, but they had
precious little private space or private life:

> There was an old wooden bed in the Katthult kitchen, on which Lina
> slept. In those days Småland was full of old beds in kitchens where maid-
> servants slept on knobby mattresses, with flies buzzing all around them.
> So why shouldn't it have been the case in Katthult as well? Lina slept
> soundly on her bed. Nothing could rouse her before half past four in the
> morning, when the alarm clock woke her and she had to get up and go
> do the milking. (15)

Many farmhands did not even have as much as a bed they could call
their own and, since they rarely had the money to get married, often
treated the farm family's children as their own. Emil's close tie with the
farmhand Alfred mirrors that situation. And when the maid Lina is out-
raged at Emil, who repeatedly ruins her few moments of intimacy with
Alfred, this too is a reflection of the lives of maids that Lindgren captures
in her essay "I Remember. . . ." For those rare opportunities to make love
occurred only when the master and mistress had been invited out for a
family dinner, because only then could a farmhand join a maid on the
kitchen sofa in the pitch-black kitchen, where maids all over Småland
slept, and often enough they had to share that sofa with another maid.

No noble paupers can be found in Lindgren's work, and none of her
books can be blamed for embellishing the fate of simple people and outcasts in turn-of-the-century Sweden. The naivete imposed by the perspective of the child may hide from the reader the full extent of suffering
or the social consequences of poverty, especially in the Noisy Village
books, but for Mischievous Meg and Emil, paupers and drunks are a fact
of life that they have to deal with. Incidentally, their "naive" impressions
and actions bring out the hypocrisy and social injustice even more clearly to the adult reader, as does the child in "The Emperor's New Clothes."

Rasmus, the orphan who teams up with a vagabond, is an exception
to the other children in the Småland books in that he encounters hardship firsthand. But even in *Rasmus and the Vagabond* the hardships are
only the backdrop for the protagonist's glorious and adventurous summer roaming the Swedish countryside with his friend and father-to-be,

Paradise Oscar. As mentioned earlier, vagabonds—that time's homeless and hoboes—were part of Lindgren's childhood. They roamed the countryside and slept in the family's hayloft almost every night. These men (for they were all men) brought a whiff of adventure into farm life and carried with them an air of thrills and mystique as they entered the kitchen asking for some milk and bread. They were intruders into the safe haven of the kitchen and were greeted with a blend of fear and curiosity by the small group of Ericsson children who gaped at them. Lindgren's tale about these men, "Godnatt, Herr Luffare" (Good night, Mr. Vagabond), was made into a short film in 1988 by Ingmar Bergman's son Daniel. Daniel Bergman's beautiful rendering of this story is true to the original in most respects. It aptly transfers to the screen the story's atmosphere of thrill and wonder and lingering sadness once the vagabond has left and the show is over.

The voice and structure of this short story belong to the folktale; it begins with an interdiction, tension rises with its violation, but the tale ends happily. Both parents leave, and the children are alone in the house one night shortly before Christmas. They are sternly warned not to open the door to strangers, but they accidentally let a cold and hungry tramp into their kitchen. He tricks them into serving him some food and, in turn, treats them to much excitement and magic. Dr. Seuss's story *The Cat in the Hat,* well-known to young American readers, has a similar plot development. Cat and tramp are initially welcomed by the children with a mixture of terror and anticipation, and when each leaves the children feel relieved and sad at the same time. Both come from nowhere without being summoned and vanish into nowhere, but while present they perform the most amazing feats. While the Cat in the Hat is a figure that remains in the realm of fantasy and imagination, Lindgren's vagabond is very real, as is the mixture of terror, marvel, and enjoyment he elicits in the children. Just like the vagabond's ambiguous appearance—real and fantastic, scary and funny at one and the same time—the fictional childhood world of Småland is both anchored in reality and created in Lindgren's imagination, springing from her desire to improve on reality.

In *Rasmus and the Vagabond* the perspective is reversed from the kitchen looking out to the outdoors looking in, and the whiff of adventure that enters the kitchen with the vagabond becomes the dominant feature of this summer vacation, mystery, and orphan story. The loveless life in the orphanage that Rasmus escapes takes a decisive turn for the better when he meets Paradise Oscar. To make sure the reader savors the full extent of Rasmus's final happiness, Lindgren shows her readers poverty and depravity in a family setting in all its ugliness. The first farm Rasmus and Paradise-Oscar come to asking for food is a poor one, where "there was a smell from the garbage pails over by the sink which were destined for the pigs, and sour rags and a strange undefinable house smell" and a "whole raft of fat, pasty-faced" children, who gape at the strange intruders (61). Life on the road seems infinitely healthier and better when compared with the unhealthy, enclosed life in that kitchen. The contrast, one of Lindgren's unfailing narrative techniques, becomes even clearer when we look at the preceding scene with Rasmus asleep on the ground: "He was lying on a floor of thyme, breathing in the good, spicy smell. The warmth of the sun also brought out the fragrance of the juniper bushes. These were summer smells and all his life they would bring back to him this summer day on the road" (59).

The Swedish countryside on a lovely summer day is painted in the brightest colors and most idyllic manner. It mirrors Rasmus's jubilance over his escape from the cold prison atmosphere of the orphanage, which finds its apogee in the strong and soft arms of Oscar's wife, Martina. This embrace and what it implies is the fulfillment of all his dreams and desires. He has found a home where he is treated with love and respect, for Martina, unlike many other grown-ups, does not make conversation just to be nice to him; she takes him seriously. Just then, Paradise Oscar's place seems like real paradise. A closer look reveals that the picture is not perfect. His new home comes with scant material resources, the fence is in need of repair, and hard labor waits on Nielsen's farm. But even these attributes can assume a warm glow in the moment of extreme and sublime happiness that Rasmus feels: "Yes, it was a day of miracles. He had a lake and a cat and a father and a mother. He had a home. The walls of the cottage were worn and shiny, almost like satin. What a beautiful house it was! With a thin, dirty little hand, Rasmus lovingly stroked the walls of the house that was his home" (192).

This special glow of happiness and exuberance that turns the worn cottage into a beautiful house tinges all the Småland books, which, like most of Lindgren's work, reflect the author's dreams of, and the reader's desire for, a happier and more humane life. The world would be a better place if all were as strong, loving, tolerant, humorous, and unconcerned with material wealth as Rasmus and his parents and almost all the main characters in her books. Because the world is not this better place, Lindgren feels compelled again and again to build up fictional counter-worlds for her young readers to stage the victory of good over evil, joy over gloom, courage over fear, freedom over oppression, the beautiful over the ugly, the playful over the somber.

The mean, ugly, and boring side of life is never denied, but Lindgren keeps it well-hidden from the eyes of her young readers. The narrator's and the protagonists' attitudes are positive through and through. Lindgren does not place shattered or abusive homes and neglectful or stifling parents into the center of action, as some recent children's authors have done. Such characters exist in her fiction only as marginal figures or as a point of departure to be replaced by a loving, respectful relationship either in reality or in the world of imagination. The mental geography of the Småland books is arranged in concentric circles around a safe center of love and trust at home from which the protagonists undertake forays into the big, always exciting, and sometimes nasty world beyond. Meanness, ugliness, and danger are relegated to the periphery, but through their presence they provide depth and fullness to the stories. The lives of the destitute and social outcasts, the falseness and pretentiousness of society remain as tangential and as present as the almost daily visits of the hoboes.

By limiting her perspective to the small world of a free and unencumbered childhood, Lindgren can make life into one big exciting adventure while still remaining truthful. Presentiments of disaster and evil are readily pushed aside and banished to the periphery, and a celebratory, playful mood saturated with love and laughter resides in this small world, which is tangible and yet ineffable, since it merges reality and fantasy. The small world of happiness and security may be a subterfuge, but one that is vital for our understanding and endurance in the big world that is painful, chaotic, and incomprehensible. It is a mere extension of those moments in time when existential loneliness is forgotten, human frailty is accepted, and life can be lived to its fullest. In this strangely realistic utopia Lindgren merges the best elements of modern child-rearing practices with the dearest wishes of the child within, which despite cultural and age differences still correspond to the desires of her readers around the world.

Lindgren has received many letters from young readers who want to know the exact location of Noisy Village, because they agree with Anna who feels sorry for the people who don't live there; they, too, want to move there. Lindgren has always been wise enough to answer that Noisy Village cannot be found on a map. The Noisy Village of her books is a world of make-believe, inspired by real experiences, which has become manifest in the imaginations of millions of children. In this respect, it is a truly a utopia, an imaginary place. The three small farmhouses that served as the setting for the stories can still be found in Sevedstorp, a small community close to Vimmerby, Lindgren's hometown. A replica of

Having escaped from the toolshed through the chimney, Emil disturbs a peaceful Saturday night in Lönneberga. Illustration by Björn Berg from *Nya hyss av Emil i Lönneberga* (*Emil's Pranks*).

Noisy Village, devoted to the famous characters and places from Lindgren's books, even exists at a theme park in Vimmerby.

Lindgren has always been vehemently opposed to commercial exploitation of her fictional characters. According to Kerstin Kvint, her literary agent, she insists that clauses be added to her book and film contracts prohibiting the sale of paraphernalia associated with her fictional characters. The theme park in Vimmerby is an exception to this rule, and it inspires visiting children to act out the stories in the books, much as Lindgren had done when she was a child, although without ready-made props. In the small town of Vimmerby, Astrid Lindgren's town, as it is officially promoted in a colorful brochure, children and their families can still find the sites where the Noisy Village children lived and played, where Emil and Meg got into mischief, where the Bergson gang roamed, and where Pippi made fools of honorable policemen and society ladies and bought forty pounds of candy. Lindgren's beautifully restored home—now surrounded by a growing suburban development—the mayor's house, the store where Anna and Lisa of Noisy Village and Pippi went shopping, and even the owl tree still stand. These sites are now, and have always been, perfectly ordinary sites, a reminder of the enchanting power of Lindgren's narrative.

Pippi playing tag with two policemen on the roof of Villa Villekulla. Illustration by Ingrid Yang Nyman from *Pippi Långstrump*, the original Swedish edition of *Pippi Longstocking*.

Chapter Three

Happy Anarchy:
Pippi Longstocking and
Karlsson-on-the-Roof

On second thought, however, perhaps there is a humorous temperament; a paradoxical view-point that combines profound compassion for human beings with profound irreverence for their institutions and behavior. A humorist, instead of worshiping sacred cows, would rather milk them.

    —Lloyd Alexander, "No Laughter in Heaven," *Horn Book Magazine*

Compensatory Fantasies

Two of Astrid Lindgren's best-known and most-beloved fictional charac-ters are without doubt Pippi Longstocking and Karlsson-on-the-Roof. In the United States, wild and wonderful Pippi is by far the better known of the two. Since the publication of *Pippi Longstocking* (1945), *Pippi Longstocking Goes on Board* (1946), and *Pippi in the South Seas* (1948), Lindgren's stories about Pippi have been reprinted and adapted to the screen and stage countless times all over the world. In the United States alone, the Pippi Longstocking books have been reprinted twenty-four times, and further reprints seem likely. After its first publication in Sweden, *Pippi* was broadcast on Swedish radio as early as 1946, and the story was staged as a play the same year. The first Swedish feature film about Pippi followed in 1949, and since then three more Swedish film adaptations of *Pippi Longstocking* have appeared. The 1988 Columbia Pictures film *The New Adventures of Pippi Longstocking* will probably not be the last in a long series.

Without exaggeration, one can say that *Pippi Longstocking* has become a modern classic in children's literature. Astrid Lindgren may not be the household name in the United States that she is in Sweden and in Northern Europe, but one need only introduce her as the author of *Pippi Longstocking* to get knowing nods and smiles. In fact, she is identified on the covers of the English translations of most of her works as the author of *Pippi Longstocking*. According to Lindgren's German publisher, Friedrich Oetinger Verlag in Hamburg, the Pippi books have been translated into fifty-six languages, and 4 million copies have been sold in Germany alone. The total number of Lindgren's books sold worldwide approach 40 million, the lion's share of which belongs to the books about *Pippi Longstocking*.[1]

What makes Pippi so attractive to readers of varying cultures, creeds, and languages? The stories' humor, tempo and suspense are the most obvious reasons. But these qualities alone would not have made the stories about Pippi Longstocking as influential and as world famous as they have become. It is rather that Pippi's superhuman qualities make her an ideal outlet for readers' compensatory fantasies and turn her into a vicarious playmate, a role she fills for Tommy and Annika, the children next door. Pippilotta Delicatessa Windowshade Mackrelmint Efraimsdaughter Longstocking is as outrageous as her name promises. She is the strongest, nicest, funniest, smartest, and richest girl in the whole world. Intangible yet real, she represents a most unusual combination of hero and consummate entertainer. When Pippi fights bullies, strong men, and thieves and saves little children from a burning house, she does it with bravura and even madcap sassiness. The lovely parties and outings she arranges for her playmates all contain hair-raising, discomfiting elements. By incessantly telling the most outrageous, nonsensical tales and by playing with words and meanings, Pippi outsmarts teachers and professors and ridicules narrow-mindedness and conceit.

Pippi Longstocking blends diverse cultural and literary patterns and conventions. The abundance of situation comedy and Pippi's clownish appearance seem inspired by slapstick comedies familiar from the movies of the 1930s and 1940s. Intermittently, Pippi resembles the folktale's trickster and imp, rascals like Tom Sawyer, and magical mother and fairy figures like Mary Poppins and Peter Pan. But any hint of heroism, mythmaking, and sentimentality is immediately undercut by humor.

With *Pippi Longstocking* Lindgren paid tribute to and overcame the nineteenth-century girl's book. Pippi's assertiveness, her red hair, freckles, and de facto orphanhood bear traces of Lucy Maud Montgomery's *Anne of Green Gables,* one of Lindgren's favorite books during her own childhood, as mentioned in the previous chapter. But Pippi is Anne taken to the extreme. The name of Pippi's abode, for example, is a playful reference to Grönkulla, the name of Anne of Green Gables' home in the Swedish translation.[2] Grönkulla, which means Green Hills, becomes Villekulla in Pippi Longstocking. Villervalla in Swedish means disorder or chaos, and chaos is exactly what Pippi introduced into the girl's book. When *Pippi Longstocking* first appeared in Sweden in 1945, the book upset readers' expectations by inverting value patterns, role models, and the stereotypical uniformity and predictability of the traditional girl's book. Just as Pippi resolutely puts her horse on the porch of her house because "he'd be in the way in the kitchen, and he doesn't like the parlor,"[3] Lindgren turned a few things upside down and brought new life to that old, dilapidated house of the traditional book for girls.

Pippi could not be farther removed from the heroines of nineteenth- and early twentieth-century girl's books in her behavior and her state of mind. She loves her freckles and her tattered clothes and makes not the slightest effort to suppress her wild imagination or to adopt good manners. An independent, emancipated girl, she can and does mock and parody the narrow-mindedness of bourgeois norms and values, and defies all authority with exuberant irreverence. Pippi's tomboy predecessors may have balked at conventions as well, but Pippi plainly refuses to adapt to the norms of the establishment with the ultimate consequence that she refuses to grow up. Her success depends in large part on her magic powers. Very likely it is the ingenious constellation of power and parody, in which Pippi undermines and makes fun of the powers that be and prevails in a carnivalesque celebration of life.

Karlsson-on-the-Roof (1955) has not achieved the same popularity as Pippi internationally or in the United States. Actually, Karlsson has led rather a shadow existence here. There are countries where he actually supersedes Pippi in popularity, namely Russia and the former Eastern bloc countries. In the former Soviet Union alone, 2.5 million copies of *Karlsson-on-the-Roof* have been sold, with the book further popularized by Russian film and stage productions.[4] It is tempting to hypothesize about the difference in reception and popularity of these two books. Availability plays a major role, and as Vivi Edström explains in her book about Astrid Lindgren, Karlsson-on-the-Roof was in 1957 the first of her characters introduced in the Soviet Union.[5] Without doubt, socio-cultural and ideological differences also affect the stories' impact on readers and alter their appeal. Maybe a history of forced solidarity and an official discourse that suppressed private initiative and egocentrism contributed to the appreciation of this selfish, self-centered, and unreliable fictional character who lives for one thing only: his own pleasure. Be that as it may, both Karlsson and Pippi are humorous and farcical fantasy characters who are loved because, psychologically, they fulfill the readers' desire for pleasure, power, fun, and excitement.

Like most Småland books, the stories about Pippi and Karlsson are episodic in character. In all three volumes about Pippi, readers follow her escapades, which are hilarious, nonsensical, and exhilarating. In *Pippi Longstocking* Pippi plays tag with policemen, eats up a whole whipped-cream cake, and scares off two thieves who want to steal her gold coins. *Pippi Goes on Board* has her buy eighteen kilos (approximately forty pounds) of candy for the town's children, take Tommy and Annika, very normal children and her best friends, to a deserted island, and go to the circus where she ends up performing herself. And in *Pippi in the South Seas* Pippi gets the better of sharks, bandits, real estate investors, teachers, and society ladies by using her wits and turning the language inside out.

In *Karlsson-on-the-Roof,* which has more of a story line, Eric, the youngest boy in a middle-class Stockholm family, feels misunderstood and inferior; he longs for attention. He fills his lonely hours with pranks and fantasies, which come alive in Karlsson, a tubby, little "Man in his Prime," with a propeller mounted on his back. Karlsson and Eric sneak up on people, tease Eric's siblings, take dangerous walks on the rooftop, fly around the neighborhood, masquerade as ghosts, and chase two dim-witted robbers, Guffy and Ruffy. Karlsson lives in a little house on the roof of Eric's apartment building, which, incidentally, is in just as much disarray as is Pippi's Villa Villekulla, but with one decisive difference. The chaos he has created in his house is the result of his lackadaisical attitude, whereas Pippi's chaos stems from her boundless creative energy. The adventures of Karlsson-on-the-Roof in the English version end with Eric's eighth birthday party, when Eric receives the present he has longed for intensely, a puppy to call his own and cherish. Not even Bimbo, the puppy, can take the place of Karlsson, however, who appears at the birthday party to stuff himself with cake (just as Pippi does at Mrs. Settergren's) and to shock Eric's parents and siblings.

Vivi Edström calls Karlsson an immoral Pippi who selectively portrays the selfish and bullying qualities and nasty quips Lindgren had deleted from her original Pippi manuscript. Even the nonsense verses that Lindgren had to cut from the Pippi manuscript reappear in a fresh guise in the two sequels to *Karlsson-on-the-Roof, Karlsson på taket flyger igen* (Karlsson-on-the-Roof flies again, 1962) and *Karlsson på taket smyger igen* (Karlsson-on-the-Roof sneaks again, 1968) (Edström 1992, 126). Neither sequel has been published in the United States, and, consequently, American readers hear only about some of Karlsson's pranks and miss the nonsense rhymes entirely. (Patricia Crampton translated the second part of the Karlsson trilogy for Methuen Publishers in London, where it appeared under the title *Karlson Flies Again* in 1977.)

In mood and setting the books about Pippi and Karlsson are fairly different, but conceptual similarities invite comparison. Like Pippi, Karlsson symbolizes childhood's easy transgressions between fantasy and reality, its desire for instant gratification, and its delusions of grandeur. Both books oscillate between the colorful world of fantasy and play and the rather ordinary, conventional everyday life of well-educated middle-class children. Both burst with crazy ideas and sweep readers along into a world that is full of rambunctiousness and excitement, merriment, and pranks. Pippi and Karlsson are brilliant distillations of those aspects of childhood that are suppressed, denied, and eradicated in the process of socialization. Thus, Pippi and Karlsson fulfill young readers' dreams by letting them live out repressed feelings vicariously. Together with Pippi and Karlsson readers can for a moment forget the anxiety, boredom, and feelings of dependence, envy, and helplessness they encounter in their daily lives and instead give in to their desire for pleasure.

With Pippi and Karlsson Lindgren created a dream come true for a "child's will to power," a phrase coined by Bertrand Russell, whose thoughts in turn are based on Alfred Adler's theories that inferiority complexes and compensatory drives create neuroses. Lindgren acknowledges Russell's influence on her thinking in the letter that accompanied her first manuscript to Bonniers Publishing house in 1944: "In Bertrand Russell . . . I read that the preeminent instinctive drive in childhood is the drive to grow up, or rather the will to power, and that the normal child will surrender to fantasies reflecting this will to power. I do not know if Bertrand Russell is right, but I tend to believe it, judging from the almost sickly popularity that Pippi has enjoyed with my own children and friends their age" (Strömstedt, 250–51). Pippi and Karlsson both live completely independent lives in their own delightfully dilapidated houses, both feast on candy and cream cakes, and, above all, both talk back and make fun of those adults who are in the habit of reprimanding children and having the last word. Both project childhood fantasies and childish feelings of omnipotence, but they do it in very different ways.

The differences between Karlsson-on-the-Roof and Pippi Longstocking hinge on the ages of the main protagonists as well as the narrative perspective. Despite all of his fantastic qualities, Karlsson is a much more realistic figure than Pippi. In just about every respect he is a scaled-down version of her. He lacks Pippi's heroic qualities and he is not as smart, courageous, loving, strong, or fault-free. Befitting his stature and character, his house and sphere of influence are also much smaller. While Pippi roams the globe in spirit—and later in action when she takes Tommy and Annika to the South Seas—Karlsson pretty much limits his excursions to one part of town. Fat and complacent, Karlsson is a demythified Peter Pan who does not take Eric to never-never land but only on short airborne excursions to the roof of his apartment building and around the immediate neighborhood. His sphere of action coincides fully with Eric's everyday experiences and reality.

Pippi's power is universal and natural—she is simply stronger and richer and more clever than the rest—whereas Karlsson's superhuman quality seems contrived and is based purely on pretense. His self-appraisal as the "World's Best Karlsson" and shouts of "Hooray, how clever I am!" only underscore his pretentiousness and complacency. Karlsson's superlative claims to be the World's Best Steam Engineer, Stunt-Flyer, Meat Ball Maker, Building Erector, Thinker-Upper, Rooster Painter, Nurse Maid, Fire Putter-Outer, Magician, Grandchild, and Tricker are repeatedly revealed as untrue. His claim to be the World's Best Cake-Eater is at least debatable, for, whenever he can, he stuffs himself with goodies and candy, which he lures Eric into giving him as a bribe or, on one occasion, as "medicine," under the pretext of being the World's Illest.

When something goes wrong, as it invariably does, he never takes the blame. His favorite saying, "It's a small matter," attests to his nonchalance. Even his claim to fame, his ability to fly, is purely mechanical, as it turns out, for he simply has a propeller strapped to his back—not maintenance-free, by the way—with which he buzzes through the air like a little live helicopter. Next to the truly glamorous Pippi, who is altogether trustworthy—even to Tommy and Annika's mother—despite her tall tales and lies, Karlsson seems an inflated, self-absorbed, pompous busybody. Karlsson lacks Pippi's lightness and her electrifying enjoyment of life. He tends to be egotistical, sulky, and self-pitying at times, and despite his flying stunts this pot-bellied little man remains rather ponderous and clumsy.

More so than Karlsson, Pippi pulls the reader right into compensatory dream worlds. Reality occasionally intrudes into fantasy, but generally the reality plane remains as blurry and nondescript as Tommy and Annika's house or parents. Pippi is unquestionably the focus and main character of the Pippi Longstocking books, Tommy and Annika are not. In *Karlsson-on-the-Roof,* on the other hand, Eric is the main character and his family and environment are the primary plane into which the fantastic in the form of Karlsson intrudes, when he suddenly comes flying in through the open window. Lindgren makes it clear at the outset of each of these books who is to be the focus of attention. *Pippi Longstocking* opens: "Way out at the end of a tiny little town was an old overgrown garden, and in the garden was an old house, and in the house lived Pippi Longstocking. She was nine years old, and she lived there all alone" (11). Tommy and Annika only enter the scene four pages later. *Karlsson-on-the-Roof* starts out quite differently: "On a perfectly ordinary street in Stockholm, in a perfectly ordinary house, lives a perfectly ordinary family called Ericson. There is a perfectly ordinary Daddy and a perfectly ordinary Mommy and three perfectly ordinary children—Bobby, Betty, and Eric."[6] Eric, whose Swedish name "Lillebror" literally translates into "little brother," is the youngest member of the family. Sometimes he feels left out, pushed aside, belittled, and misunderstood, and on these occasions his compensatory alter-ego, Karlsson, lets him forget his disappointments. With Karlsson at his side, Eric attracts the attention of the others and easily succumbs to delusions of power.

An infantile little flying man in the prime of his life, Karlsson-on-the-Roof represents childhood at its best and worst. In the company of Karlsson, Eric displays naive thoughtlessness in innocently cruel games that Lindgren remembers from her own childhood. Dressing up as ghosts to sneak up on his big sister, who is necking with her boyfriend, is one of these scenes that has echoes in Emil and Noisy Village books. In her recollections, Lindgren regrets the involuntary cruelty of children who are not able to foresee the consequences of their action, a matter that still weighs heavily on her adult conscience ("I Remember . . . ," 156). In his "Karlsson" state Eric breaks things, sneaks around and spies on people, and sulks when he feels cheated, yet he himself cheats, avoids work whenever possible, and escapes all responsibility. Karlsson's displays of nastiness, his inflated self-image, his gluttony and greediness, his stubbornness and defiance, his constant lying and phoniness, his lack of self-control, and his manipulative manner are expressions of the self that are not sanctioned by society. But Lindgren asks her readers to be forgiving of these weaknesses, because these are very human and very "childish" qualities.

With *Karlsson-on-the-Roof* Lindgren presents a side of childhood and human nature that is far from standard in children's books and farther still from the childhood ideal embodied by Pippi. The urban child Eric is also far removed from the comparative freedom and adventure experienced by the rural children of Noisy Village. In fact, with Karlsson, Lindgren has created an antihero with whom some readers have difficulty identifying. He reveals a side of childhood that many older readers would rather forget and that they dislike. On the other hand, his unrestrained, impulsive behavior may also fascinate readers, because it belongs to the realm of the forbidden and taboo. The reason for the mixed response to this novel and to its main protagonist, Karlsson, who is both strongly loved and disliked, can be sought there. Despite his negative character traits, Karlsson has many endearing and redeeming qualities that also belong to Eric's stage of childhood, around the age of seven. He is playful, optimistic, creative, and, in his own way, for Eric at least, as seductive as Pippi.

Eric's invisible playmate and compensatory fantasy figure, Karlsson, is based on observation and deep psychological understanding of a child's feelings of inferiority and longing for power, reflecting occurrences that Lindgren herself must have experienced as a mother and housewife in her Stockholm apartment, where the novel is set. *Karlsson-on-the-Roof* is one of the few Lindgren stories in which the perspective of the adult writer seems to interfere with that of the child, and at times even dominates it. *Pippi Longstocking,* on the contrary, is written from one perspective only, that of the child. Pippi expresses the longings of Lindgren's child within, with which both her old and young readers can identify. In a 1966 interview with Ellen Buttenschøn, Lindgren talks about the intentions that lay behind *Pippi Longstocking:* "I did not want anything else when I invented her than to satisfy a wishful desire within me. The fictional character of Pippi represents my own childish longing to meet a person who has power but does not abuse it. And pay attention to the fact that Pippi never does that."[7]

Pippi, a Powerful Friend

The first book about Pippi Longstocking came about during one of the darkest times in twentieth-century Europe. Between 1941, when the fictional character Pippi assumed a life of her own in response to Lindgren's daughter's need for entertainment, and 1945, when the first episodes were published, World War II raged on the continent, and the Nazi regime in Germany provided ample evidence of the dark sides of human nature and the corrupting effect of power. Against the background of so much cruelty and misery, and responding to an intense desire to escape and improve the world, Lindgren created in the character of Pippi a human ideal able to inspire hope and happiness.

Pippi is a supergirl not only because of her strength but also because she is equally superior on account of her goodness and fairness. Through Pippi, Tommy and Annika—and the reader, as well—meet chaos and adventure in faraway places in the safe and enjoyable form of illusion and spectacle. Pippi's wild imagination, wit, and energy provide an environment that is exhilarating and at times unsettling. But Tommy and Annika know they can always trust her, for without fail she takes their side and the side of the helpless and abused in a unique show of solidarity. Pippi has been compared with Mary Poppins, and there is definitely something motherly and protective about her. Teasing, impish Pippi is also a loving, warm friend, and Tommy and Annika can be sure she will always stand by them and defend them. Pippi is their entertainer, their looking glass, and their guiding star, twinkling with wit and irony.

Pippi straddles the realm of the conventional, proper, and acceptable and the realm of the unconventional, improper, and unacceptable. She lives at the periphery of town, in a no-man's land between the small town and the wide open sea. The daughter of an angel—as Pippi unsentimentally calls her mother who died while giving birth to her—and a pirate and cannibal king, Pippi has inherited only the best traits from both and resembles neither. An angelic Pippi would have been a poor main character for a fantastic prankster story; on the other hand, her wild and revolutionary spirit does not permit abuse of power, injustice, or violence. Her parentage makes her intangible and invincible, but also down-to-earth and very human; she puts up a good fight, but is at the same time peace loving and compassionate and can secretly shed tears about a dead bird that has been kicked out of its nest.

Pippi's performances and stories may be tall, and her presence may dominate the story, but she is never domineering. The power she represents is not the static power of domination, which easily gives way to abuse. Pippi is a sworn enemy of all violence and of any abuse of power. Despite her sabre swinging and pistol shooting, Pippi practices nonviolence, and she can afford it, since she is the strongest girl in the world. A show of power and the element of surprise suffice to intimidate her adversaries. Usually, her reprisals take the form of a big shake-up. She simply throws rogues and bullies high up in the air a few times, and when they come down they respect her, keep out of her way, and even mend their ways.

In *Pippi in the South Seas,* the last of the Pippi books, Lindgren takes issue with some harsh early criticism of *Pippi Longstocking.* The stories about Pippi were in bad taste, critics said, and exerted a bad influence on readers by teaching them bad manners. Through Mrs. Settergren, Tommy and Annika's mother, Lindgren confronts those critics who shuddered at the thought of child readers carried away by Pippi's dangerous nonsense. In the book these critics take the form of society ladies in Pippi's small town, who voice their indignation at Mrs. Settergren's decision to leave the children in Pippi's care and even let them go off to the South Seas with her: "You don't mean that you're thinking of sending your children off to the South Seas with Pippi Longstocking? You can't be serious!" Whereupon Mrs. Settergren calmly replies: "And why shouldn't I? The children have been sick and the doctor says they need a change of climate. As long as I've known Pippi, she has never done anything that has harmed Tommy and Annika in any way. No one can be kinder than she" (66). The excursion into fantasy and fiction with Pippi is healthy and strengthening, just what the doctor ordered. With the fresh winds Pippi Longstocking brought into children's fiction Lindgren provided her readers with a beneficial change of climate as well. And to those who still wrinkle their noses like the ladies in the little town, Mrs. Settergren adds a further explanation: "Pippi Longstocking's manners may not always be what they ought to. But her heart is in the right place" (67).

There was a slight wrinkling of noses at Rabén and Sjögren as well at Pippi's lack of respect and impudence toward adults when Lindgren submitted her first manuscript for publication. Pippi had much rougher edges then. Ulla Lundqvist, comparing this early version of the manuscript with the printed version, shows how Lindgren gave in to some of these pressures to change Pippi (Lundqvist, 99). Lindgren revised approximately one-third of the text, and the Pippi that emerged was a little more polite, a little less chaotic and nonsensical, and a little more the innocent nature child or noble savage who criticizes civilized society by simply being what she is.

Thus, the character of Pippi, as we now know it, emerges as a unique and irresistible blend of noble savage, superhero, good friend, trickster, and clown. The trickster part of Pippi is still allowed stinging attacks on hypocrisy and abuse of power, but in the revisions much of the criticism is hidden behind a veneer of apparent compliance, childhood innocence, and nonsense. In the manuscript, for example, Pippi's visit to school exasperates and exhausts the teacher. Before she leaves, Pippi announces gleefully, while swinging from a lamp, that she is not coming back to school because she has no time for such childishness. In the final, cleaned-up version the teacher is assuaged by an earthbound Pippi's rueful explanation: "Have I behaved badly? Goodness, I didn't know that.

. . . You understand Teacher, don't you, that when you have a mother who's an angel and a father who is a cannibal king, and when you have sailed on the ocean all your life, then you don't know just how to behave in school with all the apples and ibexes" (*Pippi Longstocking*, 59).

Typically, Lindgren cleansed the manuscript of some of Pippi's nasty quips and of her excessive back talk to adults. Thus, the entire dialogue with one Mr. Lundin, who wants to take Pippi to a children's home, was cut because of Pippi's rudeness and defiance. His insulting remark, "Just look what hair this child has—maybe it will get better with age, but right now it is most certainly not pretty," is turned back on him by Pippi when she wonders what color hair Mr. Lundin might have had before becoming bald. She suggests blue, since that color would match Mr. Lundin's red nose perfectly (Lundqvist, 107). In *Pippi in the South Seas,* Lindgren no longer exerts self-censorship and instead lets Pippi talk back in a similar situation. A "fine gentleman" who wants to buy Villa Villekulla allows himself a little fun at Pippi's expense by pulling her red pigtails and comparing her head to a newly lighted match. Becoming even ruder, he blurts out: "I really think you're the ugliest child I've ever seen," and Pippi retorts tit for tat, "Well, you're not exactly a beauty yourself" (18). Swear words and references to snuff, sexuality, and alcohol were also removed from the first manuscript. They too reappeared in Lindgren's later books when she had gained greater stature and more self-confidence as a writer. Emil, for example, witnesses brawling drunkards and even—without quite planning it—gets drunk himself; he tries out snuff, and swear words are not unknown to him.

The same tendency to tidy up the text and adapt it to existing norms that we find in the first book about Pippi Longstocking can be encountered in the translation of the books from Swedish into English, compounding the effect of censorship. In a letter from 27 January 1959, the children's books editor at Viking Press suggested to Lindgren just before its publication that she delete chapter two of *Pippi in the South Seas* entirely, arguing:

> The difficulty with the teaparty episode is that Pippi really gets out of character and behaves so brashly and rudely that she's not really very funny any more. In all the other episodes of her career no matter how outrageous she is she's always kind, and the children who read about her feel this and that's one of the reasons why they love her so. But this time she isn't kind at all, just a rather tiresome "show-off." These may seem like harsh words, but I know you'll understand that we're really protecting Pippi from herself, so to speak. We'd hate like anything to have her behave so badly in public![8]

Pippi's "behaving badly in public" was precisely the point of this chapter; Pippi's "childishness" is used as a literary device by Lindgren to criticize hollow social conventions, pretentiousness, and current educational norms. Thus, to Mrs. Settergren's remark that children should be seen and not heard, Pippi replies, "it's nice if people are happy just to look at me! I must see how it feels to be used just for decoration," and she sits down on the grass with a fixed smile (23–24). Lindgren, who was herself an editor at Rabén and Sjögren at the time, stood her ground, and the chapter remained intact in the English translation. Only a few things were changed, among them Pippi's cure for her grandmother's nervousness. In the original, Pippi suggests rat poison (literally fox poison), but in the translation the medication is a harmless tranquilizer. Furthermore, Lindgren accepted the editor's suggestion to eliminate all specific references to the skin color of the South Sea Island people because of the American sensitivity to racial questions.

Overall, the English translation is fairly true to the original. The same cannot be said of the French adaptation of *Pippi Longstocking*. The editor of the first edition of *Pippi Longstocking* in France seems to have had little appreciation for the tallness of the Pippi tale. He wrote to Astrid Lindgren that the French Pippi (Fifi Brindacier) couldn't possibly be made to lift a horse—a pony would be more like it. His reasoning was that Swedish children might perhaps believe absurdities about a small girl being capable of lifting a whole horse, since Sweden had not been involved in World War II. French children, however, were much too realistic to swallow such unreasonable stuff. That is why Fifi Brindacier lifts only a pony. Lindgren in return asked the editor to send her a photo of a ten-year-old French girl lifting a pony with one hand, because that child would most assuredly have a secure future as a weight lifter.[9]

Pippi's rudeness to those who are mean and rude themselves does not detract from her innate goodness of heart toward those who need help. Pippi is not generally disrespectful; on the contrary, she has high respect for fairness and for "earned" authority. She only ridicules abusive and pretentious behavior. In Pippi's topsy-turvy world, where petit-bourgeois values like orderliness and cleanliness are definitely not prime virtues, other values, such as empathy, responsibility, and respect for fellow human beings are upheld and even reinforced by her assertiveness and underhanded criticism of power abuse and narrow-mindedness.

Pippi is free to do what her readers only dream about for three reasons: she is terribly strong, so strong that she easily lifts her horse with one hand; she is unfathomably rich, "as rich as a troll," in her words; and she is smart—an unbeatable combination of qualities indeed. Despite her poor skills in spelling and in math, she is extremely articulate and outwits everybody. Pippi certainly has the brawn, the brains, and the means to handle any situation, and she can say with the power of conviction, "Don't you worry about me. I'll always come out on top" (*Pippi Longstocking,* 14). She always does, even when she eats a poisonous mushroom or saves little children from a burning house in a tightrope balancing act. Nine-year-old Pippi's independent spirit is aptly illustrated in her exchange with her father shortly before he departs on his ship *Hoptoad* to ravage the seas in *Pippi Goes on Board:* " 'You're right, as always, my daughter,' answered Captain Longstocking. 'It is certain that you live a more orderly life in Villa Villekulla, and that is probably best for little children.' 'Just so,' said Pippi. 'It's surely best for little children to live an orderly life, especially if they can order it themselves.'"[10]

By the end of *Pippi Goes on Board,* no reader will miss the irony of this statement. Pippi certainly does not lead an "orderly life" in Villa Villekulla, where she lives with her monkey and her horse, where she sleeps with her feet on the pillow, "the way they sleep in Guatemala," and where everything is in great disarray. The way she makes herself go to bed at night is equally unorthodox: "First I tell myself in a nice friendly way; and then, if I don't mind, I tell myself again more sharply; and if I still don't mind, then I'm in for a spanking—see?" (*Pippi Longstocking,* 20). Tommy and Annika, to whom she has offered this explanation, cannot always follow Pippi's mental somersaults; they remain confused. Maybe readers are, too, but they soon learn that Pippi basically does what she pleases when she pleases, and, furthermore, they are told that Pippi always goes to bed extremely late. Given this context, Pippi's measures of self-control are pure farce, underhandedly throwing open to question the purpose of strict bedtime practices as well as spanking.

As I have pointed out, superchild Pippi is based on Lindgren's desire to create a positive counterimage to situations of power abuse that she encountered and heard about during the war years. Long before Alice Miller's psychoanalytically based findings about poisonous pedagogy and the antiauthoritarian educational wave took hold in the 1980s, Lindgren argued for a revision of strict authoritarian educational practice because of its hidden violence, which itself could in turn foster violence, an argument in line with the one Alice Miller makes in *For Your Own Good: Hidden Cruelty in Child-Rearing and the Roots of Violence.*[11] Pippi is a symbol of freedom held up against all those overeducated bourgeois children of the 1930s and 1940s whose strict and rigid socialization never allowed their bodies and spirits to move freely and develop fully. Tommy and Annika are model products of that kind of education, before Pippi enters the scene: "They were good, well brought up, and obedient children. Tommy would never think of biting his nails, and he always did exactly what his mother told him to do. Annika never fussed when she didn't get her own way, and she always looked pretty in her little well-ironed cotton dresses; she took the greatest care not to get them dirty" (*Pippi Longstocking,* 14).

This little *Übermensch,* as Lindgren herself called Pippi in 1944, in her letter accompanying the first manuscript, embodies the ideal child of modern pedagogy envisioned in A. S. Neill's Summerhill model, which was discussed in progressive circles during the 1940s. The British educational pioneer set up a progressive, experimental school in 1924 (first in Dorset, then Suffolk) based on the educational principles of freedom of choice and participatory democracy. (Neill's experiment has aroused controversy in educational circles up to our day.) Like Rousseau's educational ideal, Emile, experience, not books, has taught Pippi what she knows. She is free, happy, and strong, and at the same time full of imagination, creativity, and warmth. Her casual and natural egocentricity—reminiscent of Rousseau's *amour-de-soi*—has been allowed to develop freely, so she can approach every task with the nonchalance and self-confidence characteristic of someone whose self-esteem is not clouded by the least bit of doubt. Consequently, Pippi is free from feelings of uncertainty, fear, and inferiority that might breed violent and aggressive behavior.

Tommy and Annika's parents, as well as Eric's, embrace new educational ideas even more than do Emil's and the Noisy Village parents. Both sets of parents are generally permissive and understanding. They recognize their children's need for playful imagination and experimentation by acknowledging their fantastic playmates. Mrs. Settergren is fully aware of Pippi's beneficial influence on her children, and even Eric's parents, who are presented with a much less idealized "childishness" in the form of Eric's invisible playmate Karlsson (who breaks toys, plays pranks, and gets into trouble), learn to accept it as they acknowledge Karlsson's presence at the end of the story. In effect, *Karlsson-on-the-Roof* can be read as a manual in parenting and family relations.

Family members' interactions change over time, and the family's learning process is depicted in their gradual appreciation of Karlsson's behavior. To begin with, the whole family, and especially Eric's older siblings, think that Karlsson—the pleasure-drive side of Eric—is the most rotten, spoiled, and clumsy good-for-nothing in the world. Over time, they get used to him, accept him, and almost like him in the end. His parents even react with magnanimity when Eric talks back. When Eric is told to sit up straight at the dinner table and eat his cauliflower, he is not punished when he replies, "I'd rather be dead." And they show love and understanding in trying situations. Just as Meg's mother assures the guilt-ridden girl that she loves her no matter what, Eric's mother gives him a big hug after his life-threatening excursion with Karlsson to the roof of their apartment building, from which he descends in the arms of a fireman. She assures him, "We wouldn't be without you for anything in the world, surely you know that?" (79–80).

Lindgren's subversive humor carries much of her pedagogical message as well. To Annika's question of why she has to eat hot cereal every day, which she finds repulsive, Pippi answers, "How can you ask anything so stupid? Of course you have to eat your good cereal. If you don't eat your good cereal, then you won't grow and get big and strong. And if you don't get big and strong, then you won't have the strength to force *your* children, when you have some, to eat *their* good cereal. No, Annika, that won't do. Nothing but the most terrible disorder in cereal-eating would come of this if everyone talked like you" (*Pippi in the South Seas,* 56–57). In effect, it is Pippi who brings disorder into cereal eating and the rest of Tommy and Annika's life by willfully misunderstanding and misappropriating things to upset and question the conventional order. Her favorite method is to question the obvious by means of a queer, slanted logic, by parody, or by telling fibs, lies, and tall tales.

Tall Tales and Lies

Lindgren's stories about Karlsson-on-the-Roof are full of excitement, fun, and situation comedy. In Karlsson's company Eric gets into hilarious mischief. Together they make fun of people and play tricks on them, but Karlsson does not take it well when the joke is on him. In effect, he lacks humor. Humor is a socially acquired skill, and Eric—especially his Karlsson self—has not reached that degree of maturity. Befitting his role as the personification of an ordinary child's fantasy life and naughty alter ego, Karlsson moves only in the circles prescribed by Eric's environment and everyday concerns. Most of the time, the two stay in the apartment, dress up as ghosts, and terrify members of the family, friends, as well as three slightly dim-witted thieves. On one of these occasions Karlsson describes himself with his usual complacency as a "little motorized ghost—savage but beautiful." There is very little that can be called

The world's best Karlsson high up in the air. Illustration by Ilon Wikland from *Karlsson på taket smyger igen*, the third volume of the Swedish Karlsson-on-the-Roof books.

beautiful about this tubby little selfish fellow, but there is something savage about him; he lacks social grace. Selfish and self-indulgent, he does what he pleases most of the time; but since he is not strong or rich or clever, and since his ability to fly is his only distinguishing characteristic, his self-indulgence is rather limited. While Pippi is superhuman, Karlsson is all-too-human. In sum, he is the realistic counterpart to the noble savage Pippi represents.

"Savage but beautiful" Karlsson (as he describes himself repeatedly) enters Eric's life much as the Cat in the Hat enters Sally's and her brother's lives in Dr. Seuss's classic story. Eric is all alone in his room and bored when Karlsson comes flying through the window, and with him enters mayhem. Compared with the Cat in the Hat's cartoon-like, exaggerated creation of chaos, Karlsson's impact seems small, but the cumulative effect is still considerable. In his presence Eric's steam engine explodes, the bathtub overflows and the apartment is put under water, or the curtains are sucked up into the vacuum cleaner. Like Sally and her brother, Eric initially has misgivings about Karlsson's ideas; his conscience restrains his pleasure drive. But in the end the lure of pleasure becomes too strong, and he abandons himself to the adventure of the game.

As a rule, Eric is tricked into doing Karlsson's bidding and then thoroughly enjoys his presence, but once the fun is over he has to deal with the unpleasant consequences. Whereas the Cat in the Hat reveals himself as a figment of Sally and her brother's imagination, a vicarious thrill they experience in reading, because he can turn mayhem into order within a split second before mother comes home, Karlsson is the real, "savage" part of Eric. Invariably, Eric's excursions and experiments with Karlsson leave behind traces: a broken steam engine, a wet apartment, and torn curtains. Each disaster reveals Karlsson's claims as "the world's best" to be a lie, and his inflated self-esteem is promptly and repeatedly deflated. Superchild Pippi, on the other hand, lives up to her reputation, since she is a tall tale herself and not a representation of a child's delusions of omnipotence. She is not subject to the reality checks of parental supervision and social demands and consequently gets away with telling the most outrageous tall tales.

In her personal lore Lindgren tells us that it was her daughter Karin who invented the name Pippi Longstocking, a name so wild and crazy that the stories themselves simply had to turn out the same way. This name triggered in her mind a long row of tall tales about Pippi, who in turn delights in telling tall tales. Pippi is the material expression of Lindgren's childhood spirit—the childlike dreams and desires she shares with millions of readers—and once Pippi entered the realm of fiction, she also entered Lindgren's real life to stay. In her 1986 picture book *Assar Bubbla* (Assar Bubble), Lindgren gives expression to this phenomenon. Pippi enters Lindgren's apartment in Stockholm complete with horse and monkey, just as she entered Lindgren's life in the form of the name chosen by her daughter Karin. She takes over as she plops down in a chair with her horse in her lap, rocking it back and forth to give some real meaning to the word rocking horse. Quite a number of crazy, unbelievable things happen as a result of Pippi's visit, and it is hard to tell which of the two friends tells the tallest tales.

In this hybrid story, hovering between autobiography and fantasy, Lindgren tells us in a Pippiesque manner about the disappearance of the

Pippi Longstocking manuscript, which could have been the author's night-mare: "Now I shall tell you what a close call it was that there would not have been a book about Pippi Longstocking. It was the big thief Assar Bubble's fault, for he stole my brown briefcase. It happened on a street-car. There were streetcars in Stockholm at that time, for this happened a long time ago."[12] This short farcical tale, told in the form of an anecdote from life, does have a quality of "truthfulness," as Lindgren uses the word, when she talks about her work. For in this story there lives the author's playfulness, love of tall tales and wordplay, sense of humor, and keen sense of fairness. But it is also a great big lie. Ironically, it is Pippi who states with great relief, sitting next to Astrid at the time the stolen manuscript is finally returned, "Now you don't have to lie anymore!" (37). In a playful manner this tale—which can also be read as a "meta-tale," or a tale about a tale—introduces young readers to the ambiguous nature of taletelling. In fiction as in childhood, relationships between truth and fiction are complex, and the borderlines are permeable. Just as Pippi, the fantastic figure, is anchored in everyday reality, *Assar Bubbla,* too, straddles both realms and makes the readers wonder where fantasy ends and reality begins.

The most profound and pervasive traits in *Pippi Longstocking* are the heroine's penchant for the extraordinary and her nonchalant treatment of the distinction between fact and fiction, between truth and lies. In Pippi's world of fiction, truth and lies are indiscernible. One can never be quite sure whether she is serious or not. She tells one fib or tall story after another, does everything backward, and laughs at others and herself. She does not even spare her own birthday party, which becomes a parody of the already parodied coffee party at Mrs. Settergren's. In a social environ-ment that cannot tolerate blurred lines between fact and fiction Pippi is an anomaly and a challenge. As a matter of fact, neither Tommy and Annika nor the reader/listener can ever be quite sure of her. The Pippi stories elude total comprehension because of their inner contradictions and ambiguities, which add to their lasting attraction. Their playful inter-mingling of sense and nonsense, their denial of any demarcation between the two make reading the episodes a challenging pleasure.

Pippi's awe-inspiring ability to straddle the no man's land between fact and fiction stands out in the chapter "Pippi Sits on the Gate and Climbs a Tree" from *Pippi Longstocking.* Sitting on the gate Pippi tells a girl who is looking for her father an incredible story about Hai Shang from Shanghai, whose ears are so big he can use them for a cape and who has more children than he can count. Peter, one of Hai Shang's children—and Pippi comments on the oddness of the name—is pigheaded and does not want to eat the swallow's nest his parents serve him for dinner. The story parodies the "Suppenkasper" story in Heinrich Hoffmann's *Struwwelpeter*. Like the boy Kasper's soup plate in Hoffmann's story, the swallow's nest rides in and out of the kitchen from May until October, for Peter will get nothing else to eat until he has eaten what he is served. Peter steadfastly refuses to eat the swallow's nest and dies of "Plain Common Ordinary Pigheadedness" (*Pippi Longstocking*, 66). Like Kasper, Peter dies, but the story's absurdity and Pippi's comments do away with the moralistic undertones of the original cautionary tale.

In this story and many others, Lindgren takes little bits and pieces from popular lore and the narrative tradition for children and combines them into a collage that becomes a new story, often with a very different subtext. Another source of inspiration for the Hai Shang story may have been an episode in the popular Swedish film *Intermezzo* by Gustaf Molander, released in Sweden in 1936. In this film, a little girl's uncle tells her a story about a Chinese eating birds' nests which both confounds and amuses her. There are more turns to the Hai Shang tale, however, as Lindgren focuses on the reception of the story. The girl who listens to the story at first says, "Nonsense!" but is immediately reprimanded for not believing what Pippi tells her. A second later she is scolded for believing that a child can live without food from May until October: "To be sure, I know they can get along without food for three of four months all right. But from May to October! It's just foolish to think that. You must know that's a lie. You mustn't let people fool you so easily" (*Pippi Longstocking*, 67). The girl leaves utterly confused, and Tommy, Annika, and the reader/listener, too, may be a little dizzy from Pippi's somersaults of logic.

The incongruity of the tall tale, in which events are disguised as facts and then taken far beyond the limits of credibility, adds to the confusion. Tall tales literally come gushing out of Pippi. Apropos of walking in a gutter full of water, Pippi asserts, "In America the gutters are so full of children, that there is no room for the water. They stay there the year round. Of course in the winter they freeze in and their heads stick up through the ice. Their mothers have to carry fruit soup and meatballs to them because they can't come home for dinner" (*Pippi Longstocking*, 16). To cheer up Aunt Laura, Pippi tells her a long and crazy story—that in fact greatly annoys her aunt—about a cow who comes flying through the window of a train and sits down right next to her. The aunt's—and very likely the adult reader's—sense of humor is very different from

Pippi's. Consequently, the aunt misses the punch line completely, which is not the cow's ability to fly or to sit down, but her choice of a smoked herring sandwich when she could have had a sausage sandwich (*Pippi in the South Seas,* 27).

Like the narrator of Knut Hamsun's *Hunger,* Pippi gets carried away with the fascination of the study. The narrator, weakened by hunger and slightly delirious, tells the most outrageous lies to a harmless and somewhat feeble-minded old man sitting next to him on a park bench. He is eying the old man's sandwiches, but soon forgets his pangs of hunger, for, as he says, "I was entirely absorbed in stories of my own which floated in singular visions across my mental eye. The blood flew to my head, and I roared with laughter" (Hamsun, 33). When she read this story on a park bench in Stockholm during one of the darkest periods of her life, Lindgren's reaction was identical. She, too, roared with laughter as she read about the fictional Happolati, fearing that people might think her insane. Later on she asserted that *Pippi Longstocking* might not have been written without that reading experience.

Certainly, the Happolati story influenced the Hai Shang story, in which Pippi makes fun of her astonished listener's credulity. Quick-witted Pippi is exasperated with the gullible girl who apparently lacks her own playful imagination: "'What's the matter? You don't really think that I'm sitting here telling lies, do you? Just tell me if you do,' said Pippi threateningly and rolled up her sleeves" (*Pippi Longstocking,* 67). Hamsun's narrator is equally infuriated in the same situation and heaps abuse on the dull old man: "'Hell and fire, man! Do you imagine that I am sitting here stuffing you chock-full of lies?' I roared furiously. 'Perhaps you don't even believe that a man of the name of Happolati exists! I never saw your match for obstinacy and malice in any old man. What the devil ails you?'" (*Hunger,* 34). Both the girl in *Pippi Longstocking* and the old man in *Hunger* quickly take to their heels in total bewilderment.

Incidentally, I have always considered this scene somewhat out of character for Pippi, since she makes fun of an innocent bystander, and a child at that. Ulla Lundqvist's research into the original manuscript provides the answer. The girl had originally been an inquisitive adult, and, under the influence of the censor's pen, Lindgren changed the adult into a child, thereby violating the subtext of her story, which is a defense of childhood and an attack aimed at adults who seem to have forgotten childhood.

Like Karlsson-on-the-Roof, Pippi not only tells tall tales, she participates in them, too. Thus, in the tradition of Superman, she subdues various strong men, saves small children from a burning house, and emerges victorious in fights with a bull, sharks, and a boa constrictor. All these heroic deeds are performed with a flair for theatricality so that the show itself, rather than the deed, becomes the focal point. Thus, the chapter heading "Pippi *Acts* as a Lifesaver" is to the point (*Pippi Longstocking*, 132, italics added). Watching a melodramatic play at the fair, she storms the stage to save the heroine from the brute villain. On the other hand, life for her is just a stage on which she herself performs her stunts and somersaults. That is why the concept of circus or theater is alien to her. Pippi does not need a compensatory entertainment industry that is part of the cultural differentiation in industrialized societies. As a result, she falls asleep during the performances of the "real" circus once she is no longer participating herself. But during her performances she keeps the audience spellbound and roaring with laughter in the best tradition of a circus clown. With her potato nose, shoes twice the size of her feet, red hair sticking straight out from her head, and a hodgepodge of ill-fitting clothes, Pippi certainly looks the part.

Humor on Many Levels

To understand the breadth of humor in Lindgren's work, one can do no better than take a close look at *Pippi Longstocking*. In this story and its sequels all expressions and functions of Lindgren's humor come together in sparklingly witty and wonderfully funny episodes. The humor in the Pippi books is one of extravagance and excess. As such it is a humor perfectly suited to the young audience Lindgren addresses, for in the excessive gesture the childlike and the humorous meet. Lindgren's colorful and concrete humor seems especially appropriate for children, who can and do laugh more often and sometimes at different things than do adults.

Lindgren has noted that while reading parts of her books to mostly adult audiences she has more than once heard the high ringing laughter of a child somewhere in the crowd of seriously attentive listeners. Lindgren knows there is a humor that adults seem to have outgrown and forgotten. She has not. Somehow, she has been able to keep the child within her alive, and she strives to amuse that child. As far as humor is concerned, she seems more partial to children than to adults. If not all adults laugh at everything that children find funny in her books, it may be deplorable, but unavoidable; when the adults laugh, the children should be able to laugh, too. After all, these are children's books. And she advises young authors:

Go ahead and write things that are *only* funny for children and not at all for adults; go ahead and write things that are funny for *both* children and adults, too; but never write anything in a children's book that your common sense tells you is *only* funny for adults. You're not writing so that reviewers will think you are clever and express yourself in a spiritual way, remember that! Many children's writers wink cleverly right over the heads of their young readers to an imagined adult reader, wink in agreement with the adults and leave the child aside. Please don't ever do it! It's an insult to the child who is to buy and read your book. (*Mina påhitt,* 250)

This attitude sets her apart from those authors whose sophisticated humor excludes those who do not understand all the references and associations—literary or otherwise—that make the text interesting for adults. The extent and complexity of the secondary literature about *Alice in Wonderland* is just one case in point. Much of the irony in *Alice* is way above the heads of child readers and addresses educated adults only. In *Pippi Longstocking,* the fun originates in Pippi. Whereas Alice is lost in a chaotic dream world in which she struggles against nonsense and in which only her common sense guarantees her a degree of normalcy, Pippi herself creates a bit of chaos to escape everyday normalcy and logic.

Admittedly, as reader-response theory has taught us, no one reception of a certain text is like another, given the different cognitive and emotional experiences each reader brings to the text. Thus, there exists no *one* Pippi Longstocking for children, either. Lindgren has succeeded, however, in keeping her narrative emotionally and cognitively appealing to both young and old. Because she knows that the pleasure derived from humor stems from the fantastic distortion of previously acquired knowledge and experience, Lindgren limits references and allusions to the cognitive and experiential horizon of children. In so doing, she can run the gamut of humorous expression from the simplest wordplay, boisterous slapstick, and nonsense to highly sophisticated parodies and delicate irony. Clever puns, parody, and gallows humor are presented in a manner children can apprehend. Lindgren is helped in this endeavor by her heavy reliance on oral narrative forms with deep roots in the vernacular storytelling tradition, which knows no age discrimination. Her humor is based on the same fundamental emotional situation on which the whole concept of Pippi Longstocking rests, namely, the desire to be strong, clever, and in control.

Much of the humor can be found in Pippi's playful manipulation of language. Substitutions and inversions, distortions and exaggerations appear in the smallest building blocks of language, in single words and names. They intrude into the sentence structure and grammatical logic, and they are equally omnipresent on the conceptual level. Pippi's errors in language or logic are funny because the child readers (and listeners) know better. They can laugh at Pippi's "stupidity" when she mispronounces words or assumes that walking backward is easier than turning around. At the same time, her humor is subversive because of its fresh, unusual look from the periphery or from below. Pippi's tendency to equate all school knowledge with "pluttification" (literally "fartification") and her capacity to outsmart the teacher during her visit at school ridicules the quantification of knowledge and formal learning outside of any practical context. When Pippi refuses to acknowledge the symbol of the letter "i" and calls it "a straight line with a little fly speck over it" (*Pippi Longstocking,* 54), she delights the reader/listener who has just accomplished the difficult task of learning to read and write; she also raises questions about the relationship between signified and signifier for those readers whose relatively stable language skills and knowledge of the semiotic framework enable them to handle the subversion of cultural codes and conventions through parody and irony.

Unfortunately, much of the playfulness and richness of connotation are lost in the English translation. Names are very often the first stumbling block. Thus, the word *pippi* means crazy or nuts in Swedish. The name of Pippi's house, Villa Villekulla, besides its associations to Green Gables (*Grönkulla*), evokes not only a playful mood with its alliterations but also a number of associations and connotations in Swedish. The Swedish *villa* corresponds the English "villa," but Pippi lives in a rather dilapidated old house. Calling it "villa" is thus in line with her propensity for exaggeration and tall tales. *Ville* can be associated with *vilja* (will, desire), and Pippi definitely has a strong will; it can also be associated with *villa bort, vilse* (confuse, confused), and *villervalla* (confusion, disarray, chaos), and upsetting order and normalcy is Pippi's favorite pastime. *Kulle* means "hill," *kul* means "fun," and *omkull* means "overturned," "toppled." Some of these connotations may be wholly accidental, yet they add to the richness and playfulness of the narrative that cannot be replicated in translation.

Lindgren's love of sounds and command of words is reflected in Pippi's experimentation with language. Pippi's inventiveness and playfulness encompasses names and words as well as objects. She delights in redefining and misusing familiar words and concepts and in discovering new ones. To name is to exercise power, and Pippi exercises this power liberally. One morning, for example, the ever-creative thinker and tinkerer Pippi invents a new word. The word is "spink." With the characteristic absence of modesty she shares with Karlsson-on-the-Roof, she considers it to be the best word she has ever heard. Now, having invented the word, a problem arises: what is she going to do with it? All she knows about "spink" is that it does not mean vacuum cleaner. That sets her off on a search for the meaning of "spink," which is considerably more high-spirited, illustrative, and fun than any crash course on Ferdinand de Saussure's arbitrariness of the relationship between signifier and signified. In her quest, Pippi manages to embarrass a few townspeople who dare not admit their ignorance (a well-known theme from *The Emperor's New Clothes*). Eventually, after many unsatisfactory attempts to find the absent signified, she settles on serendipity and decides on a whim that a beetle that happens to cross her path is the "spink." By virtue of this act of naming, Pippi undoes the authority of the "bunch of old professors," who, according to her, "decided in the beginning what all the words should mean" (*Pippi in the South Seas*, 31).

Pippi's revolt against the tyranny of logic continues on the level of sentence structure. Pippi and Lindgren keep their audience on its toes with sentences like this one: "Even if there aren't any ghosts, they don't need to go round scaring folks out of their wits, I should think" (*Pippi Longstocking*, 159). Throughout the story, common sense is turned into uncommon sense, straddling the narrow line between sense and nonsense. Tommy and Annika first spot Pippi walking on and off the edge of the conventionally acceptable, one foot on the sidewalk and one foot in the gutter, unperturbed and seemingly oblivious of her new audience. Her action is child's play, of course, but, like her parentage, it characterizes her. To top off her introductory performance, Pippi retraces her steps backward "because she didn't want to turn around to get home" (*Pippi Longstocking*, 17). This is a perfect fool's trick. By not doing the obvious, and by taking a step beyond the accepted, Pippi reveals the often invisible limits of freedom everyone accepts even in the freest of societies. In defense of her action, Pippi argues: "Why did I walk backward? . . . Isn't this a free country? Can't a person walk any way she wants to?" (*Pippi Longstocking*, 17). Thanks to her superhuman powers and wealth of imagination, Pippi can walk as she pleases. Tommy and Annika, who observe the spectacle from their securely fenced-in yard, can only look aghast and marvel at a freedom they will never possess.

Pippi wears "the popular mask of a bewildered fool" that Mikhail Bakhtin assigns to Socrates as the central hero of the novelistic, carnivalesque genre.[13] This mask makes possible Pippi's wise ignorance, with which she defamiliarizes the familiar and makes familiar the awe-inspiring and foreign. By treating the accepted social codes and discourse as a performance, she reveals the artifice of the parodied model and its claims to represent reality and normalcy. Indeed, an argument can be made that all parody and satire belong to the powerless and suppressed who find in them underhanded ways to set up a new discourse against the dominant one. Pippi is adept at that. She feigns ignorance and uses her role as outsider—a world traveler who is unfamiliar with bourgeois behavioral codes—to make fun of narrow-mindedness.

Many of Pippi's most fervent attacks on ethical and conventional codes derive their keen edge from the narrative voice of studied naivete. She imitates society ladies, teachers, and other representatives of law and social order not to become accepted into bourgeois society but to ridicule its social games by playing them to the extreme. Invited to the Settergrens for coffee and cake, Pippi misappropriates and thereby undermines the social codes of behavior. As is the custom, Pippi dresses up for the occasion. She has combed her hair, but it is even more unwieldy than usual; she has painted her face white, used a lot of red lipstick, and put on a fancy dress that does not fit. The final result is that she looks like a clown. In accordance with her image, she dives straight into the cream pie, pours sugar on the floor, gets in everybody's way, and is a perfect parody of the assembled ladies both in looks and behavior. By telling tall tales, she mocks the discourse of this social gathering.

Pippi's studied naivete on the spiritual level is paralleled by her physical performance. Like all clowns, Pippi is awkwardly graceful or gracefully awkward. She dives into pies and stumbles into puddles, yet she can walk a tightrope with ease and climbs trees and rocks as quickly and nimbly as her monkey. She has one further characteristic of a clown, an inner sadness and solitude that is hidden under a thick layer of merrymaking. The last glimpse the reader catches of Pippi from the warm comfort of Tommy and Annika's home reveals some of the loneliness of the outsider. When her two friends see her, she is unaware of being observed and is not performing; "Pippi was sitting at the table with her head propped against her arms. She was staring at the little flickering flame of a candle that was standing in front of her. She seemed to be dreaming. 'She—she looks so alone,' said Annika" (*Pippi in the South Seas,* 124).

The foremost task of a clown or storyteller is to entertain and to amuse us. As Sigmund Freud demonstrated, however, humor can also be therapeutic; and, depending on the need of the reader/listener and the cultural matrix within which it is situated, it can be either affirmative or subversive of the status quo. Moral indignation no longer colors reactions to Pippi, but two opposing views still prevail in the secondary literature and in reviews. Literary critics on the "left" like Eva Adolfsson, Ulf Eriksson, and Birgitta Holm regard Lindgren's books as fundamentally escapist and affirmative of middle-class values.[14] Astrid Lindgren's commentary reflects the wide range and the shifting opinions in the reception of the Pippi books. "When [Pippi] first appeared, she was greeted as a 'revolutionary in the nursery.' But according to later verdicts by the radicals, she is nothing but an arch-capitalist who throws gold coins around in the most atrocious way" ("Barnböcker," 75). Other critics make out the Pippi books to be a prototype of an antiauthoritarian, subversive children's novel. Winfried Freund finds emancipatory qualities in Pippi's spontaneity and in her caricatures and parodies that can lead to the "dissolution of the solidification of norms."[15]

The question of whether humor is subversive or affirmative remains controversial in scholarly research. Followers of Bakhtin and his concept of the dialogic and the carnivalesque see laughter as an emancipatory force. Roland Barthes, however, does not accept this premise unconditionally. He argues instead that the carnivalesque loses its emancipatory tendencies in a society in which there seems to be an ongoing carnival, a society which is "amusing itself to death," as Neil Postman puts it. Postman argues that the epistemology created by television, the image-based culture, "not only is inferior to a print-based epistemology, but it is dangerous and absurdist" because it lacks the structure, discipline, sense of origin, and progression mediated by print culture.[16] With her fibtelling, performativity, and defense of eternal undisciplined childhood Pippi likewise undermines print-based epistemology from within. Forty-five years ago, Pippi was an exception in her playful subversion of the dominance of "adult," linear, confining thought patterns. By the end of the twentieth century, print-based culture is no longer unchallenged, and the periphery, where Pippi resides, has become more densely populated.

For Pippi Longstocking, both views are justified. Pippi's ambiguous, elusive personality, which is full of contradictions and self-irony, cannot easily be put at the service of any hegemonic cultural or educational apparatus. Yet this is precisely what happened when the stories about Pippi were translated into the 1988 Hollywood film, *New Adventures of Pippi Longstocking*, at the expense of Pippi's original voice and character. In this film Pippi becomes a mere shadow of herself, and her original creative spark and natural exuberance are transformed into stereotyped merrymaking. Since Pippi's playful attacks on small-town mentality and bourgeois conventions are glossed over, the film affirms mainstream values and falls prey to stereotypes, which the original Pippi, by juggling with established cultural codes in a highly skilled, artistic way, continually undermines.

Pippi Longstocking, the book, has long been a part of school curricula in Sweden and abroad. Time has caught up with its spirit of revolt against the stuffy and highly regulated bourgeois childhood, and some of Pippi's irony has lost its edge. Children's need to free themselves from constricting conventions may not be quite as strong and as sharply delineated in the Western world of the 1990s as it was in 1945 when *Pippi Longstocking* was first published, for a strong wave of anti-authoritarian education has given children greater freedom, independence, and responsibility. As for the enforcement of strict educational and behavioral codes, many parents have become more understanding and permissive—in line with Eric's parents—and children have moved a little closer to the state of total freedom Pippi enjoys. They can consume quite a bit more than their counterparts could thirty or forty years ago, and forty pounds of candy is probably no longer the focus of intense desire now that it was then. But children are still far enough removed from any position of control to be able to see in Pippi the embodiment of all their desires, and her anarchistic, engaging vitality remains a wonderful and funny device for compensation and inspiration.

Pippi Longstocking, I believe, will continue to inspire and engage readers because of the character of Pippi herself. The primary audience, that is child readers, still enjoy the fun, the nonsense, and the playful inversion of the normal. Moreover, superchild Pippi provides them vicariously with the power to get back at those who hold and exert power over them. Older readers may find in Pippi a late—and more down-to-earth—successor to the romantic ideal child and may find her equally inspirational and compensatory. Her inclination to live and enjoy life to the fullest—for its own sake and for no ulterior motive—makes her a natural critic of a growth- and development-oriented society.

Pippi always comes out on top. Illustration by Louis S. Glanzman from *Pippi in the South Seas*. Reprinted with permission of Penguin Books USA Inc.

Measured against the purposiveness characterizing Western society, Pippi appears a wise fool who reads the world against the grain by making life into an endless game. She is a true "Thing-Finder" and tinkerer, misusing utilitarian objects and basically making her environment into one big Tinkertoy. Since Pippi does not see any ultimate value in either growth or development per see, it is only logical that, in the end, she decides never to grow up. This decision does not mean, however, that Pippi consciously escapes responsibility. On the contrary, superchild Pippi does not refuse adulthood altogether; she is already the very ideal of a caring, creative, and concerned person—admittedly a rather extravagant and immoderate one—who defies age barriers. Karlsson-on-the-Roof is merely an over-age child, and in his childishness he may be refreshingly funny and compensatory, but he is hardly inspirational. This may be one reason why Pippi has so far surpassed Karlsson in popularity and why most readers (and I believe not only adult readers) would want Eric to outgrow his Karlsson stage but hope that Pippi's chililug pills will work.

On the way to the land of make-believe and paradise, where spring and love are eternal.
Illustration by Ilon Wikland from *Sunnanäng* (South Wind Meadow).

Chapter Four

The Teller of Tales: *Mio, My Son,* *The Brothers Lionheart,* and *Ronia, the Robber's Daughter*

Today children no longer grow up within the security of an extended family, or of a well-inte-
grated community. Therefore even more than at the time fairy tales were invented it is important to provide the modern child with images of heroes who have to go out into the world all
by themselves and who, although originally ignorant of the ultimate things, find secure places
in the world by following their right way with deep inner confidence.
—Bruno Bettelheim, *The Uses of Enchantment*

"I can't stand seeing children suffer."
—Astrid Lindgren

The Fairy Tale Connection

Just as Pippi and Karlsson-on-the-Roof are representatives of readers'
innermost desires and compensate for their needs, so too are the main
characters in Astrid Lindgren's three great novels *Mio, My Son* (1954),
The Brothers Lionheart (1973), and *Ronia, the Robber's Daughter* (1981). In
contrast to the Pippi Longstocking and Karlsson-on-the-Roof books,
however, which are comedies in character, these three novels address pro-
foundly serious, even tragic, issues. They have an altogether different
format and address our most fundamental anxieties: the need to be loved
and valued, the fear of existential loneliness and worthlessness, the love
of life, and the fear of death. Pippi Longstocking and Karlsson-on-the-
Roof exude a lighthearted and playful mood. Tommy, Annika, and Eric
are loved and well-cared-for children whose excursions into the realm of
fantasy and imagination add excitement and wonder to their lives, coun-
teracting momentary doldrums and fits of anger and anguish. Karl
Anders Nilsson and Karl Lion (whose nickname is Rusky), the protagonists of *Mio, My Son* and *The Brothers Lionheart,* on the other hand, need

Farawayland and Nangiyala to maintain their sanity. Their excursions into the realm of fantasy are not a matter of whim or a desire for entertainment but a necessity in coping with the stress of loneliness, lovelessness, and the fear of impending death. The heroic struggles of Karl Anders and Rusky against the cruelties of life to which they have been subjected are transposed into the imaginary, reappearing there as the heroic struggles of Mio and Karl Lionheart against the powers of evil reigning in Farawayland and Nangiyala. These sublimated struggles are drawn in stark, dramatic images and powerful language. Before I proceed to scrutinize fantasy and folktale elements, narrative technique, and message in the novels, a brief plot summary is in order.

Mio, My Son is the story of Karl Anders Nilsson (the name in the Swedish original is Bo Vilhelm Olsson), who is a foster child in an exceedingly loveless and uncaring home in Stockholm. In Farawayland, he becomes "Mio" and is reunited with his father, the King, with whom he finds the respect, warmth, and love he lacks in his foster home. Told in retrospect by the protagonist, the story starts dramatically with a missing-person's bulletin issued by the Stockholm police for nine-year-old Karl Anders Nilsson. Mio remembers the day quite well. He had just finished reading tales from *A Thousand and One Nights* when he was sent on an errand. Sitting on a park bench and clutching a golden apple and a magic note given to him by a nice lady in a store, he notices an empty beer bottle with a genie trapped inside. He frees the genie, who, following the fairy-tale convention, grants him a wish. His wish is to be reunited with his father, and he travels through day and night to Farawayland, where he soon finds himself in the warm embrace of his father the King in the palace's rose garden. There he meets his best-friend-to-be Pompoo, who replaces Ben, his best friend in Stockholm, and is given his own beautiful horse, Miramis. But his carefree delight in his newfound happiness does not last long, for fate has ordained that he become the savior of Farawayland, now threatened by the evil Sir Kato. Mio takes on his role as knight and with his friend Pompoo and many magical helpers he overcomes terror and life-threatening dangers and in the end plunges his sword into Sir Kato's heart of stone. The evil spell is lifted from Outer Land, the Dead Lake and the Dead Forest return to life, the bewitched children are freed from their spells, and all return victoriously to Greenfields Island, where Mio's father the King awaits him. The magic tale ends with the assurance that Karl Anders is no longer sitting on a park bench in Stockholm and that *"all is well with Mio."*[1] What really happens to the missing Karl Anders remains shrouded in mystery.

The Brothers Lionheart follows a similar pattern. Again, the story is told in retrospect and in the first person. Karl Lion, called Rusky, who is slowly dying of a lung disease and is confined to the kitchen sofa-bed, loses his beloved brother Jonathan in a fire when Jonathan attempts to save him in a daring jump from the window of their burning house and perishes. Shortly thereafter Rusky is carried off to Nangiyala, a land of dreams and magic already familiar to him from his brother's stories. There the two brothers are reunited in Cherry Valley, where they experience peaceful bliss for only a short time because the evil Lord Tengil, who reigns over the neighboring Wild Rose Valley with the help of a cruel dragon named Katla and scores of mindless and ruthless soldiers, threatens to bring Cherry Valley under his power. Again, a long and dangerous struggle for freedom ensues in which both brothers play key parts. In the battle between the forces of liberty and the forces of oppression Tengil is killed by his own dragon, Katla. As Jonathan tries to rid Wild Rose Valley from the persistent threat Katla poses, the fire-spewing dragon manages to paralyze him. Now it is up to Rusky to save Jonathan from terrible suffering by jumping into the looming abyss, carrying Jonathan on his back. This leap, Jonathan assures us, will take both brothers to the paradise of Nangilima and reunite them forever.

Ronia, the Robber's Daughter presents a Romeo and Juliet/Robinson Crusoe plot in a combination folktale, developmental novel, and robber's tale. The setting is a large forest animated by mythical figures. Initially, the forest is large and "safe" enough to function as the hunting ground for two competing robber bands led by Matt and Borka, respectively. These two robber bands turn into each other's archenemies as more and more soldiers make parts of the forest unsafe and force Borka's band to move into the unused half of the castle, whose other half is occupied by Matt's band. The novel opens dramatically with a thunderbolt that splits the castle in two during the night Ronia is born to Matt and Lovis. The same night, unbeknownst to the members of Matt's robber band, a son, whom they call Birk, is born to the rival chieftain couple, Borka and Undis. The reader now follows Ronia's gradual discovery and mastery of her world and her sometimes painful steps toward independence. Tension starts building when she meets Birk on one of her many forays into the forest. The two continue to meet secretly and choose to move away from home to a cave in the forest for the summer. As winter approaches and life in the cave becomes impossible, heartbroken Matt begs his daughter to come home. Separated from Birk once again, Ronia clears a passageway between the two halves of the castle, setting the stage for a reconciliation between the two robber bands. Through Ronia's efforts the two bands and the two families ultimately join in a grand celebration of their union, but the joyous occasion is overshadowed by Ronia and Birk's solemn vows never to become robbers. Their choice is a very different life based on peaceful coexistence.

In *Ronia, the Robber's Daughter* Lindgren no longer uses the two-world paradigm of the fantasy tale she employed in *Mio, My Son* and *The Brothers Lionheart*. *Ronia, the Robber's Daughter* structurally bears the greatest resemblance to the folktale and can with some justification be called a modern fairy tale. In this novel readers immediately enter the timeless past of the folktale and never leave Ronia's fabulous world, which is full of magic and adventure, sadness and joy, danger and beauty. Through Ronia they experience the starkly beautiful robber's forest with its dangerous cliffs and cataracts as well as its clear and quiet lakes. In this novel Lindgren dissolves the dichotomies of black and white, good and evil. Ronia's environment combines the pastoral dreamscapes of Mio and Rusky—Greenfields Island and Cherry Valley—with the dangerous and dramatic landscape of Outer Land and Karmanyanka. Ronia herself bears closer resemblance to the wild, strong, and sincere Pippi than to Mio or Rusky. But despite the differences between *Ronia, the Robber's Daughter* and the two earlier novels, they have much in common. All three are epic novels with roots in the folktale and fantasy tradition.

I will next examine how Lindgren has made use of this tradition and altered it in form and content by integrating it into the literary discourse of the twentieth century. There are similarities between the novels' language, plot structure, setting, and content and those of traditional folktales and fairy tales, as well as those of the literary fairy tales and fantasy tales that entered children's literature around the turn of the century. Lindgren has drawn freely on the rich narrative source of the folktale, with its tricksters, ghosts, and underdogs and its themes of love, redemption, and utopian dreams; with one notable exception, she has always steered clear of the didacticism of cautionary tales in her adaptations of folktale material.

Folktales and fairy tales reach far back into oral tradition. They have been lifted from relative obscurity through waves of literary adaptations. In modern times, fairy tales were popularized in the *mode des feés* in late seventeenth- and early eighteenth-century France, and again about a century later by the German Romantics. In the hands of the Brothers Grimm these stories became almost exclusively children's fare. Folktales are the product of a lively exchange of cultures and modes of expression.

Written and oral narrative tradition, as well as high and low culture, have influenced one another, renewing the art of taletelling all along through their cross-fertilization. In the long history of folktale transmission, the merger of oral and print culture was neither new nor exceptional, but assigning the folktale tradition exclusively to children was.

Lindgren continues the tradition of renewal through a dialogue with oral and literary sources. She taps into the collected wisdom of the ages as she weaves strands from folktales, myths, sagas, and masterpieces of Western literature, integrating various cultural requisites from the Christian tradition and from Norse mythology into her own fabric. Heroic tales and Norse sagas reverberate in the novels about Mio and the Brothers Lionheart, as do the Grimm fairy tales. The artistic tale of Hans Christian Andersen and his followers are strongest in the sentimental and melancholy undertones of Lindgren's poetic prose. There are also points of contact between Lindgren's tales and the fantasy worlds of J. R. R. Tolkien and C. S. Lewis, although her fantasy worlds are devoid of the Christian perspectives characteristic of these two authors. Besides these literary influences, those of the oral taletelling tradition Lindgren breathed like air during her childhood should not be underestimated.

The influence of Nordic tradition is most strongly felt in some of her early fairy tales, in which the unearthly people from underground exert their influence on the lives of people, and where trolls, gnomes, elves, and water sprites animate nature. These creatures also appear in the oral lore of the Noisy Village children, and Ronia grows up in a nature that comes alive with goblins, fierce harpies, the Unearthly Ones, gray dwarves, and rumphobs. The blacksmith who forges the magic sword and the weaver who weaves the invisible cloth resemble Völund, the smith, and the norns from Norse mythology (Edström 1992, 194, 199).

What beyond traceable literary influences inspires an author to choose a certain topic, and how does she find the appropriate story? Lindgren allows us a glimpse into the creative impulse that led to *The Brothers Lionheart*. It consists of a series of distinct visions, images, and associations, all having to do with consolation through beauty, warmth, and tenderness, and finally all coming together to yield a story. In *Mina påhitt* Lindgren talks about an impression that touched her deeply during a train ride through the Swedish province of Värmland one cold winter morning. The rising sun had transformed the crystalline landscape into a place of unearthly beauty and instilled in her a desire to write about the experience, but other images were necessary for this seed of inspiration to grow into a concrete story. A walk in Vimmerby's cemetery brought her

the decisive impulse in the form of a gravestone with an epitaph mourn-
ing the death of two young brothers. The theme for the novel—tender
brotherly love—may have emerged during the filming of the Emil
books, when Lindgren observed the weary and exhausted young actor
who played Emil seek refuge with his older brother, who caressed and
comforted him (Strömstedt, 310–11). Finally, her winter vision in
Värmland had revived the memory of a rural road sign covered with
hoarfrost and bearing the inscription "Sunnanäg," or South Wind
Meadow. This experience had inspired her two decades earlier to write a
story of the same name, which appeared in 1959 as the title story in a
collection of short fairy tales, many of which have not been translated
into English.

In this tale, in many ways a precursor to *The Brothers Lionheart,*
images of paradise-like dreamworlds appear in connection with coldness,
depravity, and death. Two orphans, a brother and sister, live a loveless life
in poverty; not unlike Andersen's Little Match Girl, the cold and hungry
children have visions of love, warmth, and beauty during their long
walks home from school on bitter cold winter days. Andersen, writing as
much for adults as for children, brings his readers back to reality after
letting them partake in the little girl's visions of warmth, good food, and
a loving grandmother. The girl is found frozen to death in a doorway the
next morning. Lindgren, however, does not return to cruel reality; she
leaves the reader in the fantasy paradise and never returns to the two little frozen bodies in the snow. The final vignette is that of an eternal
bucolic spring in South Wind Meadow, filled with children's laughter
and games, warmth and good food, at the center of which is a loving
mother who protects and cares for all the children.

Lindgren had used the motif of a dying boy who seeks and receives
courage and strength by entering the suspense-filled fictional world of
the heroic narrative in her early, fairly conventional heroic tale "Junker
Nils av Eka" (Squire Nils of Eka), the last tale in the *Sunnanäg* collection.
In this tale the main protagonist, Nils, is seriously ill and on the verge of
death. In his feverish dreams he sacrifices his own life for that of his king,
but in real life he recovers from his illness. The outcome of the expanded treatment of the struggle-with-death motif is reversed in *The Brothers
Lionheart;* here Rusky dies as he performs his most courageous and heroic deed—leaping into the abyss—and achieves victory over the dark and
destructive forces.

Finding her own creative style—Hans Holmberg calls it her personal
fairy-tale style—and adapting the tales to the form of the novel have been

gradual processes that can be traced from Lindgren's earliest fairy-tale collection, *Nils Karlsson-Pyssling,* published in Sweden in 1949, to *Ronia, the Robber's Daughter,* published in 1981.[2] The early tales were written in a traditional vein that is reminiscent of the literary fairy tales for children written around the turn of the century and do not show the structural complexity and creativity characteristic of Lindgren's later novels. In these early tales Lindgren employs traditional popular motifs: toys and dolls come alive, protagonists enter miniature worlds, and the secondary world exists quite independently from the primary world. One figure in the early tales already foreshadows Lindgren's later use of the fabulous and fantastic, namely, the highly ambivalent Herr Liljonkvast (Mr. Lilystick) from the Land of Dusk. In the tale "I skymmningslandet" (In the land of dusk) he takes Göran, who lies paralyzed in his bed, with him into "the Land That Is Not."[3] In Mr. Lilystick's hand, Göran is freed from the fetters of his paralyzing illness as he flies over the city of Stockholm at nightfall. An amalgamation of elf, friendly man, and magician, Mr. Lilystick is as ambiguous as the twilight that is his period of operation. A product of dusk, he belongs neither to day nor night, yet he belongs to both. He is both melancholy and upbeat, and while his humorous side later expands and finds expression in Karlsson-on-the-Roof, his melancholy side has echoes in *Mio, My Son* and *The Brothers Lionheart.*

In her book *The Magic Code,* a study of the magical elements in English fantasy for children, Maria Nikolajeva perceives the development of the fantasy genre in the twentieth century as a "history of innovations and transformations, of creative reconstruction of old variables."[4] She finds that the secondary world has become more elusive and that its relationship to the primary world has become more sophisticated. Nikolajeva also finds a fundamental ambivalence in more recent English fantasy literature stemming from the clash between the rigid, archetypal structure of the archaic, mythological thinking of myth and folktale, on the one hand, and dynamic and innovative twentieth-century views of the world, on the other. These very tendencies can be observed beautifully in Lindgren's work, as well, in which a clear progression can be observed from her earliest fairy tales to *Ronia, the Robber's Daughter.* Whereas her early fairy tales show little innovation, *Mio, My Son* and *The Brothers Lionheart* display much greater complexity and sophistication in the way in which primary and secondary worlds are closely interrelated. In *Ronia,* Lindgren leaves the fantasy paradigm behind entirely by seamlessly integrating magic elements from folklore into a modern developmental novel.

Like any good teller of tales, Lindgren appropriates and molds folk-tale and literary tradition to fit her own purposes, so that worn images and structures assume a new immediacy and beauty. In the age of electronic media the culture of literacy is entering a new stage that Walter Ong has labeled "secondary orality." Lindgren still writes her fairy tales steeped in the culture of literacy, but, while doing so, also depends heavily on oral structures of mental organization and thus comes close to Ong's concept of "secondary orality." Most of the characteristics of orally based thought and expression that Ong enumerates—such as the oral culture's tendency to be redundant, aggregative, close to the human "lifeworld," agonistically toned, formulaic, empathetic and participatory, homeostatic, and situational—can be traced in Lindgren's work. Thus, Lindgren can evoke "the old oral, mobile, warm, personally interactive lifeworld of oral culture" in her epic fairy tales.[5] By superimposing this form of expression on the analytic and objectively distanced one of print culture, Lindgren succeeds in keeping alive the fairy-tale tradition and, in broader terms, the taletelling tradition itself, infusing the fairy tale with new life, as did Mme. Leprince de Beaumont, Hans Christian Andersen, Isak Dinesen, and Isaac Bashevis Singer in their ways.

Language

The three epic novels are written with the narrative economy typical of the fairy tale. We can find in them rhetorical devices such as repetition, contrast, exaggeration, concreteness, and formulaic expressions. Structurally, these novels cater to readers' expectations, yet the familiar motifs and structures that appeal to readers raised on such tales are frequently filled with new content. Lindgren's language is childproof: it is concrete, graphic, colorful, and vibrant; it allows for ambiguous situations; it is rich in expressive power because of all the connotations the images call forth; and, most important, it makes readers identify with the protagonist or situation and lets them understand the problem through feeling as well as thought. The simple poetic beauty of her stories communicates her message on the precognitive level, underscoring the arguments and actions of her protagonists. The poetry of her prose resides as much in her choice of images as in the rhythm of her language. Her prose has a unique flow that makes her stories blossom when read aloud. The natural flow and relative simplicity of her language is the result of conscious effort and painstaking labor. To achieve the perfect rhythm, Lindgren reads sentences and paragraphs aloud to herself many times. As a result, her narrative voice has an engaging immediacy.

The participatory directness of the oral taletelling style is evident in the opening lines of *The Brothers Lionheart:* "Now I'm going to tell you about my brother. My brother Jonathan Lionheart is the person I want to tell you about" (7). By addressing readers directly and emphatically, Lindgren establishes an immediate rapport and closeness with them, which is followed by her efforts to reinforce the veracity of the story she is about to tell—a tribute to today's readers, who have been taught to equate fairy tales with lies: "I think it's almost like a saga and just a little like a ghost story, and yet every word is true, though Jonathan and I are probably the only people who know that" (7).

With decades of experience as an editor of children's books, Lindgren knows how important it is to capture the imagination of her readers in the first few paragraphs; she invariably holds their attention throughout. Her novels are tightly composed, eschewing the descriptive embroidery typical of the literary tale. Instead, she makes use of the highly formulaic, metaphorical language of the folk tale, which gains lyrical and dramatic quality as the reader follows the protagonists into the fictional otherworlds of Farawayland, Nangiyala, and Ronia's archetypal forest.

By using metaphors that in turn evoke images in the reader's imagination, she reaches children—and I would argue adults as well—more easily than she might with abstract arguments. Her metaphorical language is most prominent, almost overwhelming, in the highly stylized *Mio, My Son* and lends an aura of magic to all of the novels. Formulaic expressions Lindgren has created are intermingled with popular, widely used metaphors. Mio encounters "the Bread That Satisfies Hunger," "the Well That Quenches Thirst," "the Bridge of Morning Light," "the Well That Whispers at Night," "my father the King," and "Cruel Sir Kato," and the Brothers Lionheart have to cross "the river of The Ancient Rivers." *The Brothers Lionheart* and *Ronia, the Robber's Daughter* share a freer, less poetically elevated prose. But archaisms and neologisms like "sister mine" and "what in the name of all the wild harpies have you been doing?"[6] help transport the reader into the strangeness of the otherworld and the distant past of the tale. The rumphob's insistent quizzical and nonsensical question, "Woffor did un do that?" in *Ronia, the Robber's Daughter* has already taken on a life of its own and become part of Swedish oral popular culture along with many such expressions from Lindgren's works.

Lindgren's language reflects the high degree of intensity that characterizes children's experiences of their environment and relationships. Even more than in her realistic Småland books, the immense beauty and drama of the fantasy worlds of Mio and Rusky are conjured up by a heavy use of superlatives, reiteration, and stark contrasts. Unfortunately, the flow and lyricism of the language suffer most in translation, but much of it is saved in Patricia Crampton's excellent translation of *Ronia, the Robber's Daughter.* When spring comes after a long and painful winter, Lindgren expresses it in a "resounding line of pure poetry," as Crampton observes, "some of which I had to sacrifice, some of which was, I hope, picked up elsewhere in the line: And the river roared and foamed in the frenzy of spring and sang with all its waterfalls and cataracts a wild spring song that never died."[7] Here spring evokes the euphoria of a new beginning, corresponding to the heroic and dramatic mood of this novel and the strong feeling of hope with which Lindgren concludes *Ronia, the Robber's Daughter.* This joyous restlessness of a new beginning is captured in Lindgren's description of the spring morning, with which she concludes the novel: "It is early morning. As beautiful as the first morning of the world! The new inhabitants of the Bear's Cave come strolling through their woods and all about them lies the splendor of springtime. Every tree, every stretch of water and every green thicket is alive, there is twittering and rushing and buzzing and singing and murmuring; the fresh wild song of the spring can be heard everywhere" (*Ronia,* 191).

Just as nature explodes in a frenzied and uncontrollable song of spring, Ronia can no longer contain all the energy she has damned up within her. She too explodes in her own wild, joyous spring shout, a yell as shrill as a bird. Her resounding yell is a fitting culmination for a novel that starts with claps of thunder and the screeches of harpies. It is a forceful declaration of victory over nature's—including human nature's—destructive elements.

Mio's and Rusky's experiences of the beauty of nature in springtime are comparable in intensity and poetry but very different in character. Having been transported to dreamworlds, their descriptions of cherry blossoms and rose bushes reflect the sublime quiet happiness of a wish come true. In *Mio, My Son* Lindgren resorts to a solemn rhetoric to express unrivaled beauty. Vivi Edström, who has closely examined the language of this novel, has found numerous and diverse examples of Lindgren's rich metaphorical language.[8] When Mio leaves Sir Kato's dungeon, his flaming sword cuts through iron as easily and quietly as if it were dough. Tears turn into pearls and blood; Mio's horse, Miramis, soars like a bird; and his hooves sound like thunder. Kato literally has a heart of stone and disintegrates into a pile of rocks as soon as Mio sinks his sword into his chest.

In her use of metaphors Lindgren does not shy away from the commonplace. On the contrary, most of her images are part of folklore and popular culture, and she relies heavily on their connotative power. One of these metaphors is Mio's rose garden. The garden as an image of beauty, well-being, and security goes back to the Garden of Eden and probably earlier. The rose, a well-worn metaphor of beauty and love, reflects Andy's longing for the beauty and love of which he is deprived in his daily life and the rich fulfillment he experiences in Farawayland. An exceptionally happy Sunday outing with his friend Ben's family to the Stockholm archipelago gives him a glimpse of earthly beauty. His experience of sitting at the water's edge with wild roses in bloom is one he later sublimates in his fantasy image of the rose garden. What makes Andy's dreamworld complete is the ability to share his feelings with another person (his father the King, his friend Pompoo), an experience denied him even with Ben and his family: "I had the sense not to tell Ben, but I kept thinking all the time. 'I'm sure there can't be anything in the world more beautiful than this'" (24). Only in the rose garden does he find the fulfillment of his innermost desire for warmth, closeness, and total understanding. Instead of having to keep his emotions and longings to himself, he can let down his defenses and savor the beauty, absolute love, and trusting protection his father the King offers as he clings to his hand: "No one could ever have heard or seen anything so beautiful as what I heard and saw in my father the King's garden. I stood still and clung to his hand. I wanted to feel sure that he was there, because it was too lovely to bear alone" (24).

This passage from *Mio, My Son* suggests the reason that Lindgren's stories touch so many people from so many different cultures and of all ages lies not only in what she tells but in how she tells it. Her stories grow organically out of deeply felt emotions that surface in a poetic language laced with humor and wit. It is hard to describe Lindgren's prose better than did Christine Nöstlinger, the 1986 Hans Christian Andersen Award winner, in a tribute to Astrid Lindgren on her eightieth birthday in 1987: "Your language warms us and makes us think clearly. It makes us laugh and cry and it makes us wise. It caresses and consoles."[9]

Structure

Not only in the first paragraph when Mio is still Karl but throughout the novel Lindgren refers explicitly to the fairy-tale nature of Mio's experience. Before Mio and Pompoo accompany Nonno to his grandmother's house, for instance, Mio deliberates, "In fairy tales there are always kind old grannies. But I had never met a real live grandmother, though I know there are lots of them" (45). Another prop Lindgren has borrowed

One of the many cottages in Farawayland symbolizing love and protection. Illustration by Ilon Wikland from *Mio, min Mio* (*Mio, My Son*).

from the reservoir of fairy tales to heighten her novel's power of enchantment is the cottage, which reappears in many guises. Pompoo's house, standing in the farthest corner of the rose garden, is described as "a little white thatched cottage . . . just the kind of cottage you read about in fairy tales" (*Mio,* 28). After a long walk they come to the house: "It was the kind of cottage you read about in fairy tales, too—a sweet little cottage with a thatched roof and lots of lilac and jasmine outside" (46). Totty's house in the Land on the Other Side is also a white thatched cottage: "It was just the kind of cottage you read about in fairy tales too. It's hard to explain why a house should look as if it had come straight out of a fairy tale. Perhaps it's because of something in the air, or perhaps it's the old trees around it, or the fairy-like scent of the flowers in the garden, or perhaps something quite different" (58).

The old weaver's house, a space of heightened magic in an enchanted world, has the same qualities: "In the middle of the forest we came to a cottage—one of those little white fairy-tale cottages, with a thatched roof. Apple trees grew all around it and the blossoms gleamed white in the moonlight" (77). And when Mio and Pompoo return with all the children who had been freed from their spell, including the Weaver's daughter, they see something white gleaming between the trees. "It was the apple blossoms round the Weaver's cottage. A soft drift of apple blossoms lay on the trees round the cottage which looked so like a cottage in a fairy tale" (172). The highly stylized cottage that reappears throughout *Mio, My Son* seems lifted directly out of the collective subconscious of folklore—in its Northern European variant—which merges with Karl Anders's subjective dreamworld. The repeated appearance of this image, which seems excessively repetitive as quoted here but truly enchanting in the actual reading of the novel, reflects the urgency of Karl Anders's desire for a protective and loving home. The cozy cottage in its various manifestations is a fortress of love and protection where Mio can take refuge and gather strength for his quest to destroy the evil personified by Sir Kato from Outer Land.

The little white cottage fulfills the same function in Lindgren's next novel, *The Brothers Lionheart*. The brothers cannot imagine anywhere better to live in Cherry Valley than at Knights Farm, the somewhat oxymoronic name of which, incidentally, spells out the tension-filled coexistence of idealism and pragmatism, of fiction and reality in this novel: "An old white house, not at all big, with green timbers and a green door and a bit of green ground all around, where cowslips and saxifrage and daisies grew in the grass. Lilacs and cherry trees too, in full bloom, and around it all was a stone wall . . . once inside the gate that wall felt as if it protected you from everything outside" (24). In *Ronia* the recurring theme of the mother's wolf song functions in much the same way as a guarantor of reassuring closeness, comfort, and love.

Formulaic patterns imbue the composition with a comforting predictability and stability, but reiterations are also used for dramatic effect. With a few strokes of color, Lindgren creates an image of immediate and intense atmospheric beauty reminiscent of impressionist paintings. Her description of Jonathan's and Rusky's cottage reinforces Rusky's first impression of his dreamland: "And then—then I saw Cherry Valley at last! Oh, that valley was white with cherry blossoms everywhere. White and green, it was, with cherry blossoms and green, green grass. And through all that green and white, the river flowed like a silver ribbon"

(*Lionheart,* 23). With minimalist stylistic means Lindgren creates images of serene and sublime beauty, flourishing in stark contrast to a hopeless, colorless, and depressing reality. It seems as if, with her prose, Lindgren wants to prove C. G. Jung's theory that "the unconscious content [of dreams] contrasts strikingly with the conscious material, particularly when the conscious attitude tends too exclusively in a direction that would threaten the vital needs of the individual."[10] The emphatic, melodic, and metaphoric language of Lindgren's dreamworlds, which is bridled by a tight structure, makes reading her books a familiar yet exhilarating experience.

Repetition, a complex mirroring technique, and the semantic duplicity of her narrative are examples of Lindgren's controlled and complex narrative structure in the epic tales. Lindgren's repetitive use of single motifs, such as the little white cottage, occurs on the level of sentence structure as well. In *Ronia, the Robber's Daughter,* Lovis's words "as crazy as they come" are reiterated by Ronia (95, 122), Birk repeats "I've been waiting a long time" (68, 104); and Matt's words, "It's a relief not to have to see that red head of his all the time"(160), are reiterated by Birk, "It will be a relief not to have to see that black curly head of his every day!" (176). In the case of Birk's reiteration of Matt's sentence, the words are repeated with a touch of irony, reflecting the shifts in the power relationship. Jonathan's saying in *The Brothers Lionheart,* "There are things you *have* to do, otherwise you're not a human being but just a bit of filth," functions as a leitmotif, carrying the novel's ethical message (48, 52, 130, 183).

A structural device common in folktales is the use of the magical numbers three and twelve. Examples for threes and multiples thereof abound in Lindgren's novels. In *Ronia, The Robber's Daughter* Ronia waits three days for Birk in the forest. Three messengers are sent out to fetch Ronia and bring her home. Ronia saves Birk's life three times, and he saves hers three times. In *The Brothers Lionheart* and in *Mio, My Son* there are three distinct realms in the otherworld. In *Mio, My Son* the otherworld comprises Greenfields Island, the Land on the Other Side, and Outer Land. Cherry Valley, Wild Rose Valley, and Karmanyanka roughly correspond to them in *The Brothers Lionheart,* even in their topography. In the latter novel, the world is also divided vertically into three regions. From the city and the realm of everyday reality the brothers are first transported to Nangiyala and later to Nangilima, the realms of fantasy and death. The mirror imagery in its two sets of protagonists reinforces the fundamental message in *Ronia, the Robber's Daughter* that here we are dealing with two halves—and not only the two parts of the fortress—that must be rejoined to form a whole. Two nuclear families made up of three people reside in each half, and the "extended family" consists of two times twelve robbers.

Heroes and heroines as well as minor characters in fairy tales tend to be stereotypes with few individual traits. In *Mio, My Son* Lindgren adheres most closely to stereotypical fairy tale and folktale characters, actively appropriating fairy-tale iconography and symbolic representation. Mio populates his fantasy with stock characters right out of *A Thousand and One Nights,* whose stories so nourish and capture his imagination that the fairy-tale world still resonates within him as he sits on the park bench. The world around him becomes enchanted as he is swept into Farawayland. The cast-off beer bottle next to him produces a genie, his missing father becomes a king, and he and his friend Ben become young knights on horseback setting off to destroy the evil Sir Kato. In this pursuit they are assisted by magical helpers all along. Magic golden apples, glowing messages, genies, flaming swords, and cloaks that make Mio invisible are essential for the success of their quest.

In similar fashion, Rusky appropriates bits and pieces of his brother's stories into his own fantasies. But his inspiration derives more from folktales and adventure stories than from fairy tales, which gives his compensatory dream a different voice and populates it with different, more lifelike characters. In *The Brothers Lionheart* there are representatives of the blackest evil, like Tengil, Katla, and Karm, and the whitest good, like Jonathan, the fair and faultless hero; but there are also characters who inhabit the gray zones in between. From Rusky, Orvar, and Hubert to Jossi and Park, the shades of gray deepen from off-white to the deepest charcoal.

In the realm of character portrayal, *Ronia, the Robber's Daughter* has moved farthest from the classical fairy tale. Both narrative and protagonists are historicized and psychologized. The readers follow Ronia's adventures, which are intimately linked with her growing awareness of the Self and the Other. This novel's self-reflective, developing, and changing characters roam through the forest of a timeless, ever-present past. Not one of the main characters in this novel is a stereotypical, black-and-white figure; instead, they are colorful individuals, full of ambiguities, faults, and strengths. The reader soon comes to recognize the protagonists' main traits, such as Matt's uncontrolled temper, Lovis's matter-of-factness, and Ronia's wildness, but all of them are far more complex in their behavior. What is more, all of them change and develop and respond to stimuli the way protagonists do in modern novels. While nature is animated, the magical helpers have been replaced by happy coincidence, a much more abstract phenomenon, which highlights values of responsibility, self-reliance, and cooperation between the two main protagonists, Ronia and Birk.

Despite the fact that *Ronia, the Robber's Daughter* at first appears less like a magic tale than the earlier novels, it also contains traces of the classical fairy-tale plot as defined by Vladimir Propp.[11] In *Ronia*, it seems to me, Lindgren has achieved her most natural fusion of folktale and novel, of oral and literary narrative structure. *Ronia, the Robber's Daughter* is a fairy tale that has been adapted and transformed to meet the demands and reflect the conceptual horizon of a child growing up in the late twentieth century. In accordance with Propp's fairy-tale structure, Ronia, the heroine, is given the task of growing up to be a capable member of the robber society. She is warned by her father to watch out for the river, not to get lost in the forest, and to avoid the harpies, the gray dwarves, and Hell's Gap. She repeatedly violates these interdictions and as a result comes close to death a few times, but is saved miraculously by Matt, by Birk, and by her own efforts. She leaves home and, after many trials and tribulations, returns. But unlike the classical fairy-tale hero or heroine, Ronia neither marries the prince (Birk) nor ascends the throne to become the new robber chieftain according to her father's wishes.

In *The Brothers Lionheart* Lindgren also appropriates the fairy-tale paradigm of the "overcoming of dangers and entry into the realm of glory" for the ultimate trip into the unknown.[12] There are similarities in story line in the Grimm tale "The Two Brothers" and *The Brothers Lionheart*, but they are rather tenuous, and I do not believe that the Grimm tale serves as a model for Lindgren. Both stories feature the separation of the brothers at decisive moments, their reunification, a confrontation with a dragon, and the use of wit to overcome a superior enemy. These are common structural elements in many adventure stories, however, and are more likely to prove the validity of Max Lüthi's fairy-tale paradigm than a close affinity of these two stories in particular.

One Text for Children, Another for Adults

In the early fairy tale about Mr. Lilystick, Lindgren already explores a technique of the fantasy tale, which she perfects later in her epic novels. She closely integrates child and adult perspectives into one narrative. In "The Land of Twilight" Lindgren correlates the imaginary and the protagonist's reality, making it possible to read the tale in two distinctly different ways, as an adventure story and as a realistic psychological portrayal of the imagination's emancipatory and therapeutic power. Suspension of disbelief would allow a third alternative to a reader who knowingly enters the realm of the fabulous. This duplicity provides her novels with a tension and complexity otherwise found in fantasy tales.

> For me—as an adult—it is clear that Rusky is so devastated when his brother dies that he must continue fabricating the story about Nangiyala that Jonathan tried to console him with. What happens in the book happens in Rusky's imagination, and when he dies on the last page, he dies at home in his kitchen sofa-bed. My adult self understands that, but the child in me will never accept such an interpretation; I know that everything happens just as it does in the book. Then everybody may interpret the book after his or her own fashion. (Holmberg, 79)

Lindgren makes a similar statement about *Mio, My Son.* Here, too, the adult reader believes that Karl Anders remains all alone on his park bench, while the child reader believes that Mio lives happily with his father in Farawayland. In these two novels and in many of her modern fairy tales, Lindgren provides readers with two hermeneutic choices. They can read the novel as either a fantastic adventure story or a psychological portrait of a dying boy's efforts to work through his fears and pain—or both. Whether or not readers choose to suspend disbelief, a fascinating story unfolds for them, because both perspectives are carried through with the same painstaking care in this intricately woven, double-tiered narrative.

Many direct ties and parallels exist between real and imaginary worlds in *Mio, My Son* and *The Brothers Lionheart.* In *Mio,* the memory of a lovely spring evening in the Stockholm archipelago grows into the rose garden; Karl Anders's best friend, Ben, becomes Pompoo; the old brewery horse, Charlie, is transformed into Miramis, who ambles along slowly "almost like Charlie used to do" (45–46); Pompoo's mother turns out to be "just like Mrs. Lundy [the lady from the store who gave Karl Anders the golden apple] except perhaps a little prettier" (29); and it is probably not far-fetched to see in Sir Kato Karl Anders's mean and cold foster father, who assumes mythical proportions in Farawayland. In *The Brothers Lionheart,* the brothers' old farmhouse in Nangiyala has the same layout as their home on earth. It, too, has only a kitchen, which they inhabit, and a room in which their mother will be able to do her sewing when she arrives. The sound of his mother's singing the popular song

"La Paloma" is also woven into Rusky's fantasies. Lindgren skillfully uses the double symbolism of the white dove as messenger of death and of peace. A white dove leads him to Nangiyala, and there white doves serve as Sofia's messengers in the struggle against Tengil and his terror regime.

The translator sometimes has difficulty in reproducing the full and exact counterpart of a word's semantics and symbolism. This is true for a few key terms in *The Brothers Lionheart,* such as *"saga"* and *"duva."* These two words have much richer, more encompassing counterparts in Swedish. The English equivalents of *saga* include "tale," "fairy tale," "folktale," "myth," and "saga." I believe a closer rendition of *saga* in *The Brothers Lionheart* would be "fairy tale," since that is the connotation most known to the child reader and since Lindgren refers to Jonathan as *"sagoprins,"* that is, a fairy-tale prince and not "a prince in a saga," as Joan Tate would have it. (I am well aware of the fact that the choice of the word "fairy tale" necessarily excludes the references to the Norse saga tradition which, as I have tried to show, is also present in the novel.) Similarly, the Swedish word *duva* can be translated either as "dove" or as "pigeon." Again, I would have preferred "dove," since it catches both the poetry and symbolism of *duva* that the rather pedestrian word "pigeon" lacks.

The ambiguity of the narrative perspective based on experiential levels is established in the very first lines of *The Brothers Lionheart.* The notion of subjective truth keeps the story suspended between the immanence of experience and its symbolic expression. In *Poetics of Children's Literature,* Zohar Shavit introduces the concept of the "ambivalent text," a text that crosses borders between two distinct systems.[13] Shavit speaks to the divided condition of children's book authors in general, that is, the fact that all children's books are produced, censored, sold, bought, written, and sometimes read by adults for children with the child in mind. But the ambivalence reaches deeper yet, for many authors of children's books claim to write for the child within and with this child's voice. Lindgren certainly belongs to this group of writers, but few have reflected so openly on the ambiguous nature of their creative impulse and brought it to the fore in their fiction.

In *The Brothers Lionheart,* Lindgren speaks simultaneously with two voices, each one originating in a very different narrative mode and genre: the fairy tale or fantasy tale, on the one hand, and the novel, on the other. Thus, she seamlessly fuses two conflicting epistemological systems. By imbricating the mythical and magical with the analytical and scientific, Lindgren gives expression to two irreconcilable drives in today's adult and older child: a decentered Copernican mindset in conflict with a sensory apparatus that still functions according to the Ptolemaic system, putting the individual at the secure center and letting the world revolve around this center. Since writing is not a purely cerebral exercise for Lindgren but, on the contrary, is based on emotion and intuition, she tempers and consoles her skeptical and disillusioned adult mindset with the certitude and confidence her emotional "childlike" self craves. She writes from the vantage point of the secure center for readers whose sense of magic is still alive, but with a knowing glance at those who want to keep it alive.

Lindgren's ardent desire to change unbearable situations and to console children tips the balance in favor of the child's perspective. The child, not the adult, is the primary—or perhaps favorite—audience, although the implied reader can be both. Given these predilections and the predominance of a critical and even cynical attitude among today's children, it is not surprising to see Lindgren take great pains to reinforce the child's perspective. Through the first-person narrative the reader assumes Rusky's perspective and identifies closely with his feelings and adventures. The voice of the omniscient storyteller who addresses the child overlays the voice of the novelist, who has neither easy answers nor provides a happy ending. Above all, Rusky's repeated assertions that his story is true guides readers in the right direction.

To remove further doubts from readers' minds, Rusky assures them about Nangiyala, "And it really was exactly as [Jonathan had] told me, while he'd sat there with me in the kitchen at home. Though now I was able to see that it was true, too, and I was pleased about that" (25). On numerous further occasions Lindgren buttresses the reality of the land of campfires and stories by making Rusky look back at his former self and his former environment from the vantage point of Nangiyala: "I remembered suddenly how things had been that time when Jonathan was dead and away from me, and I was lying in my sofa-bed, not knowing whether I'd ever see him again; oh, it was like looking down into a black hole, just thinking about it" (47). And, "Jonathan liked dressing up. He used to playact for me in the kitchen in the evenings, when we lived on earth, I mean" (105). Lindgren plays with the concept of imagination, as she plays with the concept of fairy tale, by introducing yet another dreamworld in the imaginary reality of Nangiyala. When Rusky first arrives in Nangiyala, he can't "imagine anywhere better to live" (24), and on his way to Katla Cavern he says to Jonathan, "This can't be real. It's like something out of an ancient dream" (128).

Read from the adult's perspective, these same references to life "on earth" anchor Rusky's vision in his real-life experiences and can be psychologically explained as Karl Anders's and Rusky's escapist or therapeutic dreams. Behind Mio hides Karl Anders, the neglected, love-starved child, whose emphatic last utterance, *"All is well with Mio"* (179), only heightens the critical reader's awareness that all is *not* well in the end. Behind Karl Lionheart hides Rusky, the pitiful, moribund, and guilt-ridden boy who will die alone on his kitchen sofa-bed. Read from the naive or child's perspective, Andy and Rusky become magical controllers of their fate, who fight against lovelessness (Sir Kato's heart of stone) and death (the merciless black Lord Tengil) and remain victorious. In one respect, however, the adult critical reader has to acknowledge the validity of the child's perspective. Magic, illusion, and belief are *real* means of empowerment. Only the power of suggestion helps Rusky face his death in the end, and this is the power Lindgren relied on when she wrote *The Brothers Lionheart* to console the child within all of us by dissipating our fear of death.

Even though adult readers may at times suspend disbelief in the process of reading and let themselves be carried away by the current of the narrative, rationally and analytically trained minds are apt to dismiss Rusky's adventures as compensatory dreams. For the critical adult reader it is not death that provides the passage to Nangiyala but imagination, and Rusky's leap to Nangilima is but a leap of faith. The different ways by which Nangiyala and Nangilima are reached support the critical adult perspective. Rusky flies to Nangiyala without being able to answer the question of how he got there; merely wishing suffices (20). But the way to reach Nangilima is incomparably more difficult, for Rusky himself has to take the step that will pull him into the dark abyss below.

The reader's perspective may not always be clear cut; and because of it adult readers can take the view of the inner child and the critical adult simultaneously. Considering a certain willingness to mix both perspectives, it may not be surprising that twenty-three of twenty-four critics who reviewed *The Brothers Lionheart* when the novel first appeared in Sweden were shocked and dismayed at the brothers' suicide at the end of the book (according to the adult's perspective, Rusky dies a natural death at home in his kitchen and, according to the child's perspective, he jumps off the cliff with his brother from the other world of Nangiyala to the paradise of Nangilima).[14] The critics' interpretation and verdict were probably based on a half-hearted attempt at assuming the child's point of view while retaining the grown-up's concern for the well-being of the child. Be it real or imagined, a positive portrayal of suicide is still taboo in children's and young adult novels. The critics' "misreading" of the novel is unfortunately something all too common in children's literature criticism, which is blinded by educational fervor and strict guidelines for proper attitudes and behavior where children are concerned. In most recent children's and young adult books that deal with suicide in one fashion or another, the actual suicide is either averted or, when it happens, is condemned as an undesirable, unethical solution. By condoning an escape into illusion *and* a conscious acceptance of death, Lindgren puts herself at odds with the accepted norms of holding onto life at any cost. Her portrayal of death is made even more contentious by the fact that Jonathan, who asks his brother to help him die because his whole body will soon be paralyzed, is the hero of the story.

Before passing final judgment on the fraternal suicide, the reader/critic should consider the author's intention and, above all, the novel's reception by child readers. Lindgren wanted to help children combat the fear of death, and in this endeavor she has succeeded, as many letters she has received from children facing death testify. The child reader knows that Jonathan and Rusky have already died before they come to Nangiyala, and they perceive Rusky's jump from Nangiyala to Nangilima as a jump into another—and better—paradise. Moreover, it is an exact mirror-image of Jonathan's jump from the burning house, for now Jonathan is paralyzed, and Rusky has to take him on his back. Although Rusky approaches the precipice with trepidation, the jump itself has wonderfully positive qualities of relief, promise, and achievement, not only because it means ultimate redemption for Rusky but also because we are assured in the closing words of the novel that both will come to Nangilima and, more important, will remain together forever: "Oh, Nangilima! Yes, Jonathan, yes, I can see the light! I can see the light!" (*Lionheart*, 183).

Although *The Brothers Lionheart* is set at the turn of the century, when most children still believed in heaven, Rusky, the younger of the two brothers, resembles in spirit those children of the late twentieth century who face a terrifying abyss of nothingness at the end of life. Lindgren depicts this state of mind metaphorically when Rusky must jump into the abyss in order to reach Nangilima, where he will be reunited with his brother Jonathan. But his leap into death and darkness is cushioned by his belief that there is a lush meadow deep down below that holds the promise of a happy existence together with his brother, reminiscent of the fairy tale's formulaic "and they lived happily ever after."

The Promise of Paradise

I believe in children's need for consolation. When I was a child, people believed that when you die you go to heaven; that was not one of the most amusing things one could imagine, to be sure, but if everyone went there . . . That would at least be better than lying in the ground and not existing any more. Today's children no longer have this consolation. They no longer have this tale. So then I thought: one could perhaps give them another tale that can provide them with a little warmth while they wait for the unavoidable end. (Törnqvist, 30)

Astrid Lindgren made this statement in 1973 in a letter to Egil Törnqvist, who had asked her for the motive that lay behind *The Brothers Lionheart*. These words corroborate her conviction that a good children's book should offer comfort, solace, and security above and beyond entertainment, drama, fun, and excitement. There are few times when comfort and solace are needed more than in situations of utter despair and in the face of death, and those are the conditions in which the readers find Karl Anders and Rusky before their fantasies provide them with a little warmth. There are readers in such situations, and among the many letters Lindgren has received in response to *The Brothers Lionheart* are those attesting to the solace dying children have derived from the story. Those readers who need reassurance will find relief from their own personal separation anxieties in Mio's and Rusky's world of fantasy and imagination. In a letter to the editor published in the newspaper *Expressen* in 1974, Lindgren assuaged the remaining fears of her readers by removing the threat to Nangilima posed by the evil forces from Nangiyala. She assured her readers that Tengil and his men and the horrifying monsters Karm and Katla will never come to Nangilima.[15]

In the early 1970s, when fantasy and fairy tales had fallen out of favor in Sweden and the United States, and when many Western countries were on the crest of a wave of social realism, Lindgren sensed a spiritual void in the children's books and filled it with her modern fairy tale about the two Brothers Lionheart. At the same time, Max Lüthi defended children's need for fairy tales in *Once upon a Time* (1970), and Bruno Bettelheim further popularized the idea of the fairy tale's therapeutic value in *The Uses of Enchantment* (1977). Both scholars argue that troubled children need tales about existential questions with a poetic vision that offer the confidence and consolation of a happy ending, and that these tales present models for sublimation through which children can distance themselves from overwhelming and potentially harmful pressures of the unconscious. Such emotional projections as dreams and fantasies become tools for working out inner conflicts.

Drawing on Freud's and Piaget's theories of child development, and displaying deep roots in German idealist thought, Bettelheim argues that fairy tales match the mindset of children better than realistic children's books written in the relativistic discourse of the scientific age, for "what seems desirable for the individual is to repeat in his life span the process involved historically in the genesis of scientific thought."[16] In periods of stress and scarcity, Bettelheim continues, "man seeks for comfort again in the 'childish' notion that he and his place of abode are the center of the universe" (51). In other words, children, and adults as well, revert to the empowering notion of being at the center and in control, which lets them face their hardships with renewed hope and energy. Thus, taking refuge in an illusion of absolute truth and justice, love and beauty provides both the sustenance with which to persevere and a means of escaping an unbearable situation. Which of the two will predominate depends to a large degree on reader reception. In any case, the dialectics of escape and empowerment (empowerment through escape and escape through empowerment) has therapeutic value.

Lindgren's conscious or intuitive choice of the fairy-tale discourse to help children combat fears and traumas follows these same lines of thinking. What better consolation is there than denial and sublimation of an unbearable and hopeless reality, and what better paradigm than the fairy tale to express and to resolve deep-seated existential fears, like those of failure and death? Like Bettelheim, she believes in the therapeutic function of folktales and fairy tales. She does not define them as narrowly as Bettelheim, who focuses primarily on the Grimm tales. Her fairy tales are a product of twentieth-century discourse, as is her rendition of paradise, and I would argue that her tales provide a better means of identification and means of empowerment for today's children than do nineteenth-century fairy tales.

What Bettelheim asserts about the fairy-tale hero can be maintained about Lindgren's female and male heroes as well: "By identifying with him, any child can compensate in fantasy and through identification for all the inadequacies, real or imagined, of his own body. He can fantasize that he too, like the hero, can climb into the sky, defeat giants, change his appearance, become the most powerful or most beautiful person—in short, have his body be and do all the child could possibly wish for" (57).

Both Rusky and Karl Anders are carried from one extreme to the other, from ugliness, pain, and sorrow to beauty, pleasure, and bliss. Karl Anders's feeling of loneliness is intensified by the warm glow of the windows he can see from his outpost in the dark, and his intense longing for warmth sweeps him into the enchanted world, like Hans Christian Andersen's Little Match Girl. Readers identifying with Mio will fly on a miraculous horse across the sky, overcome awe-inspiring odds to defeat evil, and finally break the magic spell that evil holds on them. Readers identifying with Rusky will change from a weak and pale boy with crooked legs who can't walk into a strong, healthy, good-looking boy who can swim and ride horses with the best of them and who will do his share in defeating Lord Tengil's inhumane, dictatorial regime in Wild Rose Valley.

Fear and the need to overcome it is a central theme in all three novels. As is standard for novels modeled on the quest motif, all three heroes must and do overcome deep-seated fear and experience suffering and hardship to achieve personal growth and maturity. Mio's physical growth, measured with notches on the door frame, parallels his emotional growth as he takes the decisive step to fight Sir Kato. Rusky's courage rises with every task he undertakes so that he can face death in the end. Fear never leaves him, especially during his last decisive step, but the burden of his jump into the abyss is lightened by the conviction that he will never have to be afraid again, for fear is an existential condition of life.

Overcoming fear is also Ronia's primary lesson. Step by step Ronia learns to control her fears by provoking and facing danger. She subjects herself to life-threatening tests of daring, climbing steep cliffs and jumping across Hell's Gap, the deep gorge that divides the two parts of the robber's fort, and she repeatedly fights battles against gray dwarves and harpies, externalized images of her fear. Her progress in handling fear is mirrored in her changing attitude toward the frightful mythical creatures of the forest. Symbolizing her early childhood fears, the gray dwarfs that terrorized her and had proven to be life-threatening during her first outing into the woods later become less daunting for her, and she chases the hissing and spitting dwarfs out of Bear's Cave without much ado. Fear condemns her to immobility and to the fury of the harpies, as her foot remains stuck in a crevice in the snow. She is as exposed to fear as she is to the elements, and only Birk can rescue her from the rage of the harpies. In a dramatic battle against the raging river and Greedy Falls Ronia and Birk trick the harpies by grasping a branch that serves as a canopy for herself and Birk, although only luck prevents them from perishing in the falls. These are significant steps on her way to winning her struggle against fear, and they parallel Karl Anders's and Rusky's battles with the forces of evil.

Once the battles against fear itself are fought, the reward is paradise or the promise thereof. South Wind Meadow, Farawayland, Nangiyala, and, to a degree, Ronia's forest are not simply paradise-like otherworlds; they cater to the child's conception of paradise and project the dreams and desires of the child who has grown up in twentieth-century industrialized society. The attractions of all three places are very similar. Like Nangiyala, all are lands of "campfires and stories," resembling settings well known from adventure tales. In Nangiyala, for example, readers find everything they may lack in real life; they can roam wide-open spaces, climb and conquer wild mountains, and, most important, enjoy their independence in an old-fashioned farmhouse. Sophia, the queen of doves and their surrogate mother, provides for their livelihood but lives at a safe distance. Whereas Farawayland is filled with magical props from folktales and fantasies, Nangiyala is furnished with stereotypical props from traditional adventure books, such as secret messages, a treasure chest, and campfires. Most important of all, all heroes and their best friends have their own beloved horses, as do Pippi and Emil.

Associations of paradise with pastoral images of nature, especially prominent in *Mio, My Son*, are commonplace in our cultural tradition. Lindgren injects her own personal experience into these cultural topoi by drawing inspiration from her own childhood. Over and over again she has returned to the somewhat idealized and embellished milieu of this happy childhood as a member of a loving extended family in a close-knit, preindustrial rural community. The fantasy worlds of Karl Anders and Rusky are close-knit communities exuding a friendly familiarity and unity, where relationships extend beyond people to nature and space, "Do stars care if you play to them?" Mio wonders, and Nonno thinks they do (*Mio*, 52). This caring small world is the realistic setting for the warm and happy Noisy Village series and the wonderfully funny Emil books. Yet when the narrative takes place in a cramped urban setting, as is the case with Karl Anders or Rusky, excursions into the wide open spaces of rural and historical fantasy worlds invariably occur.

When asked by a critic why she had chosen the particular topic and setting for *Ronia, the Robber's Daughter*, Astrid Lindgren replied that she wanted to escape the forest for a while. This rather flippant answer is a measure of Lindgren's disenchantment with the approaches of literary criticism to her books, but at the same time it is an answer that gets to the core of her choice, because in this novel Lindgren returns to her childhood forests in Småland one more time. The setting, as always, engenders memories of a free and happy existence, although it is not free from hardships, challenges, and dilemmas, and they assume a much greater role in this novel than in any of her realistic Småland stories.

The forest is a staple prop in many fairy tales. For Little Red Riding Hood, Hansel and Gretel, and Snow White it symbolizes the unfamiliar and dangerous unknown, and is often the home of witches, wolves, and other evil creatures. *Mio, My Son* and *The Brothers Lionheart* remain in that tradition. Especially for Mio, but also for Rusky, a harrowing ride through the forest precedes the final face-off with the ultimate power of evil. For Ronia, on the other hand, the forest is home after she has outgrown early childhood, a place she knows and loves well, always full of adventure and beauty, but also real danger. Her forest, too, has mythical qualities, but it is not reduced to a literary trope as is Mio's; it is real at the same time. Ronia's attitude toward her environment as she matures reflects that of Lindgren. Her initial possessiveness toward her surroundings—which she reveals when she does not want to share "her" forest with Birk—slowly gives way to the realization that the forest and all of nature is shared by everyone. Hence it should not be appropriated thoughtlessly but rather cared for with love and respect. The message that this process of matura-tion carries has its equivalent on the personal plane in Matt's changing relationship with his daughter. He, too, along with the reader, has to learn the lesson that caring does not preclude sharing.

Ronia's forest is a place that is becoming rare in a postindustrial urban society that controls and exploits nature to the extent that it is no longer nature that is dangerous, but rather its manipulation. For children of the late twentieth century, who are increasingly alienated from the expan-sion and the natural rhythm of nature and who live in highly structured and ever smaller and more confining units of time and space, the forest in *Ronia, the Robber's Daughter* becomes—as Astrid Lindgren intended it to be—an escape, a place to get away to.

Lindgren's fairy-tale novels are not among her light-hearted, humor-ous stories; the existential issues she addresses in them are far too serious. But humor and irony lend a distinct sparkle to these novels as well. Humor is least prominent in *Mio, My Son* and most apparent in *Ronia, the Robber's Daughter*, which in every respect is her ultimate work. Not only is it her last great novel, but in it she combines the wisdom of the ages with modern feminist ideas. By incorporating folktale elements into the modern novel, she skillfully fuses two narrative perspectives, the empathy of a participant and the distance of a detached observer, in a playful yet urgent appeal for a better world.

In *Ronia, the Robber's Daughter* Pippi's playful criticism—the double-voicedness Bakhtin found in the dialogic interplay of voices that humor and irony impart to the narrative—resurfaces. According to Bakhtin, the "authentic folkloric roots" of the novel as a genre are found in humor (Bakhtin, 21). Lindgren draws nourishment from these roots as she writes her heroic tales about Mio, the Brothers Lionheart, and Ronia, but at the same time she manages to keep the aura of the epic intact despite her use of humor in *Ronia, the Robber's Daughter.* The secret behind the successful blend of down-to-earth humor and epic distance lies in Lindgren's selective use of ridicule, for Lindgren dismembers the traditional heroic epic while she writes a new one. Her satiric puns never dismember the realm of magic she establishes in *Ronia, the Robber's Daughter.*

Noddle-Pete, one of the twelve robbers in Matt's castle and his close friend and confidant, is the prime representative of the subversive, critical countervoice. An adaptation of the classical trickster figure from the folktale, Noddle-Pete wields considerable power on account of his age, wit, and wisdom. Like Pippi, he dons the mask of the bewildered fool and reveals Matt's double moral standard with his feigned ignorance and ironic quips. On the surface Matt seems proud of his feats and defends his robber's life, but deep down inside he is vaguely aware of ethical wrongdoings. Not for nothing does he want to hide his source of livelihood from Ronia as long as possible to safeguard her innocence. The glory of being a robber is finally demythified when Ronia overhears Noddle-Pete ridicule Matt's self-representation as another Robin Hood. When Matt defends his trade, saying that he takes from the rich and gives to the poor, Noddle-Pete sniggers, "Oh, my goodness, yes, that's true enough! You gave that poor widow with the eight children a whole sack of flour, remember? . . . You have a good memory, you have, Matt! Let's see, that must have been ten years ago. Oh yes, of course you give to the poor. Every ten years, give or take a year" (46–47).

Noddle-Pete's and not Matt's voice prevails in the end, when Ronia and Birk denounce the life of a robber, and Noddle-Pete is also the one who holds the secret promise of a better future for Ronia and Birk. *Ronia, the Robber's Daughter* is a robber's tale with an unusual message, namely, that robbery, whatever its long-standing familial traditions, is cruel and unjust. Lindgren tells a thrilling tale about robbers, but at the same time she undermines its very foundations by deconstructing its message from within. Similarly, she tells great fairy tales but leaves open the possibility for a realistic interpretation of the story. It is this ambiguity that makes Lindgren's stories so fascinating for readers who have long outgrown childhood.

Just how Lindgren appropriates the fairy-tale paradigm for her own purposes is evidenced in the final paragraphs of *Ronia, the Robber's*

Mio and his best friend, Pompoo, ride the wonderful horse Miramis across Greenfield Island in Farawayland. Illustration by Ilon Wikland from *Mio, min Mio* (*Mio, My Son*).

Daughter. Like Noddle-Pete, Lindgren whispers tales into her readers' ears and hopes they will react much like Ronia does. Ronia has her doubts about the trustworthiness of Noddle-Pete's story, to say the least. What if the story is nothing but an illusion? What if there are no dwarfs guarding a silver mine up in the mountains? But then she reconsiders, "And who knows, it may not be just a fairy tale!" (175). She realizes that she holds the promise in her hands. The robbers will go on in their old ways, but *she* can change things. Noddle-Pete's story itself becomes a secret treasure she will guard. His story empowers and energizes her as does spring, because it is something to believe in, something that will make the prospect for the future clearer and brighter.

With this un-fairy-tale-like self-reflection, Lindgren leaves the door wide open for a belief in the wonders of the real world as she pulls the reader out of the fairy-tale past and into an unresolved but promising future at the very end of the book, trusting that her readers will take hold of the promise. This move is reinforced by the change in the last paragraph from narrative past to present tense (except, in the Swedish original, where Lindgren returns to the past in the very last sentences of the book). Lindgren leaves her readers with the encouraging notion that a life of harmony and nonviolence, given plentiful natural resources, is not just fantasy, but can become reality, if one believes in it now and acts accordingly. In *Ronia, the Robber's Daughter* the emancipatory traits of the fantasy seem to outweigh its escapist tendencies, but both are an undeniable part of Lindgren's fiction. Just as robber band history is rewritten when Matt and Borka start reminiscing about their joint childhood ventures in the castle's pigsty, Lindgren encourages her readers to adopt new narratives, tales, myths, or fantasies to make sense of the world. It may be just a fairy tale, but it is the only hope we have in a world that combines robber-like exploitation and advanced technology.

Sofia sends her messenger doves to Wild Rose Valley to undermine and undo the cruel Lord Tengil's despotic regime. Illustration by Ilon Wikland from *Bröderna Lejonhjärta*, the Swedish edition of *The Brothers Lionheart*.

Chapter Five

Courage and Compassion: Ethical Dimensions in Lindgren's Work

The children of today will someday take over the chores of our world, if there is still something left of it. They are the ones who will decide about war and peace and in what kind of society they want to live. In a society where violence steadily increases or in one where people live together in peace and harmony.

—Astrid Lindgren, *Something about the Author*

Improving Life through Fiction

Especially in her fantasy tales, but to a degree in her realistic stories, Astrid Lindgren takes her readers to a better place and a better way of life. Villa Villekulla, Farawayland, and Ronia's forest let readers escape into a dreamworld of wish fulfillment, and in a sense they do the same for the adult author. These fictional places are projections of Lindgren's visions of a better society and a more humane life for both children and adults. As such they serve not only as an escape but as an inspiration for her readers. In this chapter I will take a closer look at precisely this inspirational part of Lindgren's fiction, in other words, the ethical dimension of her work.

A constant in Lindgren's character and her fiction is her abhorrence of violence and abuse. Hitler's and Stalin's reigns of terror were as unbearable to her as are the neglect and abuse of children, domestic animals, and the environment—in general, the disrespect of people and things considered inferior. Her horror of all these manifestations of cruelty and insensitivity have found expression in her stories, for never does Lindgren present a scene of neglect or cruelty unbalanced by a projection or a promise of better times. Specific issues and concerns vary from book to book depending on topic and genre and on changing social conditions, to which Lindgren has responded with the artist's sensitivity. The life conditions and the status of children have changed dramatically since

Lindgren's childhood. Her work reflects these changes, but despite her sensitive and acute responses to shifts in social and political conditions the tenor of her writing has remained the same. Extending over almost half a century, Lindgren's work displays a rare cohesion through her ringing indictment of abuse and her appeal to her readers to find the courage and compassion to change the world.

Jonathan Lionheart's maxim that there are things that you just have to do if you want to be called a human being and not just a bit of filth and Pippi Longstocking's declaration that people with great power also have the greatest obligation to be good and responsible not only function as leitmotifs in their respective novels but are also guiding ethical principles for all of Lindgren's writing. These two adages are emblematic of Lindgren's deep devotion to humanity and her commitment to civility in her work and her life.

In her desire to reinforce and foster courage and compassion in her readers, the precondition for a more peaceful, just, and humane world, Lindgren uses a two-pronged approach, addressing those in control and those being controlled. Attaining a better world requires the concerted effort of both. The powerless are called upon to stand up against oppression and abusive treatment, while those in power are reminded of the fact that power can corrupt. Both are urged to respect the dignity of all life and love all living creatures on earth, starting with themselves. Pippi, who is in the remarkable position of belonging to both sides—she is a child, yet eminently powerful—bases both ethical principles on supreme self-confidence. Although Lindgren writes stories for children, her ethical appeals reach beyond the scope of the child audience. Clearly, Pippi's declaration is aimed at those who have the power to oppress and abuse because of their strength and position—be they children or adults—and adults are always in a position of power in their function as parents and educators.

When asked what she would have liked to be, given another chance in life, Lindgren responded that she would have loved to be an activist in the early days of the social democratic movement in Sweden, fighting for the rights of the underprivileged.[1] This statement not only satiates our curiosity about Lindgren's alternative career choices; it is symptomatic of the humanism and social commitment that form the backbone of her entire work. Lindgren has in a sense become just that, an activist for the powerless and underprivileged. In her fiction, she fought for social justice and the pursuit of happiness—and against the abuse of power—in the name of children long before the relatively bland codification of children's rights by the United Nations in 1959 and the more radical demands of children's rights activists in the 1970s. With her crusade for peace and her animal rights campaign in the late 1980s, Lindgren pursued her activist career further by becoming publicly engaged.

Lindgren, like wise women and men of time immemorial, has taken refuge in storytelling to solve riddles and teach lessons. The length of her stories can range from a novel to a short anecdote or tale; their function remains the same, that is, to touch the innermost core of our beings and to provide an inspiring and consoling narrative for a world in need of improvement. "I don't consciously try to educate or influence the children who read my books," Lindgren observes. "The only thing I would dare to hope for is that my books might make some small contribution towards a more caring, humane, and democratic attitude in the children who read them" ("Lindgren Talks," 5). This is a cautious statement, and few authors today dare attribute more influence to their writing. In addition, Lindgren's remark undercuts any implied assumption of didacticism in her work. Her stories are not cautionary tales or moralizing fables, but carry within them the complexity and inscrutability of folktales—hence her preference for this genre. Even more to the point, Lindgren's humanism, in the broadest sense of the word, and her social activism are so much a part of herself that they could never constitute a pose. Lindgren's attempt to improve life on earth by instilling human kindness and empathy in her readers and by making life a little more bearable has remained a constant, from *Pippi Longstocking* to *Ronia, the Robber's Daughter.*

Never Violence: Peaceful Conflict Resolution

Lindgren strongly believes that how we educate children will greatly influence the world of the future and that what children need most is love and trust. She contends that children who are treated lovingly by their parents and caretakers will in turn love their parents. This mutual love and trust will help them establish a "loving" relationship with their environment that they will retain during their entire life. "And this is good," Lindgren continues, "even if the child does not become one of those who govern the fate of the world. But if one day, contrary to expectations, the child should belong to those powerful people, then it is a joy for all of us if its attitude has been determined by love and not violence, for even the character of statesmen and politicians is formed before they are five years old—this is a horrifying fact, but it is true" (*Something,* 38, 133).

Her message seems simple: if we want to make the world a kinder place, we have to treat children with kindness, gentleness, and respect, since they will shape future societies in the spirit in which they themselves have been shaped. If we teach children violence or treat them with violence and disrespect, the world will continue to be filled with violence. Violence begets violence. That is why we who have the power over children as parents or educators should refrain from violence and model peaceful behavior.

Corporal punishment is one form of violence many parents have committed unwittingly or even with good conscience, since it was the commonly accepted practice. By refashioning an old tale, "The Old Man and His Grandson," in the Brothers Grimm collection, Lindgren contributes to breaking the vicious circle of abuse. When she received the German Bookseller's Peace Prize in 1978, she told the (overwhelmingly adult) audience the following:

> I would like to tell those . . . who so loudly call for stricter discipline and tighter reigns what an old lady once told me. She was a young mother at a time when one still believed the saying from the Bible "spare the rod and spoil the child." At the bottom of her heart she didn't really believe this, but one day her son did something for which, in her opinion, he had earned a sound thrashing, the first in his life. She directed him to go to the garden and to find a rod himself which he should then bring to her. The little boy went out and did not return for a long while. Finally he returned crying and said, "I couldn't find a rod, but here is a stone which you can throw at me." Then the mother began to cry too, for suddenly she saw everything through the eyes of the child. The child must have thought: "My mother really wants to hurt me and she can also do this with a stone." She took her little son into her arms and then they both cried together for a while. She then placed the stone on a shelf in the kitchen and left it there as a constant reminder of the promise which she had made herself in this hour: "Never violence!" (*Something*, 38, 134)

By modeling ways of peaceful conflict resolution and conviviality, Lindgren has surely helped raise the level of sensitivity to abusive treatment of children in Sweden, where corporal punishment was allowed in school until the late 1950s and where a law was passed in the 1980s forbidding parents to strike their children. The message of nonviolence is most forcefully expressed in the books that most openly deal with violence and destruction, such as *Mio, My Son* and *The Brothers Lionheart*. In *The Brothers Lionheart* Lindgren moved one step further away from the traditional dragon-killer quest on which both books are based. Whereas

Mio hated the idea of having to take the sword in his hand and kill evil Sir Kato to break the spell—and relieve Sir Kato himself from the pain and suffering of a heart of stone—Jonathan flatly refuses to arm himself and kill Tengil or Katla. Both heroes show no signs of the heroic-aggressive behavior that is commonplace in traditional quests and nineteenth-century retellings of fairy tales. Still, Lindgren placates her readers' fear, satisfies their hunger for excitement, and instills in them hope and courage.

Courage assumes center stage in *The Brothers Lionheart*. As their name suggests, the brothers have ample courage and big hearts. Jonathan represents these qualities in an idealized form, whereas Rusky's long struggle against fear—following his ideal as he follows his brother—is a more realistic portrayal of the human condition. Jonathan differs from his namesake, King Richard I Lion-Heart, in at least one important respect. He is a champion of nonviolence. Jonathan, who dares to confront the dragon, is neither the valiant dragon-slayer of traditional fairy tales and sagas nor a powerful and ruthless ruler. Instead of killing the dragon, he averts the danger by trickery. All in all, this new hero does not yearn for power; instead he is a warm, tender, and caring person who would neither hurt nor kill anybody—not for lack of daring, but out of conviction.

Courage in *The Brothers Lionheart* is not synonymous with bravery and definitely not with ostentatious fearlessness. This becomes evident when a Tengil soldier named Park, bragging about his strength, foolhardily forces his horse into the swift rapids of the river of the Ancient Rivers to prove his courage. Only with Jonathan's help—and at the risk of Jonathan's life—do horse and rider survive, yet Park has not even a word of thanks. Not only is Park called a fool, but a coward as well (*Lionheart*, 156). By frivolously gambling his life on a bet he displays the same disregard for human life that is characteristic of the despotic Tengil regime as a whole. Courage in this book about death and suicide is synonymous with love and a high esteem for life.

By raising the question of pacifism, Lindgren lends considerable complexity to the struggle of good versus evil, especially because it does not remain uncontradicted. There are heroic and caring figures in this novel who do not shrink from using violence to combat oppression and abusive cruelty. Among them are Antonia, who is prepared to avenge the murder of her husband ordered by Tengil, and particularly Orvar, the intrepid rebel and freedom fighter. Orvar sees no other recourse but to use violence to liberate his country from the forces of evil. While he plans for the decisive battle, he and Rusky begin to argue. Orvar's prediction that if every-

one were like Jonathan evil would forever reign in the world is contradict-
ed by Rusky, who gets the last word: "if everyone were like Jonathan,
there wouldn't be any evil" (165). Since this poetic tale of human brotherhood is written to console children, including the child within the adult,
love, the remedy against all evil, wins out over hatred, indifference, and
death. Wild Rose Valley is freed from evil through Jonathan's nonviolent
courage, although—and here Lindgren makes a concession—Orvar's spirit of resistance proves to be a key part of the effort.

A composite of adventure and robber's tale, *Ronia, the Robber's
Daughter,* like *The Brothers Lionheart,* can be classified as quest narrative.
Like its predecessor, *Ronia* departs from the traditional path of the heroic narrative in which a solitary male leader perpetuates the paternal
order by removing and killing obstacles to his ascent to power. Ronia,
too, is born into a world of conflict and ambiguity—in her case, during
a raging thunderstorm in which the castle is split in two, leaving Hell's
Gap between. Initially, there are two sets of conflicting values, one reigning inside the family and the other in the world "outside." While caring,
love, and understanding guide life inside the castle under the auspices of
Lovis (modeled on the bourgeois family myth), the professional code of
the robbers is based on conflict and exploitation. Neither of the two
behavioral patterns is impervious to the influence of the other, however,
and conflict invades the family while the two bands' reconciliation is
based not only on pragmatic concerns of survival but on love and understanding as well.

Much like Romeo and Juliet's, Ronia and Birk's relationship eventually brings the fighting to an end, with the one difference that Ronia and
Birk do not have to pay with their lives for it. With her courageous
leaps, Ronia at first playfully bridges Hell's Gap, which symbolizes the
senseless conflict between the two robber bands. Later, at a more mature
stage of her childhood, there is little playfulness left in her effort to con-
nect the two parts of the castle by building a pathway through the rub-
ble and debris, a feat she accomplishes with much physical and
psychological suffering. She feels torn between opposing values and
incompatible demands, as when she decides to steal food from her mother's larder to keep Birk and the enemy camp alive during the winter, and
when she is forced to choose between Birk and her father. One lesson
that Ronia (and the reader) learns is that there are no easy solutions, but
solutions can be found if one works hard at it.

Through her actions Ronia offers a model for conflict resolution based
on give and take and caring enough about others to learn to understand

them. This model runs counter to the magical solutions and the rigid patriarchal hierarchy encountered in classical fairy tales, where the underdog hero prevails thanks to magical helpers and where dissenters either perish or have to find their way back into existing structures of society. The dream in the classical fairy tale, which emerged out of a rigid, authoritarian culture with stable hierarchies, had been to get to the very top through luck or cleverness and to stay there. It is replaced by a very different dream of success in a dynamic, late capitalist society based on the laws of Social Darwinism. This dream, which constitutes the subtext of all three Lindgren novels—*Mio, My Son, The Brothers Lionheart, and Ronia*—expresses the need for peaceful cooperation and a life that does not depend on the exploitation of nature or people.

Superheroes like Pippi, Mio, Jonathan, and Ronia belong to the utopian world of fantasy, but there is plenty of everyday heroism in children who stand up for their rights and protest abuse of power in Lindgren's realistic fiction as well. Tjorven in *Seacrow Island* defiantly stands up to the materialism of the rich real estate speculator just as Pippi does, and Emil reveals the true meaning of Christmas when he invites the most wretched and desolate people in Lönneberga to the big feast. Like Jonathan, Emil, too, shows courage of heart when he saves Alfred's life.

Tales of Resistance and Empowerment

Lindgren's social commitment and her call for courage of the heart permeates her realistic books as much as her fantastic tales, though the choice of genre somewhat alters the way it is expressed. Typically, this call is reflected in the protagonists' open or underhanded revolt against presumptive behavior and the abuse of authority. Pippi's and Emil's wild and joyous parodies of pretentiousness are toned down in the books about Madicken (Mardie to the British reader, Meg to the American), but this protagonist also chastises others for such vices as conceit and arrogance. Especially in the second book about her, *Mardie to the Rescue,* the heroine's sense of justice underscores the problems of human inequity and social inequality. Sometimes the protagonist's—and by extension Lindgren's—ethics are at odds with public morality, as in the episode about Mia's theft at school. Having found the headmaster's purse, Mia does not return it but instead buys chocolates and angel bookmarks, which she distributes freely to her class to gain a little recognition. To Mardie's comment, "It was terrible of Mia to take the purse as well. It's wrong to steal," her father replies, "Yes, but little children do it sometimes, and it's not right to try to knock it out of them with a cane" (78). For that is what the headmaster does in front of the whole class. It is indicative of Lindgren's ethics of compassion that Mardie's father does not get half as upset over Mia's theft as he does over the punishment she has to endure from the headmaster. Throughout the episode the narrator's sympathy is with Mia.

The issue of abusive treatment is closely linked to institutionalized abuse in the form of socially sanctioned discrimination and social disparity. Mia, called Louse-Mia by the other children because her hair is full of lice and her clothes are dirty and torn, clearly belongs to the lowest social class and feels the effects of discrimination daily. She is a fighter who stands up for her rights, which makes her into a renegade in the eyes of authority. The disgruntled head teacher can finally vent his anger after having found her guilty, and he employs the then-accepted practice of combining physical with psychological pain to break the offender's will. Mia must first confess, then ask for forgiveness, and finally she must be beaten as well. "You will thank me for it one day," is the righteous comment of the head teacher (82). This torture in the name of education, or "poisonous pedagogy," as Alice Miller calls it, is portrayed with equal disdain by Ingmar Bergman in his film *Fanny and Alexander,* through the character of the bishop/stepfather. Lindgren and Bergman belong to the same generation, and although their childhood experiences were diametrically opposed, both vehemently condemn the repression and hypocrisy of the bourgeois authoritarian educational ethic.

While Alexander's will is broken—he will never be free of fear, and memories of his stepfather will haunt him for the rest of his life—Mia's remains unbroken in spite of the fact that "there was no child he [the head teacher] could not break" (84). Mia stubbornly refuses to ask for forgiveness. Lindgren, who writes to console and inspire children, lets Mia keep her pride. Fearlessly and triumphantly she leaves the scene. Instead of delivering the expected excuse with downcast eyes, Mia stands up to the head teacher, looks straight into his eyes and says loudly and clearly "Pisspot!" before she leaves. Again, it is not Mia's expletive or her action that Mardie's father calls the most indecent thing he's ever heard but rather the headmaster's action. Lindgren's opinion about those who abuse their power over the weak can hardly be stated in more drastic terms.

The powerless and disadvantaged, often members of the working class and children, stand up for their rights in Lindgren's books, and alliances between the two are often formed on the basis of mutual understanding and common interest. Lindgren, who has always taken pride in being a farmer's daughter, empathizes with working people and uses a sharp pen to highlight the conceit of people who look down on the working class. She condemns the rigid class barriers that were prominent between masters and servants in the middle-class family at the beginning of the century, and she saves much mockery and ridicule for pretentious small-town society ladies and pompous politicians. Emil regularly gets the better of society ladies and the mayor, but a more pronounced criticism of the propensity to look down on simple folk can again be found in *Mardie to the Rescue*.

There Alma, the maid in Mardie's household, speaks up for herself if need be. Alma's insistence on having the last salmon from a fishmonger evidences Lindgren's reproof against preferential treatment on the basis of social status and title. Unfortunately for the mayor's wife, Alma is the first to claim the last piece of salmon in the shop, but the mayor's wife does not give up that easily. She uses her status to pressure Alma into relinquishing her claim: "Do you know who I am, young woman? I am the mayoress of this town!" But Alma's retort, "Well, I am the one who is going to have this salmon," leaves her speechless. In the end, Alma makes off with the salmon (15).

Alma dares speak up because she has some backing from Mardie's father, the town's newspaper editor, who is also called the "gentleman-socialist." He takes Alma along to the great charity ball organized by the mayor's wife, which constitutes an affront to the hostess and to many other townspeople. Cutting off the mayor's wife, who is remarking that servants are not invited to the ball, he asserts, "Then it is about time that there will be a change" (138). And he is savagely pleased—as is the reader—when the chimney sweep crashes the party and asks Alma, who had been frozen out, to dance. Like Cinderella and the prince, these two take over the dance floor. For Mardie, through whose eyes the reader observes the incident, this is a fairy tale come true: "They danced and danced and sang and laughed and danced as Mardie had never seen people dance before. It was beautiful, oh, how beautiful it was! For Alma was beautiful and white and the sweep was handsome and black" (142). The fairy tale's sense of justice prevails here as well, with the difference that Alma does not get her prince, for he is already married and has five children. Lindgren adapts the fairy-tale motif for her own purpose. The dream she communicates to her readers is the victory of the truly human over hollow pretense.

Many critics have found Mardie to be utterly bourgeois in behavior and values. She certainly grows up in a bourgeois household, but the cultural patterns she experiences are far from uniform. *Mardie to the Rescue* presents a cross-section of social classes, with heavy sympathies for those at the lower end of the scale, but Lindgren does not uncritically sing their praises. The mentally disturbed Lindson is outright dangerous as he walks through town snatching small children, and Mia and her little sister, Mattis, are definite cases of child neglect—dirty and full of lice and aggression as they are. Mr. Nilsson, the neighbor, is a good-for-nothing drunk with a flair for self-aggrandizement and a love of words who leaves his wife and son to fend for themselves. He is a considerably more problematic version of Paradise-Oscar in *Rasmus and the Vagabond*. Oscar only gives in to his need for freedom in the spring, when he has the urge to hit the road, in effect taking a vacation from farming, but otherwise shoulders his responsibilities; Mr. Nilsson, however, has taken a permanent leave of absence from his responsibilities.

In *Mardie to the Rescue* Lindgren allots more room to the shady sides of life than she does in most of her realistic books. A more pronounced focus on social injustice may have been Lindgren's answer to the strong movement of social realism that pervaded children's literature in the 1970s in Sweden, Europe, and the United States. Lindgren's tendency to harmonize is not carried quite as far in this book. Mr. Nilsson does not change. Lindson is finally locked up in a home to make the small town a safer place again. Mia and Mattis are deloused by Mardie's mother, but, as her father points out, this is a temporary measure that changes little in the real-life conditions under which the two girls have to live. Yet even in this book Lindgren cannot deny herself. Happiness wins out over sorrow, fear, and pain, as it does in the Alma-as-Cinderella episode. The shady side of life gives Mardie an opportunity to reflect, but it does not permanently alter her cheerful and positive disposition, for she has "a healthy young person's ability to forget anything disagreeable almost from one day to the next" (117). Mardie's unencumbered joy of life also sets the tone for this book. With the cast of characters in the Mardie books Lindgren has created a multivoiced discourse in which the only common denominator is a basic democratic humanism. Despite her clean aprons, Mardie is much too strong-minded, high-spirited, and unconventional to fit the mold of the bourgeois female heroine. As a matter of fact, Mardie, like Emil, is but a more realistically drawn version of Pippi—full of ideas, energy, joie de vivre, curiosity, and cunning. Something provocative and liberating is part of their playful experimentation with the physical, emotional, and intellectual realities of life, and this playfulness no doubt resonates in the reader.

From Pippi to Ronia: Uniformity and Development in Lindgren's Writing

Pippi and Ronia, the two strong female protagonists that demarcate the beginning and end of Astrid Lindgren's career as a children's book author, exemplify not only the growth and development of Lindgren as a writer but also developments in children's and women's life experience. This life experience has changed considerably thanks to the struggles for children's and women's rights in the Western world during the latter part of the twentieth century. Pippi's refusal to be part of the adult world she ridicules in Dadaist deconstructive fashion in 1945 is superseded thirty-six years later by Ronia's resolve to do her part to rebuild the world.

In the world of twentieth-century children's literature Lindgren is not categorized by herself or by others as a feminist author. Her prime concern remains that of children's rights; yet in her effort to give a voice to the voiceless she has often touched on feminist issues. Obvious parallels exist between the struggle for women's rights and the struggle for children's rights. A short glance at the history of childhood, motherhood, and family life, as told by Philippe Aries, Elisabeth Badinter, John Boswell, and Lloyd deMause, among others, suffices to confirm the double victimization—both as child and as female—that girls have experienced throughout the ages. In the case of girls and their fictional representation both struggles are compounded. Girl protagonists in children's literature, after all, offer models of identification for the purpose of socialization of female readers. The debilitating or emancipatory influences these protagonists exert may last a lifetime.

Despite obvious systemic differences, the movements for women's and children's rights employ similar rhetorical strategies. That is why it may be difficult at times to define Lindgren's emancipatory rhetoric as specifically feminist, counter-cultural, or child-oriented. These voices converge in Lindgren's high regard for personal integrity, community, caring, and sharing, which runs like a red thread through her entire writing. Which of these tendencies readers will bring to the fore in their analysis will depend on their focus as well as on the narrative itself. A gender-based reading of Lindgren's work would scarcely be able to bypass the two strong and self-assertive characters that flank it—Pippi and Ronia—for they invite such a reading.

Pippi's emancipatory voice reached the public four years before the publication of Simone de Beauvoir's *The Second Sex,* and I would like to argue that within its genre it became equally influential. Pippi set the stage for future female heroes who will not let themselves be confined to the domestic sphere. In Pippi Longstocking girls encountered an active and self-assertive female protagonist with whom they could identify. Her playful subversion of authority was followed cautiously in the 1960s and more vigorously in the 1970s by a whole wave of antiauthoritarian children's literature questioning traditional roles and conventional values.

Pippi's emancipatory subversion and aggressive nonviolence belong wholly to the realm of fantasy and wishful thinking, as does she herself. The liberating potential in *Pippi Longstocking* largely remains an expression of the playfulness and exuberance of childhood, a familiar romantic trope. Outwardly, the effect of Pippi's actions on social reality within the narrative seems as limited as it must have been on the immediate everyday life experiences of her readers. Nothing much seems to change in Tommy and Annika's life when Pippi is not around, nor can we trace any important changes in their attitudes. In both behavior and reasoning these two remain model children who prefer the security and comfort of the conventional. Nonetheless, as they swallow Pippi's magic chililug pills, which promise eternal happy childhood, they imbibe a permanent spark of revolt and regeneration, just as many readers must have in reading Pippi's books.

In *Ronia, the Robber's Daughter* Lindgren presents her readers with a female hero who bears much resemblance to Pippi, yet readers are confronted with two distinct concepts of childhood and femininity framed in different narratives. Both female heroes are curious, caring, courageous, and strong-willed, but while Pippi, the fantastic character in a realistic setting, represents only one side of childhood—the boundless playfulness, neglectful of time and place—Ronia, the realistic character in a timeless fairy-tale setting, is an altogether believable and complex individual.

The reader of *Ronia, the Robber's Daughter* delves into the magic world of fairy tale and adventure in which Ronia resides and follows her growth and development through the stages of childhood and beyond in a female bildungsroman. The theme of growth and responsibility, which is added to the free and adventurous childhood spirit reigning in *Pippi Longstocking,* lends this last novel its depth and importance. In both books readers follow the adventures of female heroes whose fathers have taken the law into their own hands (Pippi's father is a pirate captain and Ronia's is the chief of a robber band). Each daughter revolts in her own, unpredictable fashion. Pippi, the playful supergirl, ridicules and exposes untenable conditions with zest and courage in the realm of fantasy. Still, the concrete results of her subversive tactics remain untold. Ronia, on the other hand, needs no superhuman strength to undo her foes. She uses her muscles, acts on her convictions, and achieves concrete goals. While Pippi abrogates her growth voluntarily, Ronia accepts the challenge of the future and of adulthood. Unlike Tommy and Annika, she is not compelled to shed fantasy and playfulness like an old snake skin upon entry into the adult world; her imagination gradually loses its childish qualities but remains an important source for Ronia's vision and ambition. This portrayal of Ronia would not have been possible without the concomitant developments in society. Without the breakdown of barriers between manhood and womanhood, and between adulthood and childhood, and without the growing importance of the idea of the inner child, *Ronia the Robber's Daughter* might not have been written, at least not in its present form.

The impact of recent social change, which has affected both the feminist and the children's rights movements, has opened up possibilities for new literary discourses that support parallel changes in women's and children's social realities. *Ronia, the Robber's Daughter* is an example of the books that regenerate the genre by regendering it. This regendering goes beyond the superficial gender change of the quest hero from male to female. Feminine values and modes of expression have infiltrated the traditionally male discourse of the quest, leading to its feminization, which I see manifested in this novel. From playfully deconstructing patriarchal standards and values in *Pippi Longstocking,* Lindgren moves on to reconstruction by means of feminist myth building in *Ronia, the Robber's Daughter.* No longer is the feminist discourse deferred to fantasy and hidden in parody and trickster tale, revealing the strategy of resistance against an overwhelming force. At a time when a greater number of women are working their ways into positions of influence and power, Ronia has become a natural role model for young readers.

A Break with the Past: Women's Voices and Children's Wisdom

A feminine discourse of peaceful, nurturing coexistence and a sense of community pervade Lindgren's robber's tale. Ronia balances her autonomy and independence with an acute sensitivity to her environment and a sustained connectedness to family and community unknown in traditional quest stories. The heroic tale starts conventionally enough with Ronia's ominous birth during a thunderstorm and continues with a series of daring feats performed by Ronia, who, like Pippi, claims her right to journey into the world as a matter of course. Since Ronia is clearly at the center of the story, her counterpart, Birk, despite his virtues, pales in comparison.

In this female bildungsroman, which traces Ronia's gradual maturation to full independence within the framework of communal interdependence, the two female protagonists, Ronia and her mother, Lovis, are, by and large, stronger and wiser than their male counterparts. Lovis, whose wolf song exudes strength as well as nurturing qualities, is full of wisdom and profound affection. Nothing but a vague sense of adventure remains of the glorification of male might and power, of the feuds and open violence in traditional robber's and adventure stories. In fact, these attributes are even ridiculed when they surface. Big, tough, bragging Matt, who is also colorful and endearing, receives a fair share of ridicule, for example, when he whimpers about the bruises he has sustained during the "heroic" duel between the two chieftains. Ultimately, both women prove to be stronger and more enduring than the men. No robbers dare contradict Lovis when she chases them out into the snow stark naked for the castle's early spring cleaning. This surely is a complete reversal of values attributed to the sexes in the classical quest, where men were active, daring, and strong and women suffering, supportive, and good-looking.

Ronia's leap across Hell's Gap, the chasm separating the two parts of the castle and symbolizing the split between the two robber bands, sets her off on her as yet unconscious and undefined quest to change the world. In the traditional manner, this quest takes her away from her family and clan and out into uncharted territories in the forest, where she will spend the summer in a cave together with Birk. Her separation from her family, however, is not complete. Moreover, family ties define her attempts to gain independence and to chart her own course. Her father's unreasonably stubborn grief at having "lost" his daughter as well as her own guilt at having betrayed her parents weigh heavily on her conscience. Her inner struggle to overcome separation anxiety and to redefine her interpersonal relationships, as well as her role in society and nature, are portrayed as tasks that are just as difficult, if not more so, than any of her more flamboyant, action-oriented—and traditionally male—feats of courage. Her mental courage demands empathy, integrity, and farsightedness above and beyond daring and forcefulness. Hence, Ronia's most heroic act lies not in her attempt to save Birk's life at the risk of her own but in her attempt to reunite the warring bands and in her refusal during the bands' reconciliation celebration to become a robber's chieftain as her father desires.

All by herself and with singular persistence, Ronia changes the conditions for everyone concerned. Her bridge-building effort brings about the reconciliation of the robber bands and the rewriting of their history, erasing old dualisms, as does Lindgren with her novel. But, most important, the refusal of Ronia and Birk to continue in their fathers' footsteps will do away with the old robber ways and eventually change society fundamentally. Matt has to grin and bear Ronia's decision not to become the robber chieftain he had always wanted her to be. The ways and values of the founding fathers are overthrown and give way to change. Patriarchal authority and traditional male values of aggression and competition belong to the past and have to be replaced by a sense of community if the future is to be any brighter. The narrator tells us that this is a change for the better. Matt and Borka look forward to theft and plunder again as spring approaches, but Ronia and Birk, the narrator tells us, are "much wiser. They delighted in quite different things" (174).

Ronia picks up where Pippi leaves off. Despite her professed eagerness to follow in his footsteps, Pippi never becomes a pirate like her father. She eventually chooses a very different career. Seeing no other solution to her dilemma of retaining her wildness and freedom in a society bent on domesticating and institutionalizing her, she reverts to eternal childhood. Ronia also looks up to her father and envisions herself as a robber chieftain when she is small, but consciously chooses another path once she has reached the age of reason, realizing the cruelty and lack of social responsibility inherent in a robber's life. Ronia's father, although successful as a robber and much loved by his daughter, cannot ultimately remain her role model. Neither can her mother, who is strong and independent but nevertheless supports the robber ways. Ronia is forced to chart her own course together with Birk. Trusting their intuition, she and Birk will become the founders of a new, and, as Lindgren calls it, "wiser" world order, where the quest for possession and power is tempered by caring and nurturing and a joyful openness toward life that is expressed in Ronia's primal scream at the conclusion of the novel. In this female bildungsroman Lindgren takes her readers beyond dualism and difference to a relatively open ending and visions of a better future.

Sisterhood and brotherhood are the guiding principles of the novel *Ronia, the Robber's Daughter*. Besides the special closeness Ronia and Birk feel for each other, the idea that both belong to one big family of human beings on this planet, symbolized by the robbers' forest, also resonates in

Ronja celebrates spring with her spring yell, signaling hope for a better future. Illustration by Ilon Wikland from *Ronja rövardotter*, the swedish edition of *Ronia, the Robber's Daughter.*

their calling each other "Sister" and "Brother." Ronia and Birk change and develop as they grow up, and their fathers, who are grown men, are forced to change as well. Admittedly, they still go on in their old robber ways. They are steeped in these ways and don't know any better, but their relationship with the younger generation changes. The absolute authority of the older generation gives way to greater tolerance and understanding. Ronia does not, like the prodigal son, return begging for forgiveness following her decision to move away from home; her father has to meet her half-way and has to ask her forgiveness.

The destructive versus nurturing attitude and male versus female voice do not simply run along gender lines; likewise, the division between the more primitive life-style of the parents and the "wiser" and more advanced choice of their children is not an exclusively generational one. The vision for change originates with the oldest and wisest of the robbers, Noddle-Pete. He influences Ronia's decision to give up robbery through his underhanded and witty criticisms of the old way of life. His role very much resembles that of Astrid Lindgren, the author who writes books for children in order to entertain, console, and inspire. His voice prevails, and the optimistic message of progress, defined not in material terms but as a shift in mindset toward a more peaceful, humane society, resonates throughout the novel as it does throughout Lindgren's work. Only the future will show whether her voice will be heard and whether it will prevail.

Appendix: Feature Films Based on Lindgren's Stories

1947   *Mästerdetektiven Blomkvist* (Bill Bergson). Directed by Rolf Husberg.

1948   *Pippi Långstrump* (Pippi Longstocking). Directed by Per Gunwall.

1953   *Mästerdetektiven och Rasmus* (The masterdetective and Rasmus). Directed by Rolf Husberg.

1955   *Luffaren och Rasmus* (The tramp and Rasmus). Directed by Rolf Husberg.

1956   *Rasmus, Pontus och Toker* (Rasmus, Pontus, and Crazy). Directed by Stig Olin.

1957   *Mästerdetektiven Blomkvist lever farligt* (Bill Bergson lives dangerously). Directed by Olle Hellbom.

1960   *Alla vi barn i Bullerbyn* (The children of Noisy Village). Directed by Olle Hellbom.

1961   *Bara roligt i Bullerbyn* (Only fun in Noisy Village). Directed by Olle Hellbom.

1964   *Tjorven, Båtsman och Moses* (Tjorven, Båtsman, and Moses). Directed by Olle Hellbom.

1965   *Tjorven och Skrållan* (Tjorven and Skrållan). Directed by Olle Hellbom.

1966   *Tjorven and Mysak* (Tjorven and Mysak). Directed by Olle Hellbom.

1967   *Skrållan, Ruskprick och Knorrhane* (Skrållan, Nasty, and Grumble). Directed by Olle Hellbom.

1968   *Vi på Saltkråkan* (Seacrow Island). Directed by Olle Hellbom.

1970   *Pippi Långstrump på de sju haven* (Pippi Longstocking on the seven seas). Directed by Olle Hellbom.

1970   *På rymmen med Pippi Långstrump* (Pippi Longstocking on the run). Directed by Olle Hellbom.

1971 *Emil i Lönneberga* (Emil in Lönneberga). Directed by Olle Hellbom.

1972 *Nya hyss av Emil i Lönneberga* (Emil's new pranks). Directed by Olle Hellbom.

1973 *Emil och Griseknoen* (Emil and piglet). Directed by Olle Hellbom.

1974 *Världens bästa Karlsson* (The world's best Karlsson). Directed by Olle Hellbom.

1977 *Bröderna Lejonhjärta* (The brothers lionheart). Directed by Olle Hellbom.

1979 *Du är inte klok, Madicken* (Meg, you are crazy). Directed by Göran Graffman.

1981 *Rasmus på luffen* (Rasmus and the vagabond). Directed by Olle Hellbom.

1984 *Ronja Rövardotter* (Ronia, the robber's daughter). Directed by Tage Danielsson.

1986 *Alla vi barn i Bullerbyn* (The children of Noisy Village). Directed by Lasse Hallström.

1987 *Mer om oss barn i Bullerbyn* (More about the children of Noisy Village). Directed by Lasse Hallström.

1987 *Mio, min Mio* (Mio, my son). Directed by Vladimir Grammatikow

1988 *New Adventures of Pippi Longstocking.* Directed by Ken Annakin.

1988 Short films produced by Svensk Filmindustri based on Lindgren's early tales: *Kajsa Kavat* (Brenda Brave), *Nånting levande åt Lame-Kal* (A live Christmas present), *Godnatt, Herr Luffare* (Good night, Mr. Vagabond), *Ingen rövare finns i skogen* (There are no robbers in the forest), *Hoppa högst* (One jump too many), *Allrakäraste syster* (My very own sister), and *Gull-Pian* (Sweet Pea).

Notes and References

All sources are cited parenthetically in the text after their first reference. All translations of passages not heretofore translated into English are the author's.

Chapter One

1. "Astrid Lindgren Talks about Herself," a special brochure prepared by her publisher, Rabén and Sjögren (Stockholm), 1987, 2.

2. Margareta Strömstedt, *Astrid Lindgren: En levnadsteckning* (Astrid Lindgren: a biography) (Stockholm: Rabén and Sjögren, 1977).

3. Astrid Lindgren, *Mina påhitt. Samuel August från Sevedstorp och Hanna i Hult* (My ideas. Samuel August from Sevedstorp and Hanna from Hult) (Stockholm: Rabén and Sjögren, 1984), 216.

4. Astrid Lindgren, "I Remember . . . ," *Signal* 57 (1988): 165.

5. Astrid Lindgren, *Emil's Pranks* (Chicago: Follett, 1971), 82.

6. Astrid Lindgren, *Mardie's Adventures,* trans. Patricia Crampton (London: Methuen, 1979), 64.

7. Astrid Lindgren, *Emil and Piggy Beast,* trans. Michael Heron (Chicago: Follett, 1973), 137.

8. Astrid Lindgren, "Godnatt, Herr Luffare" (Good night, Mr. Vagabond), in *Småländsk tjurfäktare* (Bullfighter from Småland) (Stockholm: Rabén and Sjögren, 1982), 90; see also "I Remember . . . ," 159.

9. Astrid Lindgren, *My Nightingale Is Singing,* trans. Patricia Crampton, illus. Svend Otto (New York: Viking Kestrel, 1986), 1.

10. "Astrid Lindgren," in *Something about the Author,* vol. 38, ed. Anne Commire (Detroit: Gale, 1985), 128.

11. Astrid Lindgren, *The Children of Noisy Village,* trans. Florence Lamborn (New York: Viking, 1962), 66.

12. Astrid Lindgren, *Pippi in the South Seas,* trans. Gerry Bothmer (New York: Puffin Books, 1977), 124.

13. Knut Hamsun, *Hunger* (New York: Alfred Knopf, 1924), 21. Margareta Strömstedt refers to Astrid Lindgren's reading of *Hunger* in *Astrid Lindgren: En levnadsteckning,* 20–23.

14. Christina Palmgren Rosenqvist, "Det är bra för barn med bilder" (Children benefit from images), *Vi* (We), November 1987, 5.

15. Astrid Lindgren, "Junker Nils av Eka" (Squire Nils of Eka), in *Sunnanäng* (South Wind Meadow) (Stockholm: Rabén and Sjögren, 1959), 68–106; reprinted in *Sagorna* (Stockholm: Rabén and Sjögren, 1987), 259–92.

16. Sybil Gräfin Schönfeldt, *Astrid Lindgren* (Hamburg: Rowohlt, 1987), 138.

17. Astrid Lindgren, letter to the editor, *Expressen,* 23 March 1988, 23.

Chapter Two

1. In addition to the books about Noisy Village for young readers, Astrid Lindgren has written two picture books with the same setting, published in the United States as *Christmas in Noisy Village* (1964) and *Springtime in Noisy Village* (1966).

2. Three more episodes about Emil have since been published separately in Sweden by Rabén and Sjögren, but have not been translated into English or published in the United States. They are *Emils hyss nr 325* (Emil's mischief no. 325) (1985), *När lilla Ida skulle göra hyss* (When little Ida wanted to make mischief) (1986), and *Inget knussel, sa Emil i Lönneberga* (No stinginess, said Emil) (1987). These stories continue in the same spirit as the earlier Emil books.

3. Lena Törnqvist, "Astrid Lindgren 80 år," *Barnboken* 10, no. 2 (1987): 6.

4. Quotes from this essay are from the original Swedish, "Litet samtal med en blivande barnboks för fattare," *Mina påhitt,* 246–50, translated by the author. Published English translations appear as "A Small Chat with a Future Children's Book Author," *Bookbird* 4 (1978): 9–12, and as "A Short Talk with a Prospective Children's Writer," *Horn Book Magazine* 3 (1973): 248–52.

5. Astrid Lindgren, *Emil in the Soup Tureen,* trans. Lilian Seaton (Chicago: Follett, 1970), 9.

6. Astrid Lindgren, *Mischievous Meg,* trans. Gerry Bothmer (New York: Puffin Books, 1985), 31.

7. Astrid Lindgren, *Happy Times in Noisy Village,* trans. Florence Lamborn (New York: Viking, 1963), 27.

8. Astrid Lindgren, *Bill Bergson and the White Rose Rescue* (New York: Viking, 1965), 121.

9. Margareta Rönnberg, *En lek för ögat: 28 filmberättelser av Astrid Lindgren* (A play for the eye: 28 film stories by Astrid Lindgren) (Uppsala: Filmförlaget, 1987), 10–21.

10. Astrid Lindgren, *Bill Bergson, Master Detective,* trans. Herbert Antoine (New York: Viking, 1952), 7.

11. Astrid Lindgren, *Mardie to the Rescue,* trans. Patricia Crampton (London: Methuen, 1981), 7.

12. Astrid Lindgren, *Rasmus and the Vagabond,* trans. Gerry Bothmer (New York: Puffin Books, 1987), 58.

13. Transcript from a radio program on WMAQ, Chicago, broadcast on 30 October 1960.

14. The letter is reprinted in Ulla Lundqvist's *Århundradets barn: Fenomenet Pippi Långstrump och dess förutsättningar* (The child of the century: the

Pippi Longstocking phenomenon and its preconditions) (Stockholm: Rabén and Sjögren, 1979), 17; it was first published in *Dagens Nyheter,* one of Stockholm's large daily newspapers, on 7 December 1939.

15. Interview with Astrid Lindgren in *Göteborgsposten,* 20 October 1985.

16. Lloyd deMause, "The Evolution of Childhood," in *The History of Childhood,* ed. Lloyd deMause (New York: Psychohistory Press, 1974), 1–98.

17. Birgitta Thompson, "Astrid Lindgren—The Child Who Refuses to Grow Up," *Swedish Book Review* 2 (1987): 6.

18. Astrid Lindgren, *The Brothers Lionheart,* trans. Joan Tate (New York: Puffin Books, 1985), 178.

19. Walter Benjamin, "Aussicht ins Kinderbuch" (View of the children's book), in *Kinder, Jugend, und Erziehung* (Children, youth, and education) (Frankfurt: Suhrkamp, 1969), 60.

Chapter Three

1. *Oetinger Almanach* 24 (1987–88): 168.

2. Vivi Edström, "Pippi Longstocking: Chaos and Postmodernism," trans. Eivor Cormack, *Swedish Book Review,* supp., 1990, 24.

3. Astrid Lindgren, *Pippi Longstocking,* trans. Florence Lamborn (New York: Puffin Books, 1988), 19.

4. Kerstin Kvint, "Astrid Lindgrens lansering utomlands" (Launching Astrid Lingren's books abroad) *Barn & Kultur* 5 (1987): 114.

5. Vivi Edström, *Astrid Lindgren—Vildtoring och lägereld* (Astrid Lindgren—campfire rebel) (Stockholm: Rabén and Sjögren, 1992), 119.

6. Astrid Lindgren, *Karlsson-on-the-Roof,* trans. Marianne Turner (New York: Viking, 1971), 5.

7. Ellen Buttenschøn, *Historien om et "påhit": Om Pippifiguren og Astrid Lindgrens gennembrudsværk* (The story about an idea: About the character of Pippi and Astrid Lindgren's breakthrough) (Copenhagen: Gyldendal, 1975), 61.

8. A. Duff to Astrid Lindgren, 27 January 1959, Astrid Lindgren Collection, Kungliga Biblioteket, Stockholm.

9. Astrid Lindgren, "Varför skriver man barnböcker?" (Why does one write children's books?), *Svensk Litteraturtidskrift* 4 (1983): 75.

10. Astrid Lindgren, *Pippi Goes on Board,* trans. Florence Lamborn (New York: Puffin Books, 1988), 137.

11. See Alice Miller, *For Your Own Good: Hidden Cruelty in Child-Rearing and the Roots of Violence* (New York: Farrar, Strauss and Giroux, 1990). Miller traces the roots of violence to principles ruling traditional child-rearing practices. This statement from her preface to the American edition of *For Your Own Good* could have come from Lindgren's pen: "We do not need to be told whether to be strict or permissive with our children. What we do need is to have respect for their needs, their feelings, and their individuality, as well as for our own" (xiii–xiv).

12. Astrid Lindgren, *Assar Bubbla* (Stockholm: Rabén and Sjögren, 1987), 7.

13. Mikhail Bakhtin, *The Dialogic Imagination: Four Essays,* ed. Michael Holquist (Austin: University of Texas Press, 1981), 3–4. See especially the essay "Epic and Novel," 17–28.

14. Mary Orvig, ed., *En bok om Astrid Lindgren* (Stockholm: Rabén and Sjögren, 1977), 35–53, 153–79.

15. Winfried Freund, "Astrid Lindgren: Pippi Langstrumpf: das Mädchenbuch im Zerrspiegel" (Astrid Lindgren: Pippi Longstocking: The girl in the distorting mirror), in *Das zeitgenössische Kinder-und Jugendbuch* (The contemporary children's and youth book) (Paderborn: Schöningh, 1982), 31–40.

16. Neil Postman, *Amusing Ourselves to Death: Public Discourse in the Age of Show Business* (New York: Viking Penguin, 1985), 27.

Chapter Four

1. Astrid Lindgren, *Mio, My Son,* trans. Marianne Turner (New York: Puffin Books, 1988), 179.

2. Hans Holmberg, *Från prins Hatt till prins Mio* (From Prince Hat to Prince Mio) (Stockholm: Rabén and Sjögren, 1988), 69–104; English summary, 138–39.

3. Astrid Lindgren, "I skymmningslandet" (In the land of dusk), in *Sagorna: En Samlingsvolym* (Fairy tales: a collection) (Stockholm: Rabén and Sjögren, 1987), 34–47.

4. Maria Nikolajeva, *The Magic Code: The Use of Magical Patterns in Fantasy for Children* (Stockholm: Almqvist and Wiksell, 1988), 116.

5. Walter Ong, *Orality and Literacy: The Technologizing of the Word* (London, New York: Methuen, 1982), 80.

6. Astrid Lindgren, *Ronia, the Robber's Daughter,* trans. Patricia Crampton (New York: Puffin Books, 1985), 65.

7. Patricia Crampton, "Translating Astrid Lindgren," *Swedish Book Review,* supp., 1990, 84.

8. Vivi Edström, "Stenhjärtat och eldflamman: En studie i Astrid Lindgrens bildspråk" (Stone heart and fire flame: A study of Astrid Lindgren's metaphorical language), *Svensklärarföreningens årsskrift* (Swedish Teachers Association yearbook) (1986): 36–54.

9. Christine Nöstlinger, *Aftonbladet,* 14 November 1987, 6.

10. Joseph Campbell, *The Flight of the Wild Gander: Explorations in the Mythological Dimensions of Fairy Tales, Legends, and Symbols* (New York: Harper Collins, 1990), 5.

11. Vladimir Propp, *Morphology of the Folktale,* trans. Laurence Scott (Austin: University of Texas Press, 1968), 25–65.

12. Max Lüthi, *Once upon a Time: On the Nature of Fairy Tales,* trans. Lee Chadeayne and Paul Gottwald (Bloomington: Indiana University Press, 1970), 140.

13. Zohar Shavit, *Poetics of Children's Literature* (Athens: University of Georgia Press, 1986), 63–92.

14. Egil Törnqvist, "Astrid Lindgrens halvsaga: Berättartekniken i Bröderna Lejonhjärta," (Astrid Lindgren's half fairy tale: Narrative technique in *The Brothers Lionheart*) *Svensk Litteraturtidskrift* 2 (1975): 30.

15. Astrid Lindgren, letter to the editor, *Expressen*, 26 February 1974.

16. Bruno Bettelheim, *The Uses of Enchantment: The Meaning and Importance of Fairy Tales* (New York: Random House, 1977), 51.

Chapter Five

1. Margareta Strömstedt, "Junibacken Revisited," *Barn & Kultur* 5 (1987): 104.

Selected Bibliography

PRIMARY SOURCES

Assar Bubbla (Assar Bubble). Illustrated by Marika Delin. Stockholm: Rabén and Sjögren, 1987.

"Astrid Lindgren Talks about Herself." Brochure. Stockholm: Rabén and Sjögren, 1987. See also "Astrid Lindgren Writes about Herself." Translated by Joan Tate. *Swedish Book Review* 2 (1987): 12–14.

Bill Bergson and the White Rose Rescue. Translated by Florence Lamborn. New York: Viking, 1965. (*Kalle Blomkvist och Rasmus.* Stockholm: Rabén and Sjögren, 1953.)

Bill Bergson Lives Dangerously. Translated by Herbert Antoine. New York: Viking, 1954. (*Mästerdetektiven Blomkvist lever farligt.* Stockholm: Rabén and Sjögren, 1951.)

Bill Bergson Master Detective. Translated by Herbert Antoine. New York: Viking, 1952. (*Mästerdetektiven Blomkvist.* Stockholm: Rabén and Sjögren, 1946.)

The Brothers Lionheart. Translated by Joan Tate. Drawings by J. K. Lambert. New York: Viking, 1975; Puffin Books, 1985. (*Bröderna Lejonhärta.* Illustrated by Ilon Wikland. Stockholm: Rabén and Sjögren, 1973.)

The Children of Noisy Village. Translated by Florence Lamborn. New York: Viking, 1962; Puffin Books, 1988. (*Alla vi barn i Bullerbyn.* Illustrated by Ilon Wikland. Stockholm: Rabén and Sjögren, 1947.)

The Children on Troublemaker Street. Translated by Gerry Bothmer. New York: Macmillan, 1964. (*Barnen på Bråkmakargatan.* Illustrated by Ilon Wikland. Stockholm: Rabén and Sjögren, 1958.)

Christmas in Noisy Village. Illustrated by Ilon Wikland. New York: Viking, 1964.

Christmas in the Stable. New York: Coward, McCann and Geohegan, 1962.

Emil and Piggy Beast. Translated by Michael Heron. Chicago: Follett, 1973. (*Än lever Emil i Lönneberga.* Illustrated by Björn Berg. Stockholm: Rabén and Sjögren, 1970.)

Emil in the Soup Tureen. Translated by Lilian Seaton. Chicago: Follett, 1970. (*Emil i Lönneberga.* Illustrated by Björn Berg. Stockholm: Rabén and Sjögren, 1963.)

Emil's Pranks. (No translator mentioned.) Chicago: Follett, 1971. (*Nya hyss av Emil i Lönneberga.* Illustrated by Björn Berg. Stockholm: Rabén and Sjögren, 1966.)

The Ghost of Skinny Jack. Translated by Yvonne Hooker. New York: Viking Kestrel, 1988. (*Skinn Skerping: hemskast av alla spöken i Småland.* Illustrated by Ilon Wikland. Stockholm: Rabén and Sjögren, 1986.)

Happy Times in Noisy Village. Translated by Florence Lamborn. New York: Viking, 1961. (*Mera om oss barn i Bullerbyn.* Illustrated by Ilon Wikland. Stockholm: Rabén and Sjögren, 1949.)

"I Remember . . ." Translated by Patricia Crampton. *Signal* 57 (September 1988): 155–69.

Kajsa Kavat och andra barn (Brenda Brave). Illustrated by Ilon Wikland. Stockholm: Rabén and Sjögren, 1950.

Karlson Flies Again. Translated by Patricia Crampton. London: Methuen, 1977. (*Karlsson på taket flyger igen.* Illustrated by Ilon Wikland. Stockholm: Rabén and Sjögren, 1962.)

Karlsson-on-the-Roof. Translated by Marianne Turner. New York: Viking, 1971. (*Lillebror och Karlsson på taket.* Illustrated by Ilon Wikland. Stockholm: Rabén and Sjögren, 1955.)

Karlsson på taket smyger igen (Karlsson-on-the-Roof is sneaking around again). Illustrated by Ilon Wikland. Stockholm: Rabén and Sjögren, 1968.

Madicken. Translated by Marianne Turner. Cambridge: Oxford University Press, 1963. (*Madicken.* Illustrated by Ilon Wikland. Stockholm: Rabén and Sjögren, 1960.)

Mardie's Adventures. Translated by Patricia Crampton. London: Methuen, 1979. (*Madicken.* Illustrated by Ilon Wikland. Stockholm: Rabén and Sjögren, 1960.)

Mardie to the Rescue. Translated by Patricia Crampton. London: Methuen, 1981. (*Madicken och Junibackens Pims.* Illustrated by Ilon Wikland. Stockholm: Rabén and Sjögren, 1976.)

Mina påhitt. Samuel August från Sevedstorp och Hanna i Hult (My ideas. Samuel August from Sevedstorp and Hanna from Hult). Stockholm: Rabén and Sjögren, 1984.

Min ko vill ha roligt (My cow wants to have fun). Illustrated by Björn Berg. Stockholm: Rabén and Sjögren, 1990.

Mio, My Son. Translated by Marianne Turner. New York: Viking, 1956; Puffin Books, 1988. (*Mio min Mio.* Illustrated by Ilon Wikland. Stockholm: Rabén and Sjögren, 1954.)

Mischievous Meg. Illustrated by Tanina Domanska. Translated by Gerry Bothmer. New York: Viking, 1960; Puffin Books, 1985. (*Madicken.* Illustrated by Ilon Wikland. Stockholm: Rabén and Sjögren, 1960.)

Mitt Småland (My Småland). Coedited with Margareta Strömstedt. Photos by Jan-Hugo Norman. Stockholm: Rabén and Sjögren, 1987.

My Nightingale Is Singing. Translated by Patricia Crampton. New York: Viking Kestrel, 1986. (*Spelar min lind, sjunger min näktergal.* Illustrated by Svend Otto. Stockholm: Rabén and Sjögren, 1984.)

När lilla Ida skulle göra hyss (When little Ida wanted to do mischief). Illustrated by Björn Berg. Stockholm: Rabén and Sjögren, 1984.

Nils Karlsson-Pyssling: Sagor (Nils Karlssson-Pyssling: fairy tales). Stockholm: Rabén and Sjögren, 1949.

Pippi Goes on Board. Illustrated by Louis S. Glanzman. Translated by Florence Lamborn. New York: Viking, 1957; Puffin Books, 1988. (*Pippi Långstrump går ombord.* Illustrated by Ingrid Vang-Nyman. Stockholm: Rabén and Sjögren, 1946.)

Pippi in the South Seas. Illustrated by Louis S. Glanzman. Translated by Gerry Bothmer. New York: Viking, 1959; Puffin Books, 1988. (*Pippi Långstrump i Söderhavet.* Illustrated by Ingrid Vang-Nyman. Stockholm: Rabén and Sjögren, 1948.)

Pippi Longstocking. Illustrated by Louis S. Glanzman. Translated by Florence Lamborn. New York: Viking, 1950; Puffin Books, 1988. (*Pippi Långstrump.* Illustrated by Ingrid Vang-Nyman. Stockholm: Rabén and Sjögren, 1945.)

Rasmus and the Vagabond. Translated by Gerry Bothmer. New York: Viking, 1960; Puffin Books, 1987. (*Rasmus på luffen.* Illustrated by Eric Palmquist. Stockholm: Rabén and Sjögren, 1956.)

Ronia, the Robber's Daughter. Translated by Patricia Crampton. New York: Viking, 1983; Puffin Books, 1985. (*Ronja Rövardotter.* Illustrated by Ilon Wikland. Stockholm: Rabén and Sjögren, 1981.)

Sagorna: En Samlingsvolym (Fairy tales: a collection). Stockholm: Rabén and Sjögren, 1987.

Seacrow Island. Translated by Evelyn Ramsden, New York: Viking, 1969. (*Vi på Saltkråkan.* Illustrated by Ilon Wikland. Stockholm: Rabén and Sjögren, 1964.)

Springtime in Noisy Village. Illustrated by Ilon Wikland. New York: Viking, 1965.

Sunnanäng (South Wind Meadow). Illustrated by Ilon Wikland. Stockholm: Rabén and Sjögren, 1959.

"Varför skriver man barnböcker?" (Why do people write children's books?). *Svensk Litteraturtidskrift* 4 (1983): 72–77.

SECONDARY SOURCES

Books and Parts of Books

"Astrid Lindgren." In *Something about the Author,* vol. 38, edited by Anne Commire, 121–35. Detroit: Gale, 1985.

Benjamin, Walter. "Aussicht ins Kinderbuch" (View into the children's book). In *Kinder, Jugend und Erziehung* (Children, Youth, and Education), 47–54. Frankfurt: Suhrkamp, 1969.

Bettelheim, Bruno. *The Uses of Enchantment.* New York: Vintage Books, 1977.

Buttenschøn, Ellen. *Historien om et "Påhit": Om Pippifiguren og Astrid Lindgrens gennembrudsværk* (The story of an invention: about the Pippi character and Astrid Lindgren's breakthrough). Copenhagen: Gyldendal, 1975.

————. *Smålandsk fortæller: Om hovedværket i Astrid Lindgrens smålandsdigtning Emil i Lønneberga* (Småland storyteller: about the Emil books in Astrid Lindgren's Småland narratives). Copenhagen: Gyldendal, 1977.

Campbell, Joseph. *The Flight of the Gander: Explorations in the Mythological Dimensions of Fairy Tales, Legends, and Symbols.* 1969. New York: Harper, 1990.

Cott, Jonathan. "The Happy Childhoods of Pippi Longstocking and Astrid Lindgren." In *Pipers at the Gate of Dawn: The Wisdom of Children's Literature,* 135–58. New York: Random House, 1983.

deMause, Lloyd, ed. *The History of Childhood.* New York: Psychohistory Press, 1974.

Edström, Vivi. *Astrid Lindgren—Vildtoring och lägereld* (Astrid Lindgren— Campfire Rebel). Stockholm: Rabén and Sjögren, 1992. A comprehensive look at Astrid Lindgren's authorship with special focus on stylistics.

Freund, Winfried. "Astrid Lindgren: Pippi Langstrumpf, das Mädchenbuch im Zerrspiegel" (Astrid Lindgren: Pippi Longstocking, the girl's book in the distorting mirror). In *Das zeitgenössische Kinder und Jugendbuch* (The contemporary children's and young adult book), 30–40. Paderborn: Schöningh, 1982.

Hamsun, Knut. *Hunger.* New York: Alfred Knopf, 1924.

Holmberg, Hans. *Från prins Hatt till prins Mio: Om sagogenrens utveckling* (From Prince Hat to Prince Mio: The development of the fairy tale). Stockholm: Rabén and Sjögren, 1988.

Hurwitz, Johanna. *Astrid Lindgren: Storyteller to the World.* New York: Viking, 1989. (A book about Astrid Lindgren for young readers.)

Lundqvist, Ulla. *Århundradets barn: Fenomenet Pippi Långstrump och dess förutsätt- ningar* (The child of the century: the Pippi Longstocking phenomenon and its preconditions). Stockholm: Rabén and Sjögren, 1979. (Swedish dissertation. A thorough analysis of the genesis of Pippi Longstocking.)

Lüthi, Max. *Once upon a Time: On the Nature of Fairy Tales.* Bloomington: Indiana University Press, 1976.

Miller, Alice. *For Your Own Good: Hidden Cruelty in Child-Rearing and the Roots of Violence.* Translated by Hildegarde and Hunter Hannum. New York: Farrar, Straus, Giroux, 1983.

Nikolajeva, Maria. *The Magic Code: The Use of Magical Patterns in Fantasy for Children.* Stockholm: Almqvist and Wiksell, 1988.

Ong, Walter. *Orality and Literacy: The Technologizing of the Word.* London, New York: Methuen, 1982.

Orvig, Mary. "Twenty Swedish Authors Who Write for Children and Young Adults, I." In *Culture for Swedish Children,* 21–37. Stockholm: Swedish Institute for Children's Books, 1982.

————, Marianne Eriksson, and Birgitta Sjöquist, eds. *Duvdrottningen. En bok till Astrid Lindgren* (To Astrid Lindgren: queen of the doves). Stockholm:

Rabén and Sjögren, 1987. (Collection of essays, with a summary in English and an extensive bibliography by Lena Törnqvist..)

Postman, Neil. *Amusing Ourselves to Death: Public Discourse in the Age of Show Business.* New York: Viking Penguin, 1985.

Propp, Vladimir. *Morphology of the Folktale.* Austin: University of Texas Press, 1968.

Rönnberg, Margareta. *En lek för ögat: 28 filmberättelser av Astrid Lindgren* (A play for the eye: 28 film stories by Astrid Lindgren). Uppsala: Filmförlaget, 1987.

Schönfeldt, Sybil Gräfin. *Astrid Lindgren: Mit Selbstzeugnissen und Bilddokumenten* (Astrid Lindgren: with autobiographical information and picture documents). Hamburg: Rowohlt, 1987.

Shavit, Zohar. *Poetics of Children's Literature.* Athens: University of Georgia Press, 1986.

Strömstedt, Margareta. *Astrid Lindgren: en levnadsteckning* (Astrid Lindgren: a biography). Stockholm: Rabén and Sjögren, 1977.

Wolff, Rudolf, ed. *Astrid Lindgren: Rezeption in der Bundesrepublik* (Astrid Lindgren: reception in the Federal Republic of Germany). Bonn: Bouvier, 1986.

Journal Articles

Auraldsson, Kerstin. "Astrid Lindgren." *Bookbird* 25, no. 3 (October 1987): 8–10.

Crampton, Patricia. "Translating Astrid Lindgren." *Swedish Book Review,* supp., 1990, 83–86.

Edström, Vivi. "Astrid Lindgren: en plädering för livet, mot våld och förstening" (Astrid Lindgren: a plea for life, against violence and petrification). *Allt om böcker,* 6 May 1985, 40–45.

———. "Pippi Longstocking: Chaos and Postmodernism." Translated by Eivor Cormack. *Swedish Book Review,* supp., 1990, 22–29.

Hoffeld, Laura. "Pippi Longstocking: The Comedy of the Natural Girl." *The Lion and the Unicorn* 1 (1977): 47–53.

Kvint, Kerstin. "Astrid Lindgrens lansering utomlands." *Barn & Kultur* 5 (1987): 111–14.

Metcalf, Eva-Maria. "Astrid Lindgren—Rebel for Peace." *Scandinavian Review* 78, no. 3 (1990): 34–41.

———. "Astrid Lindgren's *Ronia, the Robber's Daughter:* A Twentieth-Century Fairy Tale." *The Lion and the Unicorn* 12, no. 2 (1988): 151–64.

———. "Tall Tale and Spectacle in Pippi Longstocking." *Children's Literature Association Quarterly* 15, no. 3 (1990): 130–35.

Ritte, Hans. "Astrid Lindgrens Kindheitsmythos: Beobachtungen zu ihren Bullerby-Büchern" (Astrid Lindgren's childhood myth: observations about her Noisy Village books). *Vetenskaps-societeten i Lund: årsbok* (1980): 39–55.

Slayton, Ralph. "The Love Story of Astrid Lindgren." *Scandinavian Review* 63, no. 4 (1975): 44–53.

Strömstedt, Margareta. "Junibacken revisited." *Barn & Kultur* 5 (1987): 103–5.

————. "Astrid Lindgren: Subversive Storyteller." *Scanorama,* December 1989/January 1990, 10–20.

Thompson, Birgitta. "Astrid Lindgren—The Child Who Refuses to Grow Up." *Swedish Book Review* 2 (1987): 3–9.

Törnqvist, Egil. "Astrid Lindgrens halvsaga: Berättartekniken i *Bröderna Lejonhjärta*" (Astrid Lindgren's half fairy tale: narrative technique in *The Brothers Lionheart*). *Svensk Litteraturtidskrift* 2 (1975): 17–34.

Törnqvist, Lena. "Astrid Lindgren 80 år" (Astrid Lindgren is 80). *Barnboken* 10, no. 2 (1987): 6.

Udal, John. "Richard Kennedy and the Case of Pippi Longstocking." *Junior Bookshelf* 42, no. 2 (1978): 75–77.

Index

The Author

Eva-Maria Metcalf is Assistant Professor of German at Hamline University. Born in Germany, she received her undergraduate degree from Stockholm University and her Ph.D. in German from the University of Minnesota. She is a member of the Children's Literature Association and currently chairs its International Committee. She has published several articles on Swedish and German children's literature in *Barnboken, Children's Literature Association Quarterly,* and *The Lion and the Unicorn.*

The Editor

Ruth K. MacDonald is associate dean of Bay Path College. She received her B.A. and M.A. in English from the University of Connecticut, her Ph.D. in English from Rutgers University, and her M.B.A. from the University of Texas at El Paso. She is author of the volumes on Louisa May Alcott, Beatrix Potter, and Dr. Seuss in Twayne's United States and English Authors Series and of the book *Literature for Children in England and America, 1646–1774* (1982).